SPECIAL MESSAGE TO READERS

This book is published under the auspices of

THE ULVERSCROFT FOUNDATION

(registered charity No. 264873 UK)

Established in 1972 to provide funds for research, diagnosis and treatment of eye diseases. Examples of contributions made are: —

A new Children's Assessment Unit at Moorfield's Hospital, London.

•

Twin operating theatres at the Western Ophthalmic Hospital, London.

•

A Chair of Ophthalmology at the University of Leicester.

•

The establishment of a Royal Australian College of Ophthalmologists "Fellowship".

You can help further the work of the Foundation by making a donation or leaving a legacy. Every contribution, no matter how small, is received with gratitude. Please write for details to:

**THE ULVERSCROFT FOUNDATION,
The Green, Bradgate Road, Anstey,
Leicester LE7 7FU, England.
Telephone: (0116) 236 4325**

**In Australia write to:
THE ULVERSCROFT FOUNDATION,
c/o The Royal Australian College of Ophthalmologists,
27, Commonwealth Street, Sydney,
N.S.W. 2010.**

I've travelled the world twice over,
Met the famous: saints and sinners,
Poets and artists, kings and queens,
Old stars and hopeful beginners,
I've been where no-one's been before,
Learned secrets from writers and cooks
All with one library ticket
To the wonderful world of books.

VOW OF COMPASSION

When Mother Dorothy, Prioress of the Order of the Daughters of Compassion, inherits a considerable estate from her godmother, nobody can guess that the death of one old lady will lead to one of Sister Joan's most puzzling cases. Linked with the first death is an apparent suicide and the disappearance of an abused child. In the local hospital suspicion and fear stalk the wards and, in the convent, that fear is reflected — for someone is watching and waiting. With the help of her friend, Detective Sergeant Mill, Sister Joan sets out to trap a dangerous killer.

Books by Veronica Black
Published by The House of Ulverscroft:

A VOW OF SILENCE
VOW OF CHASTITY
MY NAME IS POLLY WINTER
VOW OF SANCTITY
MASTER OF MALCAREW
VOW OF PENANCE
A FOOTFALL IN THE MIST
VOW OF FIDELITY
VOW OF POVERTY
VOW OF ADORATION

VERONICA BLACK

VOW OF COMPASSION

Complete and Unabridged

ULVERSCROFT
Leicester

First published in Great Britain in 1997 by
Robert Hale Limited
London

First Large Print Edition
published 1998
by arrangement with
Robert Hale Limited
London

British Library CIP Data
Vow of compassion.—Large print ed.
Ulverscroft large print series: mystery
2. Detective and mystery stories
3. Large type books
I. Title

ISBN 0–7089–3972–4

Published by
F. A. Thorpe (Publishing) Ltd.
Anstey, Leicestershire

Set by Words & Graphics Ltd.
Anstey, Leicestershire
Printed and bound in Great Britain by
T. J. International Ltd., Padstow, Cornwall

This book is printed on acid-free paper

1

The wards were quiet this September night. Sleep enfolded many of the occupants of the white-curtained cubicles while slumber's younger sister, relaxation, slowed the breathing and soothed the muscles of those deputed to keep alert. It had been an unusually busy day with three babies deciding to arrive at the same time in the small maternity wing and two suspected heart attacks in the geriatric ward. Added to that had been a steady stream of minor accidents through casualty and a muddle in the administration office which had resulted in a healthy young man who had recovered nicely from a hernia operation being scheduled for a hip replacement while a limping old lady had spent the day asking plaintively when she could expect to be wheeled into the theatre. Fortunately it had been sorted out before any harm was done at the expense of red faces all round, but Ward Sister Sophie Meecham had been driven to gulp down a couple of aspirins before she had felt able to trot briskly into the manager's sanctum and assure him that there had been a blip on the computer.

“And God bless computers!” she muttered, giving Clarrie a friendly pat.

Computers could be blamed for everything and the beauty of it was that a computer couldn’t be fined or sacked and never burst into tears when receiving a severe dressing down.

Now all was still and peaceful. Sophie rose from her chair and switched off the desk lamp, moving to the window that looked out over the car-park and the main street to the moors that rose into the star-hung sky. She had worked in this small Cornish town for three years now and never ceased to thank her good fortune in having been selected to work at St Keyne’s Cottage Hospital.

‘Cottage’ was an anachronism really, but the old name had stuck even after the hospital had become a fundholding concern. The patients here were mainly local people who often knew one another and the medical staff by name, and in her off-duty hours Sophie could leave the town behind her and walk up on to the moors which stretched past the housing estate and the new supermarket and left all the buildings behind as they raced in a tangle of blowing grass and rich heather towards the sea. One day, she had promised herself, she would walk as far as the sea and scramble down the rocks into one of the pebbled coves that made the coastline at once enchanting and treacherous. So far she had only made it as far as the Convent of the Daughters of Compassion that stood proudly on the high moor with its grounds spreading over the dips and swells of the landscape.

Sophie, who had had hardly any contact with nuns, had paused shyly at the gates, seeing that they were invitingly open and that a well-weeded drive ran up to the main door. The building hadn't looked like a convent, she'd thought, or rather it didn't look like her idea of a convent. It must once have been a house, its stone walls ivied, its ground-floor windows mullioned. She had pictured carriages driving up to the front door and grooms helping down ladies in billowing crinolines and velvet cloaks.

A grey-habited nun, mounted on a pony, had suddenly ridden round from the back of the mansion, her short black veil revealing a crop of black curly hair, a pair of blue jeans showing incongruously beneath the hem of her skirt. She had checked the pony and smiled, eyes darkly blue in a round, rosy face.

"Good afternoon. Isn't it a lovely day? May I help you?" Her voice had been pleasant with the hint of the North in her slightly flattened vowels.

"I was just walking past," Sophie had said, adding doubtfully, "Sister?"

"Sister Joan. I'm taking Lilith for her bit of exercise. If she doesn't get it she sulks. If you walk on round to the kitchen Sister Perpetua will give you a cup of tea."

"Sophie Meecham. I'm a nurse at St Keynes Hospital."

"How are you?" The nun sounded as if she'd really wanted to know as she'd leaned and offered a firm handshake from a small, square hand. "You look very fit. Is walking a hobby of yours?"

"When I can. Walking in cities isn't the same though, is it?"

"No, it certainly isn't." Sister Joan had gathered up the reins again, said pleasantly, "Don't overtire yourself and do pop round to see Sister Perpetua. She is the soul of hospitality."

She'd cantered off then over the moor and Sophie had watched her out of sight before she'd begun to retrace her own steps. The prospect of a cup of tea had been inviting but she was too diffident to march boldly round the back and ask for one. Out of the ward, away from the milieu where she knew herself to be efficient, her confidence drained away with shyness creeping in.

Since that day she had skirted the convent

walls many times but not paused there. She had glimpsed Sister Joan again, too, on several occasions, once with an Alsatian puppy frisking round her heels, once with a taller, thinner nun at her side. Sophie hadn't liked to attract attention. Nuns, she knew, weren't encouraged to fraternize with lay people though she'd heard the Order was only a semi-enclosed one.

"They work at various things," one of the hospital staff had remarked, having just waved off an elderly nun who'd come in with a suspected heart murmur. "I don't think they make much money because most of their time is taken up with praying and doing domestic work."

"I'd not like to have to clean that big house," one of the student nurses had said.

"It used to belong to the Tarquin family who were squires here once," someone else had said. "The nuns bought the estate and the Tarquins died out. Not many private people can afford to keep up a place like that any longer."

Standing now at the window, Sophie could look out towards the blue-black mass of the moor with its patches of moonlight that revealed in stark outline an occasional thorn tree. It wasn't possible to see the building from here but she could imagine that from one window a lamp would welcome wanderers.

"Sister Meecham?" One of the student nurses tapped on the door. "Time for ward rounds."

"Thank you, Sister Williams. I'll be there directly."

Fancy fled before the call of duty. Sophie smoothed down her already creaseless skirt and moved towards the door, clipboard in hand.

Other members of staff occasionally grumbled at the necessity of ward rounds, declaring that they achieved nothing except to wake up the patients who slept lightly. Sophie liked the long quiet walk along the dimly lit corridors, through the wards where the white curtains were like tents ranged neatly at each side of the shining central aisles. She liked the softly murmured voice of the ward nurse seated at her desk with a shaded lamp to help her write up her case notes.

At her heels Sister Williams was a mute shadow. She would be a good nurse, Sophie decided, half turning to give her an encouraging smile. She moved gently and she had the unbeatable combination of a friendly voice and a strong back. Few people realized that nurses needed a strong back almost as much as an intelligent mind and a reassuring manner.

The three new babies were all sleeping, making the little snorting noises that newborn infants make when they first begin to breathe fresh air. Babies smelt so sweet. Sophie thought sometimes that it would be lovely to have one of her own, but first she would have to find a father for it. In her romantic mind he already existed — tall and fair with surgeon's hands and the faint sharp scent of Dettol on his crisp white coat. So far he hadn't put in an appearance but at thirty-four she still had time.

They processed through the men's ward where, as usual, one of the ambulatory patients had gone into the sluice and coaxed a cup of tea from Sister Foster who never could deny a man anything. Sophie gave them both a reproving frown and a little shake of the head. They walked on past the empty cubicles of the casualty unit and the visitors' waiting-room and the ground-floor toilets to the surgical ward.

There were two broken legs, a cracked pelvic bone, a slight concussion and broken collar bone, and two or three awaiting operations in this section. Sophie checked a pulse here, smoothed a coverlet there, her gaze taking in details without seeming to do so. The lad with the concussion seemed slightly restless. She'd have a word with the ward nurse about him. Concussions could be tricky. She made a mental note to change the dressings after breakfast on the gallstones case over in the corner. The operation had proved more invasive than had been hoped and the patient, a middle-aged woman, would require careful monitoring.

The old lady who was due for the hip operation which had been postponed to the following day because of the computer blip, slept in the end bed. Sophie paused, leaning forward slightly, her smooth brow suddenly corrugated, her own breath held for a moment.

"Sister Williams, draw the curtains closed," she said quietly, bending lower to switch on the bedside light.

The round white circle of light illumined the face devoid of personality now, the mouth slightly contorted, the right hand clenched tightly in a last spasm.

"Is she — ?" Sister Williams came to her side.

"Get one of the duty surgeons and another nurse. Then bring the resuscitator, though I fear she's past it. Go on now, Sister."

She gave the girl a little push, wondering not for the first time if it was really sound policy to give all the nursing staff the title of

Sister. It was supposed to inspire confidence in the patients who might feel apprehension at being treated by a student but Sophie felt privately that inexperience couldn't be masked by a title. Well, this would be Sister Williams's first death. At least it had been a quiet one though the contorted mouth was disturbing.

She stood back as the doctor came in, white coat flapping. The two nurses wheeled the resuscitator between the other beds and the ward nurse emerged from the toilet, looking startled and affronted, skirt rustling as she hurried to join them.

"You were not at your desk, Sister." Sophie spoke quietly, not yet blaming.

"I needed the toilet, Sister. My stomach's been a bit queasy," Sister Collet said. "I checked the patients an hour ago. They were all sleeping."

"You couldn't have checked very closely," the doctor said brusquely. "She's been dead at least two hours. Already beginning to stiffen. Mind you, this damned ward is chilly. The heating should be higher."

In overheated wards germs flourished. Sophie, who would have cut off her head sooner than contradict a doctor, murmured meekly, "Yes, Doctor. I'll make a note of it."

"Hip replacement, wasn't she? Due for surgery in the morning. Are these her full case notes?" He unhooked the clipboard from the foot of the bed.

"Yes, Doctor. She had a heart murmur which was causing some concern," Sophie said. "She was rather a highly strung old lady and there was some concern as to how well she'd stand up to surgery. However, she was in such constant pain that it was considered worth the slight risk and she was fully aware of the situation."

"God forbid that my patients should be fully aware of their situations," he muttered, flicking impatiently through the typed notes. "Seventy-five. She was no spring chicken. Wasn't she scheduled for theatre this morning?"

"There was a blip on the computer, Doctor. By the time it was discovered it was too late to get it done today."

"She was quite upset about it," Sister Collet put in respectfully.

"More upset than we realized. She fretted herself into a heart attack," he said, putting back the clipboard. "There's nothing to be done here. Better get her down to the mortuary and the bed stripped. No sense in worrying the patients. Get another patient transferred before morning."

"There are no surgical cases, Doctor," Sophie began.

"Then transfer someone from geriatrics. They're pretty crowded there, aren't they?"

"Yes, Doctor." Sister Collet looked helplessly at her colleagues.

"Might not an elderly person be rather upset to find themselves on the surgical ward?" Sophie ventured.

"Don't you believe it, Sister!" he grinned. "The old duck'll have a marvellous time hearing all about everybody else's operations."

And the other patients on the surgical ward would probably not notice that the end bed was occupied by a different person, Sophie thought. Or if they did they'd assume that the hip-replacement lady had simply gone down to theatre or had her operation postponed. In hospital, death was something that occurred elsewhere, out of sight. Sophie stood back as a trolley was wheeled in and the bedclothes stripped cleanly from the frail, night-gowned figure. Her face was serene but there was a fine film of moisture across her eyes.

* * *

"Isn't September a lovely month?" Sister Teresa opened the kitchen window and leaned out, sniffing the breeze with relish.

"Especially after such a blazing summer," Sister Marie agreed.

"Oh, summer was lovely too," Sister Teresa said. "I felt a real urge to sunbathe."

"Which I hope you resisted," Sister Perpetua said, coming in and fixing the two lay sisters with a gimlet green eye. "Sunshine can be dangerous."

"So can all pleasures if you believe everything you're told these days," Sister Marie said daringly.

As a first-year novice she was not yet fully professed and generally managed to subdue her lively tongue.

"It's a good job that so many are forbidden to us then," Sister Teresa said.

"That's quite enough, Sisters!" The infirmarian checked her own smile and spoke firmly. "Sister Teresa, you're not here to hang out of windows you know. And Sister Marie, if you want to pass through to your final year as novice you'd better find something useful to do. That sink looks grubby."

"Right away, Sister Perpetua!" Sister Teresa withdrew her head and went over to the sink, running hot water energetically into the already shining bowl.

It was a lovely morning, Sister Perpetua

thought, leaving the two younger members of the community to get on and retracing her steps into the small dispensary where she kept the variety of herbal remedies with which she dosed her fellow nuns when something trifling assailed them. Thanks be to God they were all in good health, though Sister Mary Concepta had to rest more these days. Sister Perpetua began to pound some spices together, tipping them into the glass jar from which she would later extract a teaspoonful or so to enliven a tisane or a cup of hot ginger. Ginger was good for the stomach and poor Mary Concepta suffered sometimes from attacks of nausea. It seemed most unfair since she ate like a bird and never indulged herself on feast days whereas Sister Gabrielle ate the most odd combinations of food sometimes and boasted that at eighty-eight the most she had to endure was a touch of flatulence. Or, to put it another way, the rest of the community had to endure it, Sister Perpetua mused, and found herself laughing.

"What's the joke?"

Sister Joan came in with Alice, the half-grown alsatian at her heels. For a wonder Alice was walking sedately, mindful of her status as guard dog. She had just seen off a couple of wood pigeons that had soared away in a flurry of wings and alarmed cries, only to be scolded by Sister Joan with, "Not birds, Alice! Burglars! Burglars and muggers and two-legged foes, not birds and other animals! And good guard dogs don't bark. They show their teeth and snarl very softly and threateningly." Whereupon Sister Joan had shown her own white teeth and made a growling noise and Alice had immediately forgotten the scolding in the expectation of a new game.

"I was just thinking that Sister Gabrielle can eat anything without ill effect while Sister Mary Concepta has to watch her diet," Sister Perpetua said.

"Oh." Sister Joan looked slightly puzzled, trying to see the implicit jest, and decided to change the subject. "I was thinking that Sister Gabrielle will be eighty-nine soon, and next year ninety. Ninety is rather special, don't you think?"

"Hundred is more special," Sister Gabrielle said, coming in and tapping her stick for emphasis. "You can save the celebrations for then."

"Another eleven years," Sister Joan said teasingly. "How will we endure them?"

"Don't be impertinent," Sister Gabrielle said with a chuckle. "I came in to tell you that Mary Concepta has a queasy stomach this morning. She fancies a drop of that ginger wine you keep."

"I'll heat up some at once, Sister," Sister Perpetua said. "Would you like a tiny glassful yourself, Sister Gabrielle?"

"I'll stick to tea," Sister Gabrielle said, stumping out again. "Alice, come and have a biscuit."

Alice promptly switched allegiance and trotted after the thickset figure of the old woman as she returned to the infirmary where she and her younger companion spent most of their time when they were not fulfilling their religious obligations.

It was a pleasant room with a pair of large windows that looked out on to a rock garden Sister Martha had built and planted. Two chairs were drawn up before a small fire, the only room to contain one save in the severest weather. There were flowering plants along the windowsill and spanking fresh white covers drawn over the two low beds. Sister Mary Concepta looked a trifle pale but she never had much colour at the best of times and the smile she turned upon Alice was long-suffering. Sister Mary Concepta was of a natural sweetness of disposition and never grumbled, a fact of which she reminded people from time to time. Sister Gabrielle grumbled constantly.

Of the two Sister Joan secretly preferred the latter. If she'd been confined for several years in the same room as Sister Mary Concepta she suspected that she'd have grumbled a bit too.

"How are you feeling, Sister Mary Concepta?" she asked guiltily.

"A little sickly, Sister Joan, but one can't really complain on such a lovely morning," Sister Mary Concepta said gently.

"You shouldn't have eaten that pickle last night," Sister Gabrielle said briskly, going to the biscuit tin. "Sit, Alice! Sit! There's a good girl. Cheese and pickle for supper is death to the digestive system. I don't know what Sister Teresa was thinking about."

"I'm afraid it was my fault," Sister Joan said. "Sister Marie had the toothache and went to lie down with an aspirin and a hot pack on her cheek and I helped Sister Teresa to cook the supper."

"You burned the potatoes," Sister Gabrielle said in a resigned tone.

"Worse! I burned the fish."

"So we were reduced to cheese on toast and pickles! Sister Joan, it was kind of you to help Sister Teresa but you never could cook so next time get someone else to help and you go paint a picture or something!" Sister Gabrielle said.

I wish! Sister Joan said inwardly, going out into the short passage that connected the kitchen wing with the main hall.

There had been a time when she had dreamed of making her living as an artist. A very long time ago, she reflected. She had been wise enough to know early on that her talent would never be touched with genius but Jacob had encouraged her to make the most of her inherent gift, had taught her to live life fully too. And then real life had intruded, reminding them both that their religions were not mutual but exclusive, and that neither could bend sufficiently to accommodate the religious demands of the other. Jacob had gone out of her life and she had embraced a new life and never felt a moment's conscious regret about her decision. But the painting she did regret because it would increase the shaky income of the community if Mother Dorothy allowed her to use her canvasses and brushes for something more than the occasional Bring and Buy Sale.

"How is it, Sister," enquired the prioress, emerging from the antechamber to her parlour as she almost invariably did whenever the thought of her came to mind, "that whenever I meet you I have the strongest suspicion that you're wasting time?"

Sister Joan might with justice have pointed out that she'd already spent three hours at prayer, scrubbed out the stable and taken Alice for a walk but Mother Dorothy had on her unyielding face, eyes cold behind their gold-rimmed spectacles, small frame rigid. Now wasn't the time for arguing. Now was the time for getting down on one's knees and kissing the floor. Sister Joan did so, wrinkling her nose at the smell of floor polish.

"It's your turn to go hospital visiting, Sister," Mother Dorothy said. "You'll drive down into town in the van and buy some groceries on the way back. Last night's supper was somewhat inadequate."

"That wasn't Sister Teresa's fault, Mother," Sister Joan said. "I burnt the fish."

"I thought that Sister Teresa was not at fault. She's always so careful," Mother Dorothy said. "You will remember the incident in general confession, Sister."

"Yes, of course, Mother Prioress."

"Very well." The prioress went past, sunlight glinting on her deep purple habit. The habit denoted her position and would be worn by her until a new prioress was elected. Elections took place every five years, no prioress being allowed to hold office for more than two terms. They were, however, permitted to sew a narrow purple band on to the sleeve of their grey habit for each term served.

"A bit like the army really, isn't it?" Sister Bernadette had joked when she had first made application to join the Order.

Now she was nearing the end of her first year as a postulant, a mute figure in the heavy boots, pink smock and large white bonnet that effectively crushed any remnants of vanity, permitted to talk only to the prioress and the novice mistress. Recalling her own time as postulant in the London convent Sister Joan marvelled that she'd ever got through it.

Hospital visiting wasn't an activity she particularly enjoyed. Happily her turn came round only three or four times a year. She went obediently, said the right things, distributed holy pictures and the sweet-smelling posies of herbs that Sister Martha made up and felt immense relief when the whole embarrassing business was over. Had she been a patient in hospital just recovering from an operation or pumped full of drugs then the last person she'd want to see was a nun with holy pictures and a large basket of herbs.

If she went on thinking in this manner she'd have even more to confess at the general confession on Saturday evening. She hurried upstairs to her cell to get her cloak from the hook behind the door and, as usual, paused for an instant to look round the tiny room and marvel that for nine years, first at the London house and now here, she had slept every night on a horsehair mattress with grey blankets and one pillow, the white coverlet which was only spread by day neatly rolled to the foot of the bed. A small table with a deep drawer held her underwear within it and her toothbrush, toothpaste, comb, flannel and soap on top. A bowl and ewer on the floor was filled with cold water and had a small towel folded by it. A shelf contained a few books and a mug with some pens stuck in it. The tiny window was barred and a solitary candle in a tin candlestick stood on the windowsill to be lit only in a case of extreme emergency.

The cells had once been decently sized bedrooms over the kitchen wing and what was now Mother Dorothy's parlour. They had been divided into six smaller rooms, the dividing walls of hardboard so that one could hear the snores and night mutterings of one's neighbour. Sister David slept to one side of Sister Joan and snored infrequently but noisily; the prioress occupied the slightly larger space at the other side and slept silently. At the other side of the narrow passage Sisters Perpetua, Katherine and Martha slept in the three remaining cells. At the end of the passage two bathrooms provided the twice-weekly bath allowed, one in cold water, the other in hot. Everything was grey and white and Spartan and unchanging. Cells were for sleeping in and for writing up one's spiritual diary which would be read after one's death and deposited in the library. Sister Joan hoped that wherever she went after death would be a good long way away from earthly comments since she had no wish to spend eternity with her ears burning.

"Are you still here, Sister?" Mother Dorothy stood in the doorway staring at her.

"I'm just going, Mother," Sister Joan said quickly.

"Sister Martha has the herb basket ready and the holy pictures," the prioress said. "Don't forget to give the pictures first to the older children. Sister Teresa will give you the list of groceries she requires and the money for them. One further thing — "

"Yes, Mother Dorothy?"

"My godmother, Mrs Louisa Cummings, is at St Keyne's having a hip-replacement operation," Mother Dorothy said. "Perhaps you would look in on her and give her my regards?"

"Yes, Mother." Staring at her superior, Sister Joan said impulsively, "Your godmother! I never thought of your ever having had one!"

"You think I came into the world wearing the habit, did you?" Behind the gold-rimmed spectacles the pale eyes were amused. "She was very kind to me when I was a child, but then she married and moved away and we exchanged only an occasional postcard for many years. However she was widowed some years ago and has no children so I am the nearest thing to a relative she has."

"She lives in the district?" Sister Joan wondered how on earth Mother Dorothy had managed to refrain from rushing over to visit her.

"No, in Devon, but she was informed that she could have the hip replacement done here more speedily. I assume she will return to Devon for her convalescence."

"We could invite her here."

"We?" Mother Dorothy's sparse eyebrows climbed towards Heaven. "Sister, this is a convent. We are not a nursing Order and we none of us has the right to invite visitors here save for the gravest and most urgent of reasons. I myself don't care to set a precedent in this matter. Hurry along now."

"Yes, Mother Prioress."

And hallelujah to you too, Mother Prioress. Sister Joan grimaced as she went down the wide curving staircase and through to the kitchen to collect the shopping list. It was considered a virtue to practise detachment but wasn't there something about a virtue being carried too far?

"Sister Martha has the herbs and the holy pictures," Sister Teresa said. "Who will you take with you?"

"Hasn't Mother Dorothy said?"

"She's left it to you," Sister Teresa said. "Sister Martha has the apples to pick and Sister David is working in the library and Sister Katherine has the new vestments to finish, and I've the potatoes to finish — "

"And Sister Marie isn't allowed off the premises unless she's ill."

"She's trying not to complain but her toothache's started up again," Sister Teresa said. "I thought you could take her to the dentist. He's awfully kind about fitting us in at short notice."

"Right! Sister Marie it is," Sister Joan said cheerfully. "Tell her to get a move on."

Outside, Sister Martha came up with two large baskets of herb posies, each one tied neatly with coloured thread. In her wake shambled the ungainly figure of Luther, face bright with doglike devotion.

"Morning, Sister Joan!" He stuck out a huge hand. "Sister Martha and me is going to pick apples."

"Without Luther I simply couldn't manage," Sister Martha said. "He knows which ones are ripe now and which ones must be left a while longer."

"Sister Martha showed me," Luther said proudly.

He was a gangling figure, round faced and amiable though he could be obstinate when he imagined his pride was hurt. He had Romany blood but none of the sharp intelligence of his cousin, Padraic Lee. In the past he'd been up before magistrates who failed to understand that his unnerving habit of following women never went further. Helping out at the convent delighted him and kept him out of trouble because he could follow Sister Martha round all day. The sight of her tiny frame always a few yards ahead of his huge one was so usual that people had ceased to notice it.

Sister Marie arrived just as Sister Joan was getting into the van. From the kitchen came Alice's furious and indignant barking at being left behind.

"Sister Perpetua thinks I ought to see the dentist," she said, "but it's stopped aching again."

"It always does," Sister Joan said with a grin. "By the time you're in his surgery you'll believe that you imagined the whole thing. Nevertheless!"

Sister Marie climbed up to the passenger seat.

The track from the convent into town ran across the moor. Over on the right the pile of rusting metal and other refuse that marked the site of the Romany camp was just visible. The track veered away towards the small stone building once used as a school but now occupied by Brother Cuthbert who was on an extended sabbatical from his monastery in the Highlands. The tonsured red head wasn't visible this morning and Sister Marie said, "I can't imagine the place without Brother Cuthbert now. Do you think that his prior will let him stay here?"

"I think he might. Brother Cuthbert is considered a bit of a loose cannon back in his monastery." Sister Joan, who was a bit of a loose cannon herself, spoke sympathetically. Not that she could compare herself with the young friar. Brother Cuthbert was too innocent to fit easily into a community. She was too awkward. Innocence, she mused, wasn't a fault to which she could lay claim.

She dropped Sister Marie at the dentist's and drove on towards the Cottage Hospital.

It stood on the outskirts of the town, a reasonably spacious car-park in front of the main building with the smaller additional units surrounding it. It had expanded in the years since Sister Joan had come to Cornwall but the main building still retained something of the cosy atmosphere of the original institution.

"Good morning, Sister." The nurse on the reception desk looked up. "Just visiting, are you?"

"It's my turn," Sister Joan said. "Is it all right if I start over in the children's ward?"

"No problem, Sister." The nurse added with unexpected sensitivity, "You'll be ready for tea then."

Seeing small children who ought to be running and playing and getting into mischief confined to bed or hobbling round on mended limbs was always hard to bear. Sister Joan, who had never been particularly maternal, steeled her heart, put a bright smile on her face and went through the swing doors into an artificially cheerful environment with cut-outs of cartoon characters trying to hide X-ray equipment.

She went round, forbidding herself to hurry, persuading one reluctant little girl that the herbs were to smell not eat, though she was certain they would be harmless enough, assuring another that she had proper legs like other people. In one corner of a room a small girl crouched, arms wrapped tightly about her knees, face bruised and adorned with sticking plaster.

"And what happened to you?" Sister Joan enquired.

The child gave a long shudder and swivelled her whole small person round to face the wall.

"She was abused by her foster parents." A young nurse touched Sister Joan lightly on the arm. "The bruises she made herself, banging her face against any hard surface she can find. Creating pain to shut out pain. I'll take the posy and the picture for her and see if I can get to give them to her later. Amy isn't responding to kindness because in her four years she's never known any, but we go on trying."

"What happened to the foster parents?"

"Remanded for trial. They both ought to get a good long stretch in prison."

"They both ought to be shot!" Sister Joan said low and vehemently.

"The sad thing is that Amy loves them," the nurse said. "She keeps asking when she can go home. Ah well! Tomorrow's another day."

She went away on her low, rubber-soled

shoes, consciously efficient and impersonal. There were other children who needed her attention.

Back in the main building, the nurse on reception brought her a cup of coffee and a biscuit.

"No biscuit, thank you. Just coffee." Sister Joan perched on a stool and drank deeply.

"You're never slimming!"

"No, but snacking between meals isn't allowed. We have bread, fruit and a coffee for our breakfast and that suffices until lunchtime. Is there any patient in particular I ought to see?"

"I don't think so. The new mothers might appreciate a visit. They go home today."

"And I have to see a Mrs Louisa Cummings," Sister Joan remembered. "A hip-replacement case? She was transferred from Devon."

"Was she a friend of yours?"

"No, I never — Was?" Sister Joan looked up sharply.

"She was — that is to say she died last night. Heart attack." the girl said.

"She was what?"

"Nothing. She had a heart murmur and then her operation was delayed because there was a blip in the computer and a couple of patients got muddled up, but she died of a heart attack. We found her."

"We?"

"Ward Sister Meecham — she's head ward sister — came round with Sister Williams, one of the student nurses around midnight. I was on duty in the surgical ward. Oh, I'm Sister Collet. Tracy Collet. I'd been in the toilet, but not for very long. Dr Geeson said she'd been dead for at least two hours."

"And you were on duty then?"

"Yes. I left the desk a couple of times but I was never away long, a minute or two. She was in the end bed furthest away from the desk. I never heard her make a sound."

"Then she died very quickly and peacefully," Sister Joan said. "I'm sure you can't be blamed."

"She died very peacefully," Tracy Collet said. "That's just the trouble. Excuse me, Sister. That's my beeper. I'm wanted on the ward. Enjoy your coffee."

She was gone in a rustle of starched skirts. Sister Joan drank her cooling coffee and found herself frowning.

2

"Sister Joan? You wanted to see me?" The young doctor gave her a brusque handshake and a nod, designed to let her know how busy he was.

"Dr Geeson, it's very kind of you to see me at short notice," she began.

"What can I do for you? You look healthy enough!"

He had the brisk tone of a man diverted from more important duties.

"A lady called Louisa Cummings died late last night," Sister Joan said.

"The hip-replacement, yes. Heart attack. Were you acquainted with her?"

"No, not at all, but our prioress, Mother Dorothy, was her godchild. She asked me to look in on Mrs Cummings during my visit here today so naturally she'll be very shocked to hear the news. I wondered if you could possibly give me any further details."

"No more than any of the nurses," he said. "Sister Williams, one of the student nurses, alerted me just after midnight. The old lady had clearly suffered a heart attack. She had been dead at least two hours. Her case notes showed that she'd been treated by her own GP for some time for possible angina. Yesterday there was a muddle in the hospital computer and as a result her hip-replacement was delayed. She'd been very agitated about that and she was also apprehensive. You may tell your prioress that she died almost instantaneously."

"If she'd died about two hours before then it seems odd that nobody noticed her sooner."

"Nothing odd about it at all," he said with an edge of irritation. "The nurses do a quick check every couple of hours or so. At midnight the ward sister who's on duty does general rounds with one of the student nurses. Ward Sister Sophie Meecham's on duty this week. Sister Williams — she will attain the dizzy heights of ward sister once she's qualified — went with her."

"And Ward Sister Tracy Collet was on that particular ward. She's on reception this morning."

"When she should be off duty. We're short of staff, Sister. Some of the nurses have to do double shifts once a month, but if you've your mind tending towards compensation you can forget it. We do our job properly."

"I wasn't forgetting that you're all dedicated people," Sister Joan said.

"And efficient." He looked at her crossly. "We don't put patients at risk, Sister. Sister Collet had no reason to check on her patients more than once in every two or three hours. What's the point in disturbing them if the patients are sleeping peacefully?"

"You wouldn't know about the funeral arrangements?"

"Not my department. If you phone later on and ask for the almoner then you'll receive the requisite information."

"Thank you, Dr Geeson."

She shook hands again and retraced her footsteps down the corridor with the vague feeling that she ought to ask Tracy Collet a couple more questions. That odd remark about having been too peaceful a death for example. It had probably meant nothing in particular, Sister Joan thought, glancing at the fob watch pinned to her bodice and remembering that she still had Sister Marie and the groceries to collect.

"It's an impacted wisdom tooth," Sister Marie informed her, emerging from the dentist's as Sister Joan arrived. "He's given me painkillers but he thinks I ought to go into hospital to have it out because there's a nasty infection there."

"Has he made the arrangements?" Sister Joan enquired.

"He'll phone when he's got a firm date. Did you have a nice visit?"

"I got through it," Sister Joan said. "We'd better get the groceries, Sister, and then head home. We'll only just make lunch."

Not that missing lunch would be a great sacrifice! Soup and a salad sandwich followed by a piece of fruit was the unvarying menu.

Mother Dorothy was in her parlour when they reached the convent. Sister Joan left Sister Marie to carry in the shopping and hurried through to the antechamber beyond which double doors led into what had once been a large and elegant drawing-room.

It still retained traces of that elegance in the silk panels set at intervals into the pine-clad walls, the finely moulded ceiling with gilded cornices, the long white velour curtains at the French windows, but the polished floor was bare of carpet, the Adam chimneypiece surrounded a bare grate; a row of steel filing cabinets stood against one wall; a handsome flat-topped desk and chair and a row of stools had replaced the sofas of an earlier age.

"*Dominus vobiscum.*" Mother Dorothy answered Sister Joan's tap-tap on the door with the customary salutation used when the prioress was in her own domain.

"*Et cum spiritu tuo.*" Sister Joan knelt

briefly, then rose, hands clasped at waist level within her wide sleeves according to custom.

"You completed your hospital visit?" Mother Dorothy settled her spectacles more firmly on her nose.

"Yes, Mother Prioress. I took Sister Marie with me because her toothache has been very painful. She's been advised to go into hospital to have an impacted wisdom tooth removed."

"Is that necessary?"

"Apparently there's an infection. The dentist says he'll contact the hospital and make the arrangements. There's usually a waiting list for minor ops so Sister Marie may have to wait a week or two."

"Anything more?"

"Your godmother, Mrs Louisa Cummings." Sister Joan hesitated. "I'm very sorry, Mother, but she died of a heart attack late last night before the hip replacement could be carried out. I spoke to a Dr Geeson who has advised that you telephone the almoner later on. She will know about funeral arrangements etc. I'm very sorry, Mother Dorothy."

"Auntie Lou dead." Only the unexpected diminution of the name betrayed feeling. Mother Dorothy crossed herself slowly, murmuring the accepted formula. "May her soul and the souls of all the faithful departed rest in peace."

"Through the mercy of God. Amen." Sister Joan crossed herself too. "I'm sorry to bring you such news, Mother Dorothy."

"We hadn't met for many years, but she was very kind to me when I was a child. Thank you, Sister. I'll ring the almoner later on today and also Father Malone. I imagine he will be offering the requiem mass. I shall attend it myself if my duties permit. You'd better go and help Sister Teresa to lay out the lunch. Sister Marie won't be feeling well. *Dominus vobiscum.*"

"*Et cum spiritu sancto.*"

Glancing back as she left the parlour Sister Joan saw that her superior had risen and moved to the window where she stood gazing out, shoulders tight with unexpressed pain.

It wasn't until the following afternoon that the prioress referred again to the death, waiting until her nuns were ranged on the stools before her desk in readiness for the afternoon talk which occupied the hour between three and four every weekday and usually consisted of the exploration of a spiritual or moral theme. This month they were going to concentrate on the seven deadly sins and the consequences of committing them. Mother Dorothy, however, surveyed the expectant faces before her measuringly before she said, "I had intended to begin analysing greed today which is, I am convinced, a natural outcome of our present materialistic society, but something has occurred of which you must be informed. By coincidence the event has some bearing on today's subject. My godmother, Mrs Louisa Cummings, died very recently at St Keyne's Hospital from a heart attack. She was seventy-five years old and had, I understand, had heart problems for some time. We had not met for several years but we did maintain an occasional correspondence."

"May I offer condolences on behalf of the rest of us?" Sister Perpetua said.

"Thank you, Sister. You're very kind." Mother Dorothy inclined her head and was interrupted by Sister Hilaria, who sat next to her novice, her somewhat prominent grey eyes fixed on the large crucifix behind the desk.

"I often think," she said in the lightly accented voice that was so much at variance with her gaunt face and frame, "that we ought to offer congratulations when someone dies. They are after all going into a better life."

"And leaving the rest of us behind," Sister Gabrielle said. "I, for one, will be highly offended if you all start congratulating one another when I go."

"Then we should condole with people when children are born," Sister Katherine reasoned, "since they've just come from Heaven into a very troubled world."

"Sister, the newborn are sparks of divinity intended for Heaven after their lives on earth," Sister Mary Concepta objected.

"Seems a bit of a waste of time when you think about it," Sister Teresa said thoughtfully. "I mean if we're all destined for Heaven then why get born at all?"

"We have to earn our place there," Sister Martha said.

"But if the Mercy of God is infinite then we'll all get there anyway," a voice murmured.

"Speak for yourself, Mary Concepta!" Sister Gabrielle said. "If that's true there are certain people in the afterlife with whom I certainly won't be hobnobbing!"

Mother Dorothy's small wooden gavel tapped on its block.

"May we keep to the point, Sisters?" She paused for an instant to collect her thoughts, then went on, "Death is never easy for those who are left behind. My godmother had no family to mourn her. She was childless and had been widowed for several years. I spoke to the almoner and also to Father Malone who will conduct her funeral service tomorrow morning. I have also heard from her solicitor. She has left her property to me. You see now how apt our subject for discussion today is."

"Was she a millionairess?" Sister Katherine asked.

"No, Sister, but her husband left her fairly comfortably provided for," Mother Dorothy said with a rebuking glance. "She owned a small house in Devon, near Plymouth, which is left outright to us, and the sum of fifty thousand pounds. It is a grave responsibility since, of course, it goes to our community."

"Wow!" said Sister Teresa and clapped her hand over her mouth.

"After the legal fees," Mother Dorothy said with another quelling glance, "her estate will total about one hundred thousand pounds. Her house which we can either sell or rent is valued at fifty thousand and we may expect fifty thousand from the rest of her estate. That is a very great deal of money, Sister, and I wouldn't feel justified in keeping the whole amount solely for our own use. I'm sure you agree with me on that?"

There were nods, some more enthusiastic than others.

"I will send twenty-five thousand pounds to the Mother House to be distributed among our other convents," Mother Dorothy said. "As for the remainder we must not be selfish with it."

There were more nods.

"I therefore propose to donate two thousand pounds to four charities and two thousand to Father Malone."

"Father Malone will be over the moon!" Sister Marie exclaimed. "He'll give most of it away, of course!"

"And that will make his pleasure the greater. I also propose to donate two thousand five hundred pounds each to the children's home and to St Keyne's Hospital. The remaining ten thousand will be placed in our bank account against future need. That, I'm sure, meets with everybody's approval?"

"What about the house?" Sister Perpetua asked.

"I have asked the solicitor to have it securely locked for the moment. Later in the year someone will be deputed to go over and check the contents and by that time we shall have more idea what to do about the property. Now, shall we begin the afternoon's discussion. Greed is a most serious sin so let us begin with a prayer to God to protect us from it."

Bowing her head with the others, Sister Joan thought with a touch of sadness that no death was entirely without gain to somebody. Yet the money and the house would be useful.

"Sister Joan." As they filed out at the end of the talk Mother Dorothy detained her for a moment.

"Yes, Mother?"

"Tomorrow afternoon I shall be going to the funeral of my godmother so you will drive me and accompany me to the service."

"Yes, Mother Dorothy."

It would be a solemn occasion but not one marked by much personal grief, she reflected. The passing of Louisa Cummings had caused no more than a ripple on the surface of the everyday.

The next day brought sunshine and a stiff breeze. Sister Martha had made a wreath of bronze and white chrysanthemums to be laid on the coffin, and Mother Dorothy appeared at the side of the van with a black mourning band around her arm.

Driving the prioress into town wasn't like driving any of the rest of the community. Even if the occasion hadn't been a solemn one Mother Dorothy would have been unlikely to bend from her customary dignity, and Sister

Joan resigned herself to a largely silent and decorous trip.

She was surprised to find several people in the church. Sister Jerome, Father Malone's dour housekeeper, was there, of course. Sister Jerome attended every service. And there was the usual sprinkling of elderly folk who were drawn to other people's funerals as if they were practising for their own. There were also a couple of nurses from St Keyne's and Sister Joan glanced at them with interest, thinking that it was good of them to come, and then that one looked familiar.

Not until they were leaving the church did she remember as the taller of the two stopped with her hand outstretched.

"Isn't it Sister Joan? We met briefly a couple of years ago. I'm Ward Sister Meecham."

"You were walking on the moor." Sister Joan shook hands. "Mother Dorothy, may I introduce Sister Sophie Meecham? She's a nurse at St Keyne's."

"I was the one doing the ward round with Sister Williams here when we found Mrs Cummings," Sophie Meecham said. "Sister Williams is a student nurse and was naturally distressed at the event. At least we can both assure you that she died peacefully."

"Thank you." Mother Dorothy inclined

her head graciously. "These occasions are always sad ones. My late godmother would have appreciated your being here."

"We brought a spray of carnations," Sister Williams said shyly.

She was a fresh-complexioned girl who would be plump later on if she didn't watch her diet. Her cap was slightly crooked and there was something endearingly puppyish about her. Her companion looked more tense and tired as if her seniority weighed her down.

"We have Mrs Cummings's possessions at the hospital," Sophie was saying. "Only what she brought with her when she came from Devon, but we weren't sure — "

"I am her sole heir," Mother Dorothy said. "Sister Joan, instead of coming to the graveside perhaps you'd be good enough to drive to the office of the — almoner?" She glanced at the nurses.

"Yes. The almoner has them ready," Sophie Meecham nodded.

"Shall I come back here then, Mother?" Sister Joan enquired.

"No, Father Malone has kindly invited me to have supper with himself and Father Stephens, and one of them will run me back to the convent later," Mother Dorothy said. "Collect the things and — perhaps you'd look through them yourself, Sister? I confess that I would find the task somewhat upsetting."

"I'll go now then, Mother. If you're sure there's nothing else I can do — ?"

"Ask Sister Perpetua to take my place at supper. I'll be back directly after recreation."

Dismissed and somewhat relieved that she wouldn't have to endure the half-hour in the cemetery, Sister Joan stood back, waiting until the coffin with its two floral tributes had been loaded into the hearse and Mother Dorothy, flanked by the two nurses, had stepped into the following car before she turned and went to get into the van again.

At least she had a sound excuse for going to the hospital again. If Sister Collet was on duty she'd ask her what she'd meant by her odd remark about Mrs Cummings having died too peacefully. The words had stuck in her mind and refused to be dislodged.

She was in luck. The same nurse was at the reception desk in the main building and looked up with a smile as Sister Joan came in.

"Are you visiting again, Sister?" she enquired.

"Not really. I'm here to collect Mrs Cummings's belongings," Sister Joan said.

"They're in the almoner's office, first right

down the corridor. Would you like a cup of tea, Sister?"

"Thank you. Will you be on duty for a while here?"

"Worse luck!" Sister Collet made a wry face. "I'm on double duty this week. Walking the wards most of the night and answering the telephone here alternate mornings and afternoons. I tell you, Sister, anyone who goes in for nursing these days has to be crazy."

"I sometimes feel the same about religious vocations," Sister Joan said, heading for the almoner's office where, after signing an official-looking paper, she was allowed to take possession of a suitcase.

At the reception desk, Sister Collet was already sipping her tea. A second cup covered by its saucer waited for Sister Joan who balanced herself on the high stool and murmured her appreciation.

"There's nothing like a nice cup of tea or coffee, especially after a funeral service," she said.

"Yes, poor Mrs Cummings!" Tracy Collet looked suitably grave. "Not that I knew her, mind you. She'd only been on the ward a few days and she wasn't the chatty sort. Rather an imperious old lady if you know what I mean. But not difficult, not really."

"She was upset that her operation was postponed, I understand."

"More irritable about it," Tracy Collet said. "She grumbled about the muddle and said she really had hoped to get the whole business over with but she'd settled down all right by the time supper was brought round. I certainly never expected her to have a heart attack about it later on, but you never can tell with old ladies."

"And you checked up on her about ten o'clock?"

"Like I told Dr Geeson. I sat at my desk at the top of the ward near the door most of the time. Then every couple of hours I'd walk up and down a couple of times, checking here and there. Mrs Cummings was asleep."

"And then you went to the toilet you said?"

"I checked the patients at ten and then again at eleven," Tracy Collet said. "One of them wanted a glass of water. The others were all fast asleep. I didn't look at anyone closely. Then I went to the toilet just before midnight. When I got back Sophie Meecham and Ceri Williams were there with Dr Geeson."

"You must've been a long time in the loo," Sister Joan said mildly.

"Longer than I wanted to be," Tracy

Collet said, "but I'd had a queasy stomach all evening. In fact I was sick a couple of times. Something I ate I daresay." She was looking slightly puzzled at the questioning.

"I wondered why you said that Mrs Cummings had died too peacefully," Sister Joan said.

"Oh, it was only that — " Tracy Collet hesitated, biting her lip. "It was only that the cover on her bed was perfectly smooth."

"She died in her sleep surely."

"Of a sudden, massive heart attack, yes, but one of her hands was clenched into a tight fist. There must've been a split second when she'd felt a searing pain. Yet the covers were all smooth."

"Her arms were outside them?"

"Yes. No, her left arm was under the covers." Tracy Collet screwed up her eyes in an effort to recreate the scene in her mind. "The right arm with the hand clenched was outside the covers but the covers were smooth. I'm sorry, Sister. It's really not important only it stuck in my head. She was lying on her back and — no, there wasn't anything else I noticed. Why are you asking?"

"Mrs Cummings was Mother Dorothy's godmother so naturally she wants to be sure that there was no pain involved."

"Apart from one last spasm, no. A split second, no more. Your Mother Dorothy can comfort herself with that."

"Right! Well, I'd better get back to the convent." Sister Joan slid from the stool and picked up the suitcase. "Thank you for the tea. I'm sure you did everything you could for the old lady, but we can't cheat death when push comes to shove. Are you feeling better yourself?"

"I'll be glad when this double-duty nonsense is over and I can sleep round the clock," Tracy Collet said. "'Bye, Sister."

In the van she put the suitcase on the passenger seat and drove sedately back to the convent. The community was still in the afternoon talk which meant that Sister Hilaria was taking the discussion. When the novice mistress chaired anything she was apt to go off into some deep metaphysical speculation and not notice that nearly everybody else was chatting. "Sister Hilaria," Mother Dorothy had once pronounced in response to a question from Sister Joan, "may strike you as completely unworldly and impractical but she is almost a living rule, Sister. If we lost the constitution devised by our founder — may her memory serve as perpetual blessing! — we could rewrite it again simply by observing the conduct of Sister Hilaria. It's very good for them to be in daily contact with one whose life is so utterly God centred."

At least the extended discussion would give her the chance to check the contents of the suitcase. Mother Dorothy had cared more for her godmother than her habit of detachment had permitted her to reveal.

She went through to the main entrance hall and across to the chapel wing opposite the prioress's parlour. The passage with its row of small windows ran past the visitors' parlour, with the grille separating Sisters from laity, to the chapel, once the family chapel for the Tarquins but now the regular place of worship for the nuns and for any member of the public who might wish to attend.

At the side of the Lady Altar a spiral staircase twisted up to the upper storey. A library had been established there, shelves of books neatly catalogued by Sister David, who spent much of her time up here, working on the Latin and Greek translations that brought a little income to the community and working also on the *Children's Lives of the Saints* which it was hoped would attract a publisher when it was completed. Sister David was up to Saint Nicholas.

"I know that some people declare he was only a bishop who had certain legends attached to his name but children ought to know who the original of Santa Claus is, don't you think?" she had queried anxiously, rabbit nose twitching.

Sister Joan lugged the suitcase into the adjoining series of attics that completed the upper floor. The attics were scrubbed and bare now, the flotsam and jetsam of years cleared out. She set down her burden near one of the skylights, squatted beside it and snapped back the locks.

Someone else had packed the case, laying underwear and two nightdresses neatly between sheets of tissue. Mother Dorothy would almost certainly want the clothes to go to a charity. The Little Way and Cafod were her favourite ones. Under the nether garments were two blouses, a pair of wide-legged trousers, a cardigan and a wraparound skirt patterned in two shades of green. There were two pairs of low-heeled shoes and a jointed, expanding walking stick. Good quality materials, conventional style. Someone had washed and ironed them. Almost certainly they had been already clean when Mrs Cummings had brought them to the hospital, but now they bore no trace of the woman who had worn them. They were merely garments, devoid of personality.

Beneath the garments, protected by more tissue and secured by two broad straps were the rest of Louisa Cummings's things: a sponge bag in a floral design with toilet accessories inside, hairbrush and comb that smelt now faintly of Dettol, a sachet of paper handkerchiefs, a box of soluble aspirin, a make-up case with powder, foundation, blusher and lipstick neatly slotted into place. Mrs Cummings had retained her feminine vanity. A block of notepaper and two pens had been slid into a plastic bag; the block was smooth and not written on. There was a roll of cotton wool, a small tube of liniment, a box containing a solitaire diamond ring and a gold wedding-ring, a photograph of a middle-aged man with a suntan — the late Mr Cummings, no doubt — two paperback books — Louisa Cummings had enjoyed thrillers — a pair of reading spectacles in a leather case, rosary beads and a Cornish Pisky, perched crosslegged on top of a thick pencil. A neat handbag with a shoulder strap was at the bottom. Sister Joan opened it with a faint shiver of reluctance. Handbags were such personal objects. Some people carried clues to their innermost selves in their handbags.

This one contained only a small bunch of keys (house keys?), a mirror, a tiny phial of eau-de-cologne and a wallet containing a credit card, a bank card and fifty pounds in loose change and notes.

One object remained: a thin exercise book with hard covers was wedged into the corner of the suitcase. Sister Joan tugged it free and opened it.

Mrs Cummings had obviously used it as a commonplace book such as the Victorians had been fond of. There were shopping lists and recipes jotted down between extracts from various poems, dates which clearly marked birthdays and other anniversaries, reminders to order fish, bits and pieces cut out from newspapers and sellotaped in. Mrs Cummings had been an active member of the Churchwoman's Catholic Guild with her name appearing regularly in items published in a local paper. Here and there among the entries, a few sentences were dated in the manner of someone who doesn't keep a regular diary but wishes to mark some days.

June, 1994, 6th day.
Harold would have been seventy-eight today. Funny to recall that he was in the Normandy Landings on his birthday. I remember how worried we all were, not knowing exactly what was going on until

it was all over. And the relief when the good news came! Seems a pity we can't celebrate it together.

Other entries were equally unilluminating though Sister Joan thought they had their own pathos. She read on here and there.

Dec 26th, 1994.
Very quiet Xmas. Dorothy sent me a very pretty scarf and a hand-painted card. Dear girl! It seems aeons since we met. Still find it hard to think of her as a prioress. Well, even the most mischievous child can astonish one.

Sister Joan repressed a snort of mirth at the idea of Mother Dorothy as a naughty little girl and turned the page.

August, 1995, 27th day.
Settled in at St Keyne's but not really happy. Nurses always in a hurry going somewhere or other, and very muddling since they all seem to be Sister So-and-So now. Doctor very young and thinks he knows it all. People these days won't listen! Tried to tell him that the tablets have been changed, but he says they haven't. Thinks that I'm a bit wanting

in wits, I daresay. Will ask him again when I get the chance.

The rest of the neatly ruled exercise book was blank. Sister Joan read the entry again and sat back on her heels, frowning. So Mrs Cummings had been under the impression that her regular medication had been changed. Possibly it had been for the good and simple reason that she had been due for a general anaesthetic within a few days and extra care was being taken. And old ladies did sometimes imagine things.

After a moment's thought she took the book through into the library and wedged it on one of the lower shelves. The rest of the stuff she returned neatly to the case. Snapping the case shut she stood up and carried it downstairs.

"There you are, Sister!" Sister Perpetua was emerging from Mother Dorothy's parlour. "Did everything go well? Where's Mother Dorothy?"

"She stayed behind to take supper with Father Malone but she'll be home directly after recreation. She asks you to take her place at supper."

"Right. Then I'd better get on. I'm trying to persuade Sister Mary Concepta to have the meal in the infirmary because she's been quite breathless this afternoon, but she can be as obstinate as Sister Gabrielle when she's a mind. What's that? Are you rushing off somewhere?" Sister Perpetua nodded at the suitcase.

"It's Mrs Cummings's belongings — what she took with her to the hospital. Mother Dorothy told me to collect it and check it through."

"Best leave it in her parlour then," Sister Perpetua said. "Then find something useful to do."

Of all the nuns that particular injunction seemed to be addressed the most often to herself, Sister Joan thought wryly. The problem was that at the moment she had no distinctive function. Prioress and novice mistress had their allotted roles; Sister Perpetua was in her element as infirmarian and wouldn't have relinquished it without a struggle; Sister Martha kept the gardens and Sister Katherine dealt with the linen; Sister David combined the offices of sacristan and librarian and the lay-sisters, Teresa and Maria, shared the cooking and the cleaning. If she had a regular task then perhaps her mind wouldn't persist in flying off at odd tangents.

Louisa Cummings thought her tablets were different. Louisa Cummings had died too peacefully, one hand clenched, the bedclothes smooth and unwrinkled.

She carried the suitcase into the parlour, set it down, hesitated and picked up the telephone,dialled the hospital and waited.

"Sister Joan from the convent here. Would it be possible for me to have a word with Dr Geeson, please?"

A voice she didn't recognize asked her to wait. Sooner than she'd hoped she heard Dr Geeson's impatient tone.

"Yes? What is it you want, Sister?"

"About Mrs Cummings's medication," Sister Joan said. "Was it changed when she came in to St Keyne's?"

"She was on digoxin, low dosage. We gave her a weaker dose since she was due for surgery. Do you need details?"

"No, that sounds fine. It's what I thought," Sister Joan said.

"I hope nobody's thinking of making any waves," Dr Geeson said irritably. "I can assure you that she'd have died whether or not the dosage had been decreased. She was agitated because of the muddle in the computer, though not to the extent that I thought might have put her at risk. Hearts are peculiar organs, Sister. They can go on for years under the most adverse conditions and then stop suddenly for no apparent reason."

"And Mrs Cummings was agitated?"

"Naturally; having steeled herself for the hip replacement, she wasn't very pleased to be delayed. If that's all, Sister?"

"Yes, thank you. Goodbye, Doctor."

Nothing to worry about then. She replaced the receiver and went through to help with the preparations for supper. Vegetable hash tonight with a fruit pie to follow. Only Alice was permitted meat.

Peeling vegetables, feeding Alice and giving her a second walk through the grounds in the hope of burning off some of her boisterous energy, laying the table, snatching ten minutes in which to write up her spiritual diary took up the time until the evening benediction, supper itself and the recreation which followed. Sister Hilaria towed Bernadette back to the postulancy since novices were not permitted to join in recreation. Sister Teresa and Marie spent the hour washing-up and cleaning the kitchen. Sister Perpetua checked up on Sister Mary Concepta who had struggled upstairs to the dining-room looking very frail indeed.

The sound of Father Malone's ramshackle old car blurred the silence, stopped and drove off again with a great clashing of gears. Mother Dorothy came in, looking, from Sister Joan's vantage point on the staircase, tired and curiously vulnerable.

"Would you like anything to drink, Mother, before we go into chapel?" she asked, coming down to floor level.

"We'll go directly into chapel. I enjoyed a very nice supper at the presbytery." Mother Dorothy was unpinning the black band on her purple sleeve. "I am glad you didn't come to the second service, Sister. I found it very impersonal, but then I'm old-fashioned, I daresay. Burial has always seemed to me to be so much gentler than cremation."

"Your godmother was cremated?"

"Apparently it was her wish. Cremation is such a final kind of thing, don't you think?" Mother Dorothy said.

3

"Sister Joan, it seems that my late godmother's will can go to probate almost at once," Mother Dorothy said, "which is pleasing since it enables her assets to be distributed without waste of time. I've received a most helpful letter from her solicitor to that effect, and he has kept his fees remarkably low in the circumstances. Not all lawyers are as greedy and grasping as they are depicted."

"St Thomas More," Sister Joan said.

"Indeed so! A very good example. Anyway, my point is that the solicitor sees no reason why matters can't be expedited. I looked through Aunt Louisa's suitcase. One must steel oneself to do such things eventually, and it is nearly a month since her death. I will place her wedding-ring below the altar in the chapel but I had thought of giving her engagement ring to the nurse who tended her during her stay at St Keyne's. It is not, as far as I can judge, a very valuable stone and it would be pleasant to think of it on the hand of a nursing sister, don't you agree?"

"I think it's a very good idea," Sister Joan said.

"The solicitor sees no reason why the gift shouldn't be made immediately. I would like you to go over to the hospital and find out who was in charge of the ward Aunt Louisa was in and give her the ring. You may drive over this afternoon and thank the medical team for their care of her."

"Yes, Mother Dorothy."

Sister Joan took the little box in which the prioress had put the modest ring and knelt for the customary blessing.

The other, however, stayed her hand in mid air, a slight frown corrugating her brow. "I would have thought," she said musingly, "that my godmother's heart would have withstood the trifling annoyance of having her operation delayed for a few hours. In her occasional letters to me she mentioned her heart condition as a nuisance more than a burden. Aunt Louisa was not a woman to suffer pain or discomfort in silence so I assumed that her ailment was being controlled by medication. Of course one can never tell."

She gave the blessing then, sketching a neat, small cross upon the air.

She isn't happy about her godmother's sudden death, Sister Joan thought, as she climbed into the van. She wants me to make a few discreet enquiries without actually telling me to do so.

The realization surprised her. Mother Dorothy had never approved much of Sister Joan's penchant for landing feet first in a mystery. Now, she had seemed to be giving her younger colleague tacit permission to ask a few leading questions. Probably to put her own mind at rest since there was no proving now that anything untoward had happened, but it denoted an interesting change of attitude on the part of her superior.

She drove out on to the moorland track, slowing and stopping as she neared the small stone building where Brother Cuthbert lodged in what he regarded as almost sinful luxury, which meant he had a few pieces of furniture, a proper toilet and a small stove on which he could boil a saucepan or in which he could bake a fish.

"Good morning, Sister Joan!" He left off fiddling with the innards of an old broken-down car that stood permanently at the side of his hermitage and came over to the van, wiping his big hands on a rag before reaching in to shake Sister Joan's hand.

"It's a lovely afternoon," Sister Joan said, gently emphasizing the last word.

"Is it afternoon already?" Brother Cuthbert laughed, ruffling up his fiery crown of hair.

"Goodness, doesn't time stand still when life's so good. I promised myself that I'd walk up to the convent today to present my condolences to Reverend Mother Prioress."

"Mother Dorothy's godmother died over three weeks ago," Sister Joan reminded him.

"Father Malone was telling me that the lady had left her property to Mother Prioress. What a terrible burden for a religious to bear!"

"She plans to share it out," Sister Joan said. "You may yet be burdened, Brother!"

"Oh, I do pray not!"

He looked so distressed that she said quickly, "As far as I know she's giving you nothing at all, but even if she does you can have the pleasure of giving it away. You could buy toys for the kids in the children's home." Privately she decided to mention that to Mother Dorothy.

Brother Cuthbert said, "You're right, of course, Sister. I always look at things from a selfish viewpoint. Yes, it would be rather fun to buy toys for the children. Well, we'll see. I'd not want to be seen as a kind of Father Christmas, but there! life has its little problems."

"Go and get yourself some lunch," Sister Joan said severely, starting up the van again.

"Lunch? Yes, yes, indeed I will."

Brother Cuthbert stepped away and called a cheerful 'God bless' as the van moved off. No doubt he was already thinking happily of dolls and train sets, she thought. In Brother Cuthbert's world everything was simple. There was no room for little girls with bruised faces who avoided human contact because they had known only blows.

She slowed down as she reached the main street of the town. Mother Dorothy hadn't requested it but it might be a good idea to have the ring valued anyway since presumably its recipient would want to get it insured. With this in mind she parked at the side of the bank and walked on the few yards to the jeweller's shop, where Mr Trevellyan presided over trinkets, clocks and watches.

"It's a very neat piece of workmanship." He screwed in his eyeglass firmly and peered at it. "Rather an old-fashioned setting. Stones not very high quality — the chips at each side of the solitaire are diamante. The gold isn't of such great value either, rather worn. But it's a pretty piece."

"How much would it be worth?"

"About four hundred pounds? For insurance purposes I'd plump for three hundred."

Behind her an amused voice said, "Going in for a bit of jewel-fencing now, Sister?"

"Good afternoon, Detective Sergeant Mill."

Sister Joan turned to greet the tall police officer who'd just come in. "No, I've not yet been driven to crime. How are you?"

"Fine." His dark eyes under the winged black brows assessed her. "You're looking well yourself. This hot summer doesn't seem to have drained your energy."

"It has been lovely, hasn't it?" Her own blue eyes sparkled. "We really have enjoyed it. We did most of our work out of doors to take advantage of the sunshine. Your boys will have enjoyed their holidays too, I daresay."

"They went off camping with friends for most of the time. A couple of parents went along too to keep an eye on them, so that was reassuring."

She had never seen his two schoolboy sons nor enquired their names. They were away at boarding-school anyway. Neither had she ever met his wife though she knew that the marriage had been through some sticky patches.

He spoke of her now, abruptly and factually.

"Samantha and I went to visit her parents for a couple of weeks."

Samantha, not Sam or Sammy. She hadn't heard his wife's name before. On the occasions that she and Alan Mill had collaborated on some mystery his private affairs had scarcely been mentioned.

"I'm sure you could both do with the break," she said. "Mr Trevellyan, can you write down the valuation for me? For insurance purposes?"

"Right away, Sister. And I'll waive my charge." Drawing a piece of paper towards him he began to write on it neatly.

"Mother Dorothy's godmother died recently," Sister told Detective Sergeant Mill, "and willed her estate to her. Mother felt that the nurse who cared for Mrs Cummings should have a memento."

"The lady who died at St Keyne's recently?"

"Yes. Did you know her?"

"Not at all, but Constable Petrie makes it his business to keep a list of local deaths. He's secretly hoping for another murder investigation, I think." The detective chuckled. "He keeps wistfully harking back to past cases. You may not realize it, Sister, but he's your second biggest fan."

His sudden teasing smile informed her who was the first. Hastily Sister Joan turned back to the counter and received the ring and the valuation.

"No problems, I hope?" Mr Trevellyan looked warily at his second customer.

"None as far as I know. I'm here to buy something for my wife," Detective Sergeant Mill said. "Something suitable for an anniversary."

"Congratulations," Sister Joan said, preparing to leave.

"Sixteen years." His face bore no particular expression. "She wears suits quite often so a brooch might be appropriate."

"The sixteenth is silver holloware," Sister Joan said. "A silver-plated vase or something like that."

"Fancy your knowing that!" He stared at her for a moment.

"We have anniversaries in the Order too. Of our final professions."

"And your next one will be — ?"

"The sixth. I made my final profession just before Christmas."

She remembered the fall of embroidered white silk against her legs as she moved up the aisle, her own quick sideways glance towards the grille behind which her family stood. Jacob hadn't been there and she'd felt a mixture of the most intense relief and the most crushing disappointment.

"And what's the appropriate gift for the sixth?" he enquired.

"Iron."

"Steel under velvet would be more

appropriate," he said. "So it's silver holloware? Show me a couple of vases or something, will you?"

"I must go. Nice seeing you again, Detective Sergeant Mill. God bless, Mr Trevellyan."

As she left the shop she heard him say carelessly, "That one will do. Looks rather elegant, don't you think?"

Sister Joan shook her head mentally at the casual tone and went back to the van where she found Constable Petrie regarding the vehicle gloomily.

"If you'd been one minute longer I'd've had to book you, Sister," he said. "On a double yellow line you are!"

"Surely not! Constable, I'm sorry but there isn't usually a double yellow line there, is there?" Sister Joan said in dismay.

"There's always a double yellow line where you park, Sister," Constable Petrie said, grinning at his own wit. "If you drive off now then I won't have seen you, will I?"

"Thank you, Constable Petrie!" Climbing behind the driving seat she asked, "Are all well at home?"

"Right as rain, thank you, Sister. The wife's expecting again. Number three this one will be."

"You must be very pleased," Sister Joan said.

"Well, to tell you truly we're both tickled pink, Sister!" He beamed at her. "My Sally is a wonderful mother, you know. Absolutely first class. Yes, we're both pleased!"

And 'my Sally' would get a gift on her anniversary chosen with loving care, Sister Joan thought with a tinge of sadness, driving away from the offending double yellow lines and heading out past the railway station and the bingo hall towards the hospital.

Nurse Ceri Williams raised her face from the list she was studying and greeted her with a smile that was still more enthusiastic than professional.

"Yes, Sister, may I help you?"

"You were with Sister Meecham when Mrs Louisa Cummings was found?" Sister Joan stopped, seeing the distress that flashed into the young face.

"I was due to make the rounds of the wards at midnight," the girl said, "so I went up to the office and told her it was time to start."

"Sister Meecham has her own office?" Sister Joan said, surprised.

"No, there's an office on the third floor of this main building," the other explained. "The hospital computer, we call it Clarrie, is kept there. Whoever's on ward rounds usually waits in the office, writes up her notes and takes telephone calls until it's time to go round. A student nurse goes round too, to get the feel of the thing so to speak."

"How many student nurses are there?"

"There were three of us, but Ann Croft had to give up the course and go home when her father was taken ill, so there's just Carol Prince and me. Carol was on holiday that week."

"And it was Sister Tracy Collet who was nursing Mrs Cummings?"

"Well, she wasn't exactly ill, Sister," Ceri Williams said. "She had a bit of a heart problem and she had a lot of trouble walking. She'd been waiting several months for a hip-replacement operation and in the end they transferred her here because there was a bed available, but she wasn't bedridden really. Sister Collet had quite a time persuading her to stay put and not go limping around the place. She was quite a — difficult old lady."

"A feisty old gal!" Sister Joan said, smiling. "Where's Sister Collet this afternoon?"

"She's on the ward, Sister. Is anything wrong?"

"I have a small token of appreciation from

Mother Prioress for her," Sister Joan said. "The surgical ward's on the floor above this one, isn't it? I remember from when Sister Hilaria suffered a slight accident and was brought here."[1]

"You can take the lift."

"I'll take the stairs," Sister Joan said. "I need the exercise."

"Was that all you wanted?" Ceri Williams detained her for a moment. "I mean — there isn't any trouble, is there?"

"What kind of trouble should there be?" Sister Joan countered.

"Oh, none." Ceri Williams looked uncomfortable. "It's only that — well, I was a bit surprised that Mrs Cummings died when she did, that's all. I mean, when someone has a heart attack they generally make a few groaning, gasping noises, and Mrs Cummings apparently didn't. Of course the other patients were asleep and Sister Collet did leave the ward a couple of times, but even so!"

"When you found Mrs Cummings how was she lying?" Sister Joan asked.

"On her back. Her mouth was slightly open. Her hand was clenched into a fist.

---

[1] See *Vow of Obedience*

She must've had a last spasm or something. I'd never been at a death before — well just after a death to be more accurate. It hits you even when you hardly know the person."

"Two hours after the death," Sister Joan said. "Yes, it must take time to get used to the more unpleasant aspects of nursing. Do you remember anything about the covers on the bed?"

"On Mrs Cummings's bed?" Ceri Williams looked puzzled. "No, I wasn't looking at the covers. Why?"

"No special reason," Sister Joan said. "I'd better get up to see Sister Collet before she goes off duty or something. Thank you, Sister Williams."

She went briskly up the stairs and emerged on the wide upper landing with arrows pointing to the various wards. The old maternity wards had been incorporated in the new maternity unit as had the former children's ward been shifted into another new building. The old wards seemed to have been transformed into a lecture room, a couple of sitting-rooms and a long narrow kitchen in which two women in green overalls were washing the floor.

Sister Joan excused herself and followed the arrows in the opposite direction towards the surgical ward. Two smaller wards intended for seriously ill patients preceded it.

The swing doors of glass gave her a good view of the long, gleaming ward with its rows of white-covered beds before she stepped through and approached the desk at which Sister Collet was seated.

She didn't look well, was Sister Joan's first thought as she raised her head, blinking slightly. Her face was pale and there were dark shadows beneath her eyes.

"Oh, Sister Joan." She rose, obviously pulling her concentration back from some private train of thought. "How nice to see you."

"Can you spare me a couple of minutes?" Sister Joan asked.

Tracy Collet looked at her fob watch and nodded. "I'm due over in the children's ward in ten minutes anyway," she said. "Sister Prince, will you take over here? They'll be bringing the teas round soon."

A dark-haired nurse halfway down the ward looked up and nodded.

"Carol Prince?" Sister Joan said.

"She's our other student nurse. Quite promising but rather apt to jolly the patients along when they just want to be left in peace. Sister Williams has a more sensitive manner. But they're both good nurses. I've a bottle of Lucozade in my locker. Would you like some?"

"It'd be a lovely change," Sister Joan said truthfully.

"Well, it peps up the energy levels," Tracy Collet said, leading the way into one of the sitting-rooms. "Sit down, Sister Joan. I'll get a couple of mugs."

The drink was golden and sparkling. Sister Joan sipped with relish.

"You wanted to see me, Sister?"

Tracy Collet had taken a chair opposite, leaning her elbows on the small table between them with an air of utter weariness.

"With rather pleasant news actually," Sister Joan said. "You nursed the late Mrs Cummings."

"Not actually nursed," Tracy Collet said quickly. "She wasn't actually ill."

"Well, you made her comfortable during the few days she was here. Anyway Mother Prioress wishes you to have a small souvenir of her godmother so she hopes you'll accept this. It was her engagement ring, not very valuable but I had it assessed for insurance purposes."

Opening the little box she held it out. To her astonishment Sister Collet took one look and burst into tears.

"Oh, please!" Sister Joan stared at her

in consternation. “It really isn’t anything to upset yourself about. I’m sure that Mrs Cummings would’ve been glad for you to have it.”

“I’m sorry!” The other groped for a tissue, held it to her eyes and scrubbed at her eyelids fiercely, her breath coming jerkily. “It’s only that — I never expected for a moment. How silly you must think me!”

“You’re probably overtired,” Sister Joan said.

“Yes, I think I must be. Shortage of staff, long hours — I do apologize.” She blew her nose vigorously on the tissue and dropped it into a wastepaper basket at the side of her chair.

“It must be exhausting work even though it is so worthwhile,” Sister Joan said.

“Oh, it can be very rewarding. This is a lovely ring!” Tracy Collet took it out of the box and slipped it on to her middle finger. “It was really good of your prioress to think of me. Look, I have to be in the children’s ward in a few minutes, but I must just write a little thank-you note. Would you like to go over there and wait for me?”

“Fine. I’ll see you there in a few minutes then.”

Sister Joan finished her drink and rose, giving the other a smiling nod as she went out. No doubt Tracy Collet wanted to compose herself before going across to the children's unit. It must be as hard for a nursing sister to learn objectivity as it was for a nun.

Halfway down the corridor she turned back into the surgical ward. The student nurse who'd been left in charge looked up from the desk, slight trepidation in her voice as she said, "There isn't anyone here who's terribly ill, Sister."

"This isn't an official sort of visit," Sister Joan said chattily. "How are you enjoying working here?"

"So far!" The girl grinned cheerfully "Mind you, I was ready for my holiday. We went to Spain."

"We?"

"Me and my boyfriend. It was all very respectable, honestly."

"I bet it wasn't really," Sister Joan said with a twinkle.

Carol Prince looked at her and giggled. "Well, it was nothing heavy," she said.

"You're Carol Prince?"

"Yes, and you're Sister — ?"

"Joan. So how do you manage to get all the work done when St Keyne's is so short of staff?"

"Everybody works flat out most of the

time," Carol Prince said. "Of course we do have some volunteer ladies who come in to make tea and bring round library books and so on."

"But they don't come in the evenings?"

"No. In the evenings we often have to do double duty," Carol Prince grimaced. "Even the doctors have to work very long shifts. I don't think that's right, do you, Sister?"

"No, I don't."

"It makes them very irritable," Carol Prince confided, dropping her voice. "Mind you, that Dr Geeson is bad tempered even when he's had twelve hours' sleep straight off! He's ever so abrupt and po-faced. Sister Collet cannot stand him! Oh, she's never said so, of course. She's very discreet, but I can tell from her manner. And he can speak quite sharply to Ward Sister Meecham too, and she's the senior ward nurse! Did you want to have a word with any of the patients?"

"Were any of them here three weeks ago?" Sister Joan enquired.

Carol Prince shook her head. "No, when I came back from holiday there were all new faces here," she said. "Most cases heal up quite quickly these days and we don't encourage them to stay bed-bound. It's very bad for the heart and anyway there's always a shortage of beds."

"With you spending your time rushing up and down the wards." Sister Joan clucked her tongue. "You must walk miles!"

"Oh, it's not so bad. Actually if you look down there you'll see a door, right by the corner bed," Carol Prince said. "We can slip down to the kitchen and make a quick cup of coffee and slip back upstairs in a jiffy. It's very handy."

"I'm sure it must be." Sister Joan gazed thoughtfully down the ward, aware that the patients had left off their own murmured conversations and were looking in her direction.

They probably think I'm here to convert them, she thought with an inward grin.

"Ward Sister Meecham is supposed to be coming to relieve me in a few minutes," Carol Prince said. "Sister Collet was due in the children's unit."

"Which is where I promised to be," Sister Joan said. "Thanks for the chat. Don't let yourself get too exhausted! I'm sure it doesn't make for more efficiency."

"You're right, Sister." Carol Prince nodded as she half rose to shake hands. "When people are tired they're apt to make mistakes — feeding Clarrie with the wrong information, not putting the right amounts on the drug register, forgetting who takes sugar in their cocoa. Nice meeting you, Sister."

Sister Joan went down the main staircase and through to the reception area. There was a youngish man in a blue overall at the desk whom she recognized.

"Mr Johns! Nice to see you again." She greeted him cordially. "I thought you'd retired."

"For about five minutes. I got very fed up just hanging around the house getting under the wife's feet so about ten days ago I offered to come back part-time. They were very glad of the offer especially as I only get expenses. There's no money available any more, Sister," he said. "Mind, you being a nun wouldn't notice."

Sister Joan smiled and went on through the main door, refraining from pointing out that even at the convent bills had to be paid, some groceries bought.

Outside, the air was unseasonably warm considering that the year was sliding towards October. The sky was a bright, hot blue, the flower heads in the border drooping. She crunched over the gravel and went into the unit, hearing the rising and falling of young voices and a more mature voice laughingly disclaiming something or other.

Someone had emerged from a car in the

car-park and came in behind her. Sister Joan, half turning, recognized one of the social workers from the children's home.

"Sister Joan, are you hospital visiting?" The square-shouldered young woman shook hands briskly.

"Not officially. How are you, Miss Fleetwood?"

Shirley Fleetwood who wasn't quite sure enough of herself not to resent being called by her Christian name looked gratified at the formal mode of address.

"Busy as usual," she said. "Not that I complain! I enjoy my work. I'm here today to assess a child called — " She consulted a paper in her hand. "Amy Foster. Cruelty case. Happily it was the foster parents and not the natural parents who were charged. Foster as with a small f."

"Surely cruelty is bad from whomever it comes," Sister Joan demurred.

"But the child hadn't bonded with them. Of course they ought to have been checked out far more carefully. We do try but a few occasionally slip through the net. It gives the department a bad name."

"It can't be awfully good for the children either," Sister Joan said dryly.

"Children are resilient." Shirley Fleetwood bestowed her faintly superior smile upon the smaller woman and went past her as a nurse approached.

"Good afternoon, Miss Fleetwood. Sister."

It was the nurse she had seen on her previous visit here. Sister Joan had the impression that she wasn't overjoyed to see either of them. Efficient, good hearted, a stickler for routine — Sister Joan firmly checked her thoughts, reminding herself that it wasn't fair to judge anyone from a few minutes' acquaintanceship.

"I'm meeting Sister Collet here," she said.

"She's not here," the nurse said. "You're welcome to wait. You've come about Amy, Miss Fleetwood?"

"How is she, Nurse?" Shirley Fleetwood asked.

"Sister." The nurse looked slightly offended. "Sister Warren. All the nurses are Sisters at St Keyne's."

"Sister Warren." Shirley Fleetwood raised her eyebrows slightly as if the pretensions of a mere nurse amused her. "Has there been any further incident of self-harm?"

"She seems to have settled in much better but quite honestly she requires able-bodied children as her companions."

The two of them went off together, briskly professional, each one guarding her territory. Sister Joan felt like yelling after them, "Who cares what other people call you, for Heaven's sake? There's a small child here who bangs her face against the wall and needs more than competence and socially correct jargon to heal her spirit!"

It wouldn't have done any good. She sat down on a bench and folded hands and lips together.

"It's Sister Joan, isn't it?" A middle-aged nurse came out of a small room nearby and crossed to greet her, hand outstretched, plump face beaming. "I nursed Sister Hilaria when she had her accident. How is she now?"

"Fully recovered, thank God! It's Sister Merryl?"

"Oh, we're all sisters now," the other said with a note of scorn in her voice. "I tell you where equality's the rule pride in one's work simply falls through the floor. I mean what's the use of working hard for promotion when every jumped-up junior can go swanning round calling herself ward sister or whatever? It's supposed to make the patients feel that they're in fully trained, professional hands. Well, let me tell you that patients aren't daft. They know who's experienced and who's not the instant the needle goes in! I made staff nurse and I'm proud of it, but who cares these days? I've been toying with the idea of going into private nursing. It would give me time to get to know the patient instead of being shifted from one section to another the way it is now."

"You didn't nurse Mrs Cummings at any time, did you?" Sister Joan broke into the flow.

"Was that the patient who came in for a hip-replacement operation and had a heart attack? No, I was doing a stint over in casualty that week. See what I mean? No chance to get really involved with the patients, to make them understand that they're individuals. I suppose it makes for detachment but it hasn't got much to do with compassion."

"You're absolutely right, Sister Merryl," Sister Joan agreed.

"Were you waiting for someone?" the nurse enquired.

"For Sister Collet. I was supposed to meet her here."

"Oh, Tracy Collet is never where she's supposed to be," Sister Merryl said impatiently. "Flits about like a moth does Sister Collet! She's a nice enough girl but she's flutter-brained. Sister Meecham now is much steadier. She never forgets to sign the poison register and then rushes back an hour later and scribbles down something illegible."

"Someone's done that recently? Sister Collet?"

"Oh, I wasn't really talking about anyone in particular," Sister Merryl said, looking suddenly embarrassed. "It's just general muddle. No old-style matron would stand for it. I'd better get on. Is the social worker here yet?"

"To assess Amy Foster, yes."

"Poor little mite!" The plump face quivered slightly. "People who ill-treat children ought to be locked up and the key thrown away in my opinion. It's a sad world, Sister Joan."

"In many ways, yes."

Rising, she consulted the fob watch pinned to her habit. Odd but there were many resemblances between nuns and nurses. Both wore uniforms designed to desex them; both wore fob watches and lived according to a routine; both were urged to practise detachment from earthly cares. Nurses were trained to regard their patients with impersonal sympathy; nuns were supposed to carry that to its logical conclusion and detach their affections from every other human being on earth.

She really couldn't justify waiting any longer. Going through the door, leaving the high-pitched chatter of the children behind, Sister Joan found herself thinking about poison registers. Someone, whether Sister Collet or another, had obviously taken something and forgotten to sign for it. That sounded inexcusably careless. However it wasn't likely that she'd learn any more by direct questioning. She'd go back to the main reception area, leave her apologies for Sister Collet and drive back to the convent.

"Sister Joan!" Sophie Meecham was running to catch her up, face flushed with exertion.

"Good afternoon, Sister Meecham."

Sister Joan paused politely, whatever else she'd intended to say driven out of her head as the other said, "Someone should've informed me that you were paying another visit but it's off duty and out of mind anyway. Is anything wrong? Why are you here?"

"Only to give something to Sister Collet," Sister Joan said, taken aback by the other's unexpected vehemence. "She was due to give me a note for Mother Prioress but she must've been delayed."

"I'm sorry. It's only that — one does like to be kept informed," Sophie Meecham said. "I didn't mean to be rude, but I pride myself as chief ward sister in keeping everything running smoothly and when visitors start wandering about — though naturally you're always welcome — "

"Who's in charge of the poisons cupboard?" Sister Joan asked.

"The poisons cupboard?" Sophie Meecham echoed. "We don't have anything like that. We have a drugs unit which is always kept locked. Anyone who requires anything must get the key and sign for what they take. Some of the more volatile substances are kept under refrigeration, of course."

"Who keeps the keys?" Sister Joan asked.

"Each of the four regular doctors has a key and I have one. There's a spare key kept in the manager's office, and his office is locked at night. Why do you want to know all this anyway? There's nothing missing from the drugs unit!"

"I'm pleased to hear it," Sister Joan said mildly.

"I'd better get back on the ward. Shall I tell Sister Collet that you've left?"

"If you don't mind. Ask her to post the note to Mother Dorothy. Thank you, Sister Meecham."

Sophie Meecham stood for an instant, poised as if she were about to soar upwards from the gravel and fly into the hot blue sky. Her mouth was slightly open. A faint quiver of her lips promised words that never came as she turned and headed in the opposite direction.

"My, oh my!" Sister Joan said under her breath. "Now what pressed her panic button, I wonder?"

She walked on thoughtfully towards the van, her mind teeming with possibilities.

4

There was nothing tangible on which to base her suspicions, only the feeling that something wasn't right, didn't gel. Seated in the library, jotting down various points that had occurred to her, Sister Joan couldn't help wondering if she'd reached the stage when anything unexplained was built up by her own imagination as a mystery to be solved. She looked down frowningly at her scribbled notes.

Louisa Cummings, 75, widow. Mild heart condition. Waiting for hip replacement. Died of heart attack after muddle over operation schedule. Cremated.
Dr Geeson, thirtyish, smart-aleck surgeon. Not as confident as he makes himself out to be? Has access to drugs.
Sophie Meecham, 30 odd, chief ward sister. Made the rounds of the wards and found Mrs Cummings. Very agitated about my asking questions.
Tracy Collet, twenties, ward sister. Felt uneasy because bedcovers were smooth.
Ceri Williams, early twenties, student

nurse. Seems pleasant.
Ward Sister Merryl, forties? Seems dissatisfied with new customs at hospital.
Carol Prince, twenties, student nurse. Seems frank and open. Not in hospital when Louisa Cummings died.

And that was it, Sister Joan mused, reading over the notes again. Nobody had any apparent motive for killing Mrs Cummings except Mother Dorothy herself. Sister Joan indulged in a brief fantasy of her superior creeping through the night-shrouded wards in order to kill off her godmother while Sister Collet was in the toilet but the picture was simply too ridiculous to sustain. In any case Mother Dorothy hadn't even known she was the chief — the sole — beneficiary.

The plain truth was that there was absolutely nothing to investigate. Old ladies did get sudden, fatal heart attacks. Obviously everything needful had been done at the time. Professional jealousies, occasional muddles in hospital routine, and the tendency of medical staff to stick together in the face of outside criticism were not in themselves suspicious.

A footfall sounded on the spiral stair. Sister Marie's head appeared, her cheek still slightly flushed and swollen.

"Sister Joan, Mother Dorothy just had a

call from the hospital to say there's a bed free tomorrow so they can fit me in for the dental treatment," she said.

"At last!" Sister Joan folded up the paper on which her notes were scribbled and put it inside the cover of her spiritual diary. "They don't seem to mind these days that people are left in pain."

"Actually it hardly hurts at all," Sister Marie said, "as long as I don't chew on that side, and I can take the occasional aspirin."

"You've taken so many recently that you're positively rattling!" Sister Joan scolded. "Does Mother Dorothy want me to give you a lift in tomorrow?"

"I have to be there by nine in the morning, and I mustn't eat or drink beforehand," Sister Marie said dolefully. "They'll probably let me go home later in the day but the bed's still available if I have to stay the full twenty-four hours. I am really not looking forward to it."

"St Appolonia had all her teeth knocked out by the Roman guards," Sister David said, appearing unexpectedly from below.

"That's not much comfort," Sister Marie protested. "Anyway I'm not a saint."

"You could pretend to be one." Sister David arrived at the top of the stairs. "I do that sometimes."

"Do you really?" Sister Joan stared at the rabbity little face under the short black veil. "Which saints do you pretend to be?"

"It depends what I'm doing at the time," Sister David said primly. "If I'm polishing in the chapel I pretend to be St Thérèse of Lisieux — she loved looking after the altar — and when I'm taking dictation from Mother Dorothy then I pretend I'm Teresa of Avila who wrote such marvellous things."

She ended on a somewhat doubtful note as if she wasn't certain whether her habit was quite moral.

Sister Joan said, "Wasn't it St Ignatius Loyola who said that if one puts oneself into a position of prayer the prayerful emotion will follow? You may attain sanctity in just that way, Sister David!"

"Heigh ho then!" Sister Marie laughed. "Make way, oh St Keyne's, for St Appolonia!"

Following them down the stairs, Sister Joan thought for the umpteenth time that her fellow nuns never lost the power to surprise her.

"I couldn't stand being cooped up with a crowd of fellows," Detective Sergeant Mill had once observed, "and I don't understand how anyone can stand being cooped up with a mob of people of the same sex and all wearing the same clothes."

Detective Sergeant Alan Mill was an avowed agnostic and wouldn't have understood anyway, she thought tolerantly. The truth was that her companions in the convent were as varied as flowers in a meadow, each one quite different from the others, yet all bound by the same vows, the same beliefs and aspirations. If he were to make that remark now she would feel confident enough to argue with him, she thought, and inadvertently heaved a sigh. There would be no discreet collaboration between convent nun and cop this time. The bald fact was that there wasn't anything to unravel.

"Sister Joan, are you doing anything in particular?" Sister Katherine was in the front hall, two large cardboard boxes at her feet.

"Nothing, Sister."

The linen mistress so seldom asked for anything that Sister Joan gave her an encouraging smile.

"I've been using some material left over from the new curtains in the recreation room," Sister Katherine said. "I've made several dresses and a couple of kilts from that and other odds and ends. Mother Dorothy agrees that it might be nice to give them to the Lee children. Mr Lee has been so very kind in supplying us with freshly caught fish."

Poached from someone else's trout stream, Sister Joan thought with an inward grin, answering aloud, "That was a lovely idea of yours, Sister Katherine. Padraic Lee does his best but it's hard for a man to try to bring up two girls by himself."

"It's such a pity his wife suffers from such bad health," Sister Katherine said.

Did she truly not know that Mrs Lee was a hopeless alcoholic? Evidently not. There was no hint of shared knowledge in the wide grey eyes, no guile in the delicate face. Sister Katherine spent her days in the enclosure, performing her religious duties with quiet grace, spending the rest of her time mending, darning, washing, ironing, and tracing exquisite embroidery on vestments and bridal gowns and first communion dresses.

"Mother Dorothy has given her permission for you to leave the grounds," she said now.

"In that case I'll drive over to the Romany camp."

She bent and picked up one of the cardboard boxes while Sister Katherine took the other.

At the van she paused. "Why not ask

Mother Dorothy if you can come with me?" she suggested. "After all, you made the garments."

"Oh, no, Sister!" Sister Katherine took a step away from the van. "I really don't want any credit for them, and I would never leave the enclosure unless it was absolutely necessary. I often think how glad you must be to get home again after one of your errands of mercy!"

Sister Joan climbed into the van brimful with undeserved glory which lasted about two minutes before she reminded herself that one cannot climb to Heaven on the opinions of others.

She turned aside on to the bumpy track that cut away towards the Romany camp. There had been gypsies on the moor for hundreds of years, and though several new-age travellers had joined them from time to time, stayed a little while and then decamped, leaving only their litter behind, the Romanies themselves had persisted down through the generations. Lees and Evanses and Treddicks and Smiths had clung to their traditions, even, she suspected, to their joyous pagan worship which ran like a dark and vital current beneath the smooth skin of newer faiths.

A small car parked awkwardly at the

side of the track and accompanied by a female figure waving her down made her heart sink.

"Good morning, Miss Fleetwood." She drew to a halt and wound down the window. "What's the trouble?"

"A puncture," Shirley Fleetwood said, "and I can't get the wheel off."

Glory be! So even self-satisfied social workers aren't perfect!

Sister Joan said, "Climb in and I'll give you a lift. I take it that you were on your way to the camp?"

"To see the Lees," Shirley Fleetwood said, climbing in and smoothing down her bob of dark hair.

"You'll not be welcome." Sister Joan set the van bouncing forward again.

"That won't be anything new!"

There was a weary amusement in the other's voice which caused Sister Joan to look at her with more sympathy.

"They're proud, independent people," she said gently. "They distrust officialdom even when it's couched in a friendly form."

"It doesn't seem to have stopped them drawing their unemployment benefit," Shirley Fleetwood said.

Sister Joan laughed. "Indeed not," she agreed. "But that doesn't mean that they stomach personal interference. Are you going to see Padraic for any particular reason or is it just a general call? I can tell you now that Padraic's two daughters are clean, bright, well fed and beloved. He's an excellent father."

"You like him?"

"Yes, I do," Sister Joan said. "He's not always acted strictly according to law but he's never done anything very serious and he's always been very kind to the community."

"It isn't really about his children," Shirley Fleetwood said. "It's about his wife. You may not know but she's — "

"An alcoholic," Sister Joan said. "You'll never get Padraic to admit it publicly. Not even privately come to that! He keeps up the fiction that she's something of an invalid."

"Invalids don't get into public brawls and smash pub windows," Shirley Fleetwood said.

"Madge Lee did that?" Sister Joan slowed and stopped as they reached the heap of rusting metal that marked the start of the camp with its caravans and trucks and tents strung out alongside a stream that rose higher up the moor and bubbled between grassy banks towards the far-off river. The lurcher dogs had set up their usual barking and were hushed by a sharp command as

Padraic strode towards the van.

"Sister Joan! Nice to see you! You've not been near us for months," he exclaimed in a mixture of reproach and welcome.

"I get most of the news from Luther," Sister Joan said, jumping down and giving him her hand. "Are Edith and Tabitha well?"

"Chirpy as crickets," he said, "and doing real well in school too. Tabitha started in the big school this month. I don't know rightly what Miss Fleetwood's doing here but she can't get us on truanting."

"Miss Fleetwood doesn't want to get you on anything," Sister Joan said. "She's here to help."

"Oh, aye." His tone was sardonic.

"Oh yes!" Sister Joan said. "She also needs a bit of help herself. Her car's got a puncture. Can you get a couple of the lads to see to it?"

"I reckon so since you're asking me, Sister," Padraic said.

He turned, yelling something in Romany to a tall lad lounging against a half-erected wooden shack. The boy uncoiled his legs, called something back and loped off.

"The car's at least a mile away," Shirley Fleetwood said.

"They'll find it," Padraic said shortly.

"Well, since you're both here you'd best have a mug of tea. It'll give you a chance to see how spanking clean I keep my vardo."

"I know you do," Shirley Fleetwood said. "I'm not here about that or about your daughters, Mr Lee."

"I reckoned not." He led the way to a large, white-painted caravan and indicated the steps leading to the open door. "You can go in if you wish."

"We can drink tea out here," Sister Joan said.

She was well aware that the Lee caravan was always spotless. Padraic cleaned, cooked, and washed for himself and his daughters and wife while the latter either made half-hearted attempts to be a housewife or lay in the double bed sleeping off her latest binge.

"Excuse me, ladies." He set two folding stools and disappeared within.

"Is this really a place in which to raise children?" Shirley Fleetwood asked in a low voice.

"It's a better place than many," Sister Joan argued. "If the town council would do something about installing proper toilet facilities then that'd be an improvement. They could use the water from the stream which is unpolluted. You might mention it to your colleagues."

"The kettle was just on the boil." Padraic brought out the mugs on a polished wooden tray, handed them round and sat, nursing his own, on the steps. Above his red neckerchief his features were sharp and brown, hewn in wood.

"I brought some dresses for Edith and Tabitha," Sister Joan said, breaking an awkward silence. "They're absolutely new. Sister Katherine made them as a small return for all your kindness to us."

"That's very good of her." Padraic who would have stolen rather than accept charity looked gratified. "Not that I expect anything for the bits of fish and such like I can supply but it's nice to be appreciated."

"They're in the van. Shall I go and get them while you talk to Miss Fleetwood?"

"No need to make yourself scarce, Sister," Padraic said. "We all know why she's here. My dear wife had a bit of an unfortunate incident last night."

"Your wife went down into the town, drank herself into a rage and started a quarrel with the owner of the pub who suggested she ought to leave his premises," Shirley Fleetwood said tersely. "She then smashed the window with a stone and cut herself quite badly in the process."

"And they took her to St Keyne's," Padraic

grimaced. "I could've tended her myself but they insisted on keeping her in. She had a couple more than she's used to taking."

"Your wife's an alcoholic," Shirley Fleetwood said bluntly. "She's getting worse because now she's started making scenes in public. You're fortunate that the pub owner refused to press charges."

"Aye, well, he owes me a few favours does Jim," Padraic muttered. "To be honest with you, Miss Fleetwood, and I'll speak plain, you've no call to come snooping out here and making a public spectacle of me and my troubles."

"Oh, don't be so silly, Padraic!" Sister Joan said impatiently. "Miss Fleetwood has come out here obviously to find out if you need any help and to discuss what can best be done to help your wife, haven't you, Miss Fleetwood?"

"I think that she ought to be transferred to a rehabilitation centre," Shirley Fleetwood said.

"She's already been in several," Sister Joan began.

"And within a month is back where she started! Mr Lee, you could sign the necessary forms to have her hospitalized in a place where they could get to grips with her problems."

"There's no place like that round here," Padraic said, "and I'll not send her far from home. I did that once and she was cruel hurt by it. I swore she'd not be sent far away again. Anyway they didn't cure anything."

"You'll have to do something," Shirley Fleetwood said. "For your children's sake if for nothing else."

"She never lays a finger on the children," Padraic said. "She knows that's the one thing I won't stand. You'll kindly leave Edith and Tabitha out of this!"

"Have you seen your wife this morning?" Sister Joan asked.

"I called in after I dropped the girls at school. They want to keep her in for a few days. She was sleeping it off same as always. She gets very low when she finds out that she's — not been well."

"She could be a manic depressive," Shirley Fleetwood said. "I believe that possibility was once suggested. Treating that might be of enormous help."

"What do you think, Sister?"

"I think that it would be a good idea to try to get to the bottom of her problems once and for all," Sister Joan said encouragingly.

"She wasn't like it when she was a girl," Padraic said in a sudden burst of confiding. "Pretty as a picture she was and hardly ever touched a drop. She'd seen what it did to her own dad. Tim Evans was only sober one day out of seven and he was only half sober then! And her mother could put it away too! It'd make your own head reel to watch."

"A tendency to drink can run in families," Shirley Fleetwood said.

"Knows everything, doesn't she?" He cocked his head mockingly towards the social worker.

"Since your wife's in hospital already there can't be any harm in having her looked over," Sister Joan said. "Look, they're not going to send her away anywhere without her and your consent. I'm taking Sister Marie over to St Keyne's tomorrow so I could look in on her myself."

"Is Sister Marie sick?" Padraic roused himself from his own musing.

"An impacted wisdom tooth. There's some infection so she's having it done in hospital."

"I'm sorry to hear about that. Toothache must be awful." Padraic whose own excellent teeth had never known a cavity looked sympathetic.

"She probably won't even stay there overnight. About your wife — "

"OK." He made up his mind, albeit reluctantly. "It won't do any harm to have her checked out, I suppose."

"And the children?" Shirley Fleetwood looked at him.

"Edith and Tabitha are just fine," he said firmly. "If you don't believe me then talk to their teacher. She's always saying what good pupils they are."

"Well, we'll leave it for the moment then." Shirley Fleetwood rose with evident reluctance. "I may have to call round again when they're at home. I hope that's all right with you."

"Wouldn't matter if it was or it wasn't, would it?" he said dryly. "You'll poke your nose in anyway."

"Believe me, Mr Lee, but I've so many cases on my books that I'll be glad to write off your family!" she retorted, evidently exasperated. "If you want my personal opinion, from the school reports we've had your girls appear to be bright and well adjusted. Clearly you're an excellent father, doing your best in difficult circumstances. Right now I've a child on my books who bangs her head against the wall because she can't stand the memories of abuse inside her head! I'd rather be concentrating on her than two children who aren't ill treated and don't need the protection of the state!"

"Got a bit of a temper on her, hasn't she, Sister?" He cocked his head again, chuckling.

"I've always said that a woman isn't a woman without a bit of passion in her! Right, so where are these clothes you mentioned?"

"In the back of the van." Sister Joan rose. "Miss Fleetwood, I'll give you a lift back to where we left your car. Will the wheel be changed by now?"

"I reckon so. Those lads know everything worth knowing about the insides of engines and the outsides too!"

They retraced their footsteps through the camp, reached the van where Padraic shouldered down the cardboard boxes.

"I'll have Edith and Tabitha write thank-you notes to Sister Katherine," he said. "You might take note, Miss Fleetwood, that I'm dead keen on my children having good manners."

"I'm sure you are, Mr Lee." Shirley Fleetwood held out her hand placatingly. Padraic shook it with an air of forgiving condescension that made Sister Joan want to giggle.

"He's a difficult man," Shirley Fleetwood said as they drove away.

"Proud as Lucifer and with some reason to be," Sister Joan said. "He really does all he can for those two girls of his. Can anything be done for Mrs Lee?"

"That's not my field," Shirley Fleetwood

said. "If you want my honest opinion then I'd say the prognosis isn't very good. If she's a manic depressive then she obviously drinks to get her spirits up but as alcohol is a depressant then she spirals downward again very fast and so she starts drinking again. I daresay that counselling and therapy — maybe aversion therapy might help — coupled with suitable medication, but the patient has to want to cooperate. We'll see."

"You mentioned the little girl — Amy Foster? I'd've thought that a new home would have been found for her by now."

"The trouble is that she was abused while she was in foster care," Shirley Fleetwood said, frowning. "She feels more secure in a place where there are other children and many carers, and the children's home would seem ideal but she's so psychologically damaged that she requires more individual attention than seems to be available."

"It seems incredible that a four year old would try to harm herself physically!"

"Unusual but not entirely unique. The child has a great deal of guilt. Most abused children do. Some recover from the experience, but others go on to become abusers themselves or to suffer all their lives from low self-esteem. It's a vicious circle."

"And little Amy Foster?"

"My case notes aren't yet complete," Shirley Fleetwood said, "but I'm not optimistic. Naturally we're trying therapy — play therapy can be very valuable. It's early days yet."

"Perhaps a few old-fashioned hugs might help," Sister Joan said, drawing up alongside the car.

"Hugging may be interpreted as a form of abuse," Shirley Fleetwood said. "As I've pointed out, hands-on touching is definitely ill advised until the child has been thoroughly assessed. It's not advisable for the carer either. At the end of the day one must maintain an objective outlook. Thank you for the lift, Sister. My car looks quite serviceable now."

She was out of the van and inspecting the wheels of her own vehicle before Sister Joan could continue the conversation. It was a pity, she reflected, as she drove on. Once or twice the efficient Shirley Fleetwood had revealed a hint of someone human beneath her cool exterior.

"Sister Joan!"

Constable Petrie was waving to her from the side of the track. She slowed and stopped.

"You've got a puncture and need a lift?" Sister Joan said, winding down the window.

"Car's parked over there," he said. "No, I

heard the van coming. Seems you got there before me. How did he take it?"

"How did who take what?" she enquired.

"Padraic Lee. About his wife."

"Well, he's not keen on the idea but he's willing to let her have therapy," Sister Joan said.

"You haven't heard then." His pleasant young face had darkened.

"Heard what? They haven't decided to charge her after all, have they?"

"Madge Lee died," Constable Petrie said flatly.

"Died?" Sister Joan echoed the last word blankly. "That's not possible. Of what? When?"

"Lord knows how she managed it," he said, "but apparently she managed to get her hands on a bottle of brandy. She'd a carrier bag with her. Padraic took a few things to the hospital for her first thing this morning. It might've been in that. Anyway she swallowed the best part of the bottle and choked on her own vomit, poor soul."

"But she was asleep. Surely someone was checking on her?" Sister Joan felt blank bewilderment.

"They'd put her in one of the side wards," Constable Petrie said. "She'd been dozing off and on so she was left in peace to come round when she was up to it. Seems she came round, grabbed the brandy and drank it straight off."

"But how could it have killed her?"

"She'd had a couple of painkillers to cope with the mother of all hangovers. I reckon the brandy on top was just too much for her. There'll be an inquest, of course. I'm on my way to ask Padraic to come over to the hospital now to clear up a few matters. Who was that?" He interrupted himself to stare after Shirley Fleetwood's car as it went past.

"The social worker."

"Poking her nose in where it probably isn't wanted, I daresay?"

"She's very well intentioned," Sister Joan said vaguely. "Constable, I simply don't believe that Padraic would smuggle a bottle of brandy into his wife. Her drinking bothered him terribly. You know that!"

"Well, I'd better tell him," Constable Petrie said reluctantly. "When I saw you I did just wonder — you being so friendly with the Lees?"

"I'll turn around and come with you," she said promptly, but with a sinking feeling.

Padraic still sat on the steps of the caravan. He had begun to take out the dresses and was holding one up, the expression on his face one of quiet satisfaction. As van and police car drew up he dropped it back into the cardboard box and rose, wary as a cat.

"'Morning again, Sister! Constable. Before you ask there's no stolen property here!"

"Constable Petrie hasn't come about that, Padraic," Sister Joan said, climbing down from the van.

"They haven't decided to press charges surely! If so I'll have a word to say to Jim about that."

"It isn't about pressing charges," Sister Joan said. "Padraic, I'm truly sorry but there's been an — something very sad has happened. Your wife — died."

The last word seemed to stick in her throat. Padraic looked at her.

"Died?" He sounded as if the word was unfamiliar, its meaning foreign. "I saw her a couple of hours ago. Not to talk to. She was asleep. Asleep, not dead."

"You took a carrier bag in with you," Constable Petrie said.

"Yes. What's wrong with that?"

"Can you tell me what was in it?"

"Change of undies, clean dress, tights and shoes, some make-up."

"Anything else?" the constable asked.

"No, nothing. I shoved in some things last night after I heard what had happened."

"You didn't go over to the hospital at that time?"

Padraic shook his head. "The girls were in bed and I didn't want to leave them. Jem Hargood came by to tell me there'd been a bit of a to-do in the pub. I didn't know Madge was there. She said that she was going over to see her sister. Fanny wed a housedweller and the two of them used to get together now and then. She said that Fanny's husband'd give her a ride back. Seems she went to the pub instead. They shouldn't've served her. Indeed they should not!"

"So you packed up some things and took them over to the hospital this morning?"

"I already said!" Padraic said belligerently. "I dropped the girls off at school and drove on to the hospital. I went in to see her for a minute and left the carrier bag by the side of the bed. She was asleep. I didn't know till I got there that she'd cut her hands. Jem didn't say else I'd've gone over last night and got someone to mind Edith and Tabitha."

"You didn't put a bottle of brandy in the carrier bag?" Constable Petrie asked.

"Brandy?" Padraic stared at them both, then said flatly, "No, I bloody well didn't! I wouldn't have a bottle of brandy in the same room as Madge if I could help it, as well you know, Sister!"

"I'm sure you wouldn't," Sister Joan said.

"But she died you say?" Padraic sat down on the steps again, drawing out one of the dresses, smoothing it absently between his fingers. "Died of what?"

"That'll be for an inquest to decide." Constable Petrie took refuge in official jargon.

"An inquest?" Padraic looked up sharply. "Must there be one? Madge would hate to have all her affairs in the local rag. She — was a very private person. Quite a lady as a matter of fact."

"Well, I can't guarantee anything." Constable Petrie looked uncomfortable. "Unless the hospital staff are fully satisfied there's not much anyone can do. You'll be needed at the hospital now anyway. There'll be the funeral and possibly a post-mortem depending on — anyway, if you don't mind — "

"I can drive you over," Sister Joan offered.

"I'll take the pickup," he said, adding, "thanking you kindly, Sister. I'd better pick up the girls from school at the same time. Sorry, but I just can't quite take it in yet. I mean she did take a drop too much now and then. But it was a sickness with her. In the family, you see. I can't rightly take it all in."

"Would you like me to follow you to the

hospital?" Sister Joan asked.

"Would you, Sister? That's very good of you. I'll get the pickup."

He went off, bewilderment surrounding him like a mist.

"He's taken it very well," Constable Petrie said, looking after him.

"He's in shock," Sister Joan said. "Look, I'll just put these boxes inside and then I'll follow you."

"Better lock the caravan for him," Constable Petrie suggested.

"Oh, the Romanies don't steal from one another," she assured him. "Only from other people when need drives them. I'll see you at the hospital."

She picked up the first of the cardboard boxes and carried it up into the caravan. This wasn't the first time she'd been in the Lee household and, as usual, she was filled with admiration for the shining apple-pie order in which it was kept. Every inch of the available space was cleverly utilized, even to the board on which Edith and Tabitha pinned their childish drawings and poems. Nobody would ever have guessed that the mother of the two children was an alcoholic who, even when stone-cold sober, would have carried off first prize as the most careless housewife in town. Dishes were ranged on the glass-fronted shelves; Madge's shoes, polished to shining perfection, stood in a row near the low double bed. A large photograph of their wedding hung framed on the wall. Setting down the second box, Sister Joan stood up and looked at it, feeling a sudden pang of grief as she saw a younger Padraic, a devil-may-care sparkle in his eyes, his arm around the slim young figure in the elaborate white dress, with a large bouquet of carnations held in front of her like a shield. What hidden stresses and strains had caused Madge to start drinking? Or had it been in her blood, legacy of a family weakness? To know all would be to understand all, she thought, turning and making her way down the steps again.

Padraic hadn't yet left. He was coming across the rough ground towards her.

"I'll need that lift, sister," he said. "The pickup won't start. Seems like it just isn't my day, doesn't it?"

"I put the boxes inside. Is that all right?"

"Boxes? Oh, the new dresses for the girls. They'll be tickled pink with them, Sister. At the age now when they start to take a real interest in how they look. I reckon it won't be long before they're giving lads the sideways glance. Well, if they're as happy with their mates as I've been they won't go far wrong."

He paused, sending her a shrewd look. "You think I'm saying that because it's not nice to speak ill of the dead? No, it's the plain truth, Sister. Madge was the light of my eyes years ago. It was after the girls were born — she had a hard time with the birthing of both of them, and afterwards she couldn't get herself together again properly. She did try though. She did try very hard. And she was never noisy or quarrelsome, Sister. That's what I can't fathom. Why did she start a brawl last night down at the pub?"

"Because the landlord wouldn't serve her?" Sister Joan suggested as they went towards the car.

"Jim wouldn't have served her anyway," Padraic said. "She must've got the drink some other place. The off-licence maybe. But she wouldn't have started a street brawl, Sister. I know my Madge and she'd never have done that!"

5

The journey to the hospital was made in silence, Sister Joan tactfully quiet, Padraic sunk in his own thoughts. The full shock of what had happened hadn't yet dawned upon him, she thought, but when it did he would need privacy in which to grieve.

When they reached St Keyne's, Dr Geeson came forward to meet them, hand outstretched, his manner marginally more sympathetic than usual.

"Mr Lee, I'm extremely sorry about what has happened," he said. "I'm afraid there was nothing we could do."

"What exactly happened, Dr Geeson?" Constable Petrie had joined them, looking grave and slightly uncomfortable.

"Mrs Lee was brought in at eleven fifteen last night." Dr Geeson sounded as if he was already giving evidence at an inquest. "She was drunk and quite abusive. That was unusual for her. Mrs Lee wasn't an aggressive person. I'm afraid her alcoholism had entered into a new phase. Anyway, she passed out shortly after her arrival here so was placed in a side ward to sleep it off.

She was checked every half-hour by one of the duty nurses in case she had vomited but she was sound asleep. This morning she woke up complaining loudly of headache. I was just going off duty but I did examine her. She was still slightly drunk; certainly she'd've been unfit to drive a car since the level of alcohol in her blood was still quite high. I told Sister Collet to give her as much water as she could drink and some dry toast together with a couple of painkillers — aspirin. She was somewhat dehydrated so it was necessary to get as much liquid down her as possible."

"And then?" Constable Petrie asked as the other paused.

"I went off duty then, snatched a couple of hours' sleep," Dr Geeson said. "I was called back at — eleven thirty. Mrs Lee had apparently suffered a convulsion and died. There was a carrier bag by the bed with a bottle of brandy — perhaps I should say a bottle with the dregs of brandy in it. Sister Williams informed me that she had come on duty at ten, relieving Sister Collet, and that Mr Lee had come earlier this morning with a carrier bag containing some things for his wife. Sister Collet informed me that she hadn't looked inside the bag."

"If she had she'd not've found any bottle

of brandy or anything else," Padraic said.

"She wasn't present when Mrs Lee actually died?" Constable Petrie enquired.

"She had looked in on her twenty minutes earlier and found her still sleeping. She had to take a message over to the children's unit and when she got back she looked in on Mrs Lee again and immediately raised the alarm. That was when I was recalled."

"The constable talked about an inquest," Padraic said. "I don't want that, Doctor Geeson. Everything splashed over the local paper and the whole town talking. It'd hurt my Madge cruelly if that happened."

There was an uneasy and sympathetic silence. Then Dr Geeson said wearily, "I've been treating Mrs Lee for alcoholism for some time. She has spent three separate periods in drying-out clinics without any lasting benefit and she attended only two meetings of the local AA group. Somehow or other, and I am prepared to accept that Mr Lee wasn't responsible, she managed to get hold of a bottle of brandy, drink most of it and that was it. I would have no hesitation in declaring that she died of acute alcohol poisoning. I see no need for an inquest."

"So you'd sign the death certificate?" Constable Petrie looked rather relieved than otherwise.

"I'll inform the coroner to that effect," Dr Geeson said. "Mrs Lee hadn't been twenty-four hours in hospital but she had previously been under my care and all the symptoms were indicative of a sudden acute onset of alcohol poisoning. The brandy bottle clinched it."

"Which I never took in to her!" Padraic repeated stubbornly.

"As you say," Dr Geeson said without emphasis.

"You'll want to make arrangements with the almoner about the registration of the death and the funeral," Sister Joan said. "You can manage all that?"

"I've been managing things for years," Padraic said. "Excuse me, Sister. Dr Geeson, I know you did what you could but she was a sick woman was Madge. A very sick woman."

"Excuse me too." Sister Joan made for the door followed by Constable Petrie.

"Seems straightforward enough, wouldn't you say?" He strolled with her across the forecourt. "Nothing to gain by holding an inquest after all. Padraic Lee will come to see it as a blessed release before long. I wonder if he did bring in the brandy. It doesn't seem likely to me but then when you remember that he'd just heard his wife was in the hospital after a brawl he might've grabbed the first carrier bag he found and shoved in some things he thought she'd need. He must've been worried, not wanting to leave the two children alone and having to wait until this morning to come over here."

"I'm sure he'd have checked the contents of the bag even if he hadn't done so last night," Sister Joan said frowningly.

"If you want my opinion, Sister," Constable Petrie said, pausing as they neared the van, "I reckon that he did put in that bottle of brandy maybe thinking that a hair of the dog that bit you is a good idea. He simply doesn't want to think that he indirectly caused her death. Now I could make a fuss, start asking a lot of questions but where's the good of it when the poor woman's gone and Padraic's left with two girls to rear?"

He waited for her reluctant agreement, wished her good day, got back into the police car and drove away.

He was right of course, she argued with herself. It would be needlessly cruel to pursue the details of what had clearly been an accident. Madge had woken up and groped in the carrier bag, found the brandy and drained the bottle deeply. Already hungover and dehydrated she had reacted immediately to what proved a fatal dose.

Suddenly she was heading back into the hospital, pace brisk, chin at an angle that her friends would have recognized as stubborn.

She headed for the stairs, a quick glance around the reception area having assured her that both Dr Geeson and Padraic were nowhere in sight. The latter would be making the inevitable sad arrangements that attended any death; the former had probably gone to catch up on his sleep.

Sister Williams was in the surgical ward, chatting to one of the patients. She excused herself as Sister Joan came in and hurried up to the desk.

"Is there something I can do for you, Sister?" she asked.

"I wondered if I might collect Mrs Lee's effects on Padraic's behalf," Sister Joan said. "It's always so upsetting having to do that when someone's just died. He's dealing with the almoner at the moment."

"They're still in the cubicle," Sister Williams said promptly. "The clothes she was actually wearing when she was brought in will be in the laundry now but the carrier bag is there."

"It must've been a dreadful shock when she was found," Sister Joan said.

"I ought to be getting used to it by now." Ceri Williams lowered her voice. "I mean very sick people do come into hospital and die, don't they? I know that in my head but it's awfully upsetting when it happens."

"And unexpectedly," Sister Joan said.

"Oh, Mrs Lee was very drunk when she was brought in last night so Sister Collet said."

"You were off duty?"

"Yes. I took over from Sister Collet this morning at ten," Ceri Williams said. "She told me that Mrs Lee was recovering from a binge in one of our side wards — cubicles really. I was to look in from time to time to make sure she was all right, but Sister Collet said that drunks were usually best left to sleep it off."

"And then Sister Collet went off duty?"

"We overlap in the duty roster." Ceri Williams explained. "One comes on at ten — that was me this morning and the one she's relieving goes off at eleven, and so on. It gives the one going off duty plenty of time to bring the incoming nurse up to date and have a final look over the patients."

"Which Sister Collet did?"

"She had to go over to the children's unit with a message," Ceri Williams said. "She told me to wait until she got back so we could go round together. So it was past eleven when we went round. To be absolutely accurate it wasn't me who found Mrs Lee. I was just behind Sister Collet when she went into the cubicle. Poor Mrs Lee was half off the bed. She must've had the convulsion and threshed about for a minute or two."

"You didn't hear her?"

Ceri Williams shook her head.

"One of the patients wanted a cup of tea. It wasn't strictly time for one but Sister Collet had just brewed up in the sluice so I went to get a cup. You can't hear much with the kettle whistling. Would it have made any difference if I'd heard something? Oh, that's just awful!"

"It wouldn't have made any difference at all," Sister Joan said. "One other thing: did you see the brandy bottle?"

"Not straightaway. It had rolled under the bed. It was caught up in the bedcovers and they were slipping down the side. There was brandy spilt all over the sheets and the floor. She must've grabbed it out of the carrier bag. One of the headsquares in the carrier was on the floor too."

"Well, I'll take the carrier bag down to Padraic Lee," Sister Joan said. "Which cubicle is it in? I can sign for it of course."

"In Side Ward B," Ceri Williams said. "We had to clean up the place once Dr

Geeson had been and she was taken to the mortuary, but it still stinks of brandy. Do you mind going and getting it yourself? I'm not really supposed to spend too much time away from the main ward."

"Fine. See you in a minute."

The side ward was a three-walled space with a white curtain providing the fourth wall. A bedstead with a flat mattress and two pillows on it, a small white locker and a chair comprised the entire furnishings. Sister Joan sniffed but only the acrid scent of strong disinfectant reached her nostrils. The carrier bag stood in the corner. She picked it up, hesitated and returned to the ward.

"I'll take this down to Padraic. I'd better sign for it, though I haven't looked inside."

"Sign here." Ceri Williams proffered a notebook. "We didn't look inside ourselves. Just put back the headsquare, that's all. It seems so heartless to start going through a dead person's belongings when they're only just gone."

"I know what you mean. What happened to the brandy bottle by the way?" Ceri Williams looked at her blankly.

"I don't know," she said. "Someone must've picked it up. It wasn't me because I ran to alert Dr Geeson."

"Who was off duty," Sister Joan reminded her.

"Yes, but he'd told Sister Collet to call him if Mrs Lee needed anything. So Sister Collet sent me over to the staff quarters to get him."

"Who was on duty?"

"Dr Meredith was but he was down in casualty. The trouble is that we're so short of staff that we're all kept perpetually on the move. Mrs Lee was Dr Geeson's patient anyway."

"And by the time you got back the bottle wasn't here?"

"I don't know," Ceri Williams said. "Yes, it must've been because I remember Sister Collet showing it to him, but I don't know what happened to it after that. It was only an ordinary bottle of brandy with a bit of liquid dribbling out of it. Sister Collet must've washed it or thrown it out. I was sent down to the mortuary with the body. Dr Geeson said it was all good experience for a student nurse."

"And when you got back to the ward?"

"Sister Collet was cleaning up. It was awfully nice of her because officially she was off duty. I took over and finished doing the floor. Sister, is anything wrong? All these questions — "

"Probably not," Sister Joan said. "Oh, one more thing! Did you see the cap? The one that was on the bottle, I mean."

"It might've been in the carrier bag," Ceri Williams said. "There were things in the waste bin that I took out to the incinerator but not a bottle top."

"Thank you for your time." Sister Joan picked up the carrier bag again. "I'd better catch up Padraic before he leaves the premises."

In the main reception hall she met Padraic just emerging from an office further down the broad corridor. He still looked shell-shocked, she thought, his face tight with the emotion he refused to allow himself to reveal.

"That's the carrier bag!" he showed a touch of animation as he saw it. "There never was a brandy bottle — never! in that bag, Sister. If there was then someone else put it there."

"Would you mind if I looked through the contents?" she asked.

"You help yourself, Sister. I'll wait by your van if you don't mind."

"My — ? Oh heavens, I forgot your lorry was out of action," Sister Joan said. "Look, take the keys and sit inside. Have a smoke. You look as if you need one. I won't be very long, but I've a couple of things to do here before I leave."

The first one was to examine the contents of the carrier bag. They were exactly as Padraic had described, only poignant because the woman for whom they'd been intended was dead. There was nothing resembling a bottle top. Sister Joan put the various items back into the carrier bag and hurried out.

The staff quarters occupied a corner of the forecourt, with entrances prudishly separate for the two sexes. Most of the permanent staff had their own homes outside the hospital premises but the staff quarters provided bedrooms where medical staff could snatch a few hours' sleep, and a couple of common rooms.

Sister Collet hadn't retired to bed despite her night on duty. Sister Joan caught sight of her seated by a downstairs window, gazing out vacantly into the border of drooping roses that was pretending to be a garden. She had obviously had a bath. Her hair looked damp and was pulled back from her face and she'd slipped into a tracksuit.

Sister Joan went in and tapped at the common-room door as she entered.

"Sister Collet, forgive me for disturbing you — " She stopped, shocked by the extreme pallor of the other's face as she turned her head. "Are you all right, Sister Collet? You must be worn out after being on duty for so long!"

"I'm overtired and can't drop off easily," Tracy Collet said tonelessly. "I suppose I ought to go and talk to Mr Lee. I saw him walking across the forecourt a few minutes ago. The trouble is that I simply don't know what to say. I was never very good with relatives."

"Padraic's still trying to come to terms with what's happened," Sister Joan said. "It was the greatest bad luck that Madge Lee got hold of a bottle of brandy in her condition, but I suppose alcoholics can be very cunning."

"When they're hellbent on a drink, yes," Tracy Collet said.

"Padraic swears that he never brought anything alcoholic in for his wife."

"Well, he would say that, wouldn't he?" The other rested her chin on her hand wearily.

"Padraic is a very responsible person," Sister Joan said. "Could Mrs Lee have got the brandy from somewhere else? Is any kept on the ward?"

"Sister Meecham keeps a bottle in the office," Sister Collet said slowly. "We're not supposed to know anything about it because she is chief ward sister, but she does have a little tipple now and again — only a drop or so, when she needs a bit of energy."

"Sister Meecham wasn't on duty last night or this morning?"

"She was on duty until eight this morning, over in the children's unit. It's more like babysitting really. She came in and went straight to bed, I think. I could call her."

"No need," Sister Joan said. "Oh, I take it that you threw out the bottle — the one with the dregs of brandy in it?"

"Sister Williams went down to the mortuary. I started cleaning up the side ward and — yes, I washed out the bottle. I'm afraid it was automatic. Dr Geeson told me to start cleaning up. The smell of brandy was awful."

"What did you do with the cap?" Sister Joan enquired.

"The cap?" Tracy Collet's face became, if possible, more expressionless. "There wasn't any — of course, I must've thrown it away. Why?"

"Oh, just clearing up a few loose ends on Padraic's behalf," Sister Joan said. "Look, it's none of my business but you ought to try to get some sleep. You don't look well at all."

"You mean that I look plain," Tracy

Collet said. "Well, that's nothing new. If you don't mind, Sister, I think I will go and lie down."

She had half risen, her fingers plucking nervously at the hem of her tracksuit top.

"Have a good long sleep," Sister Joan said encouragingly.

"If I don't get called to some emergency or other," Tracy Collet said. "That's the trouble here; when you're off duty you're still on call and when you're on duty you get stupid errands to run or a message to deliver that nobody knows anything about."

She went out, consciously straightening her shoulders as she crossed the threshold.

"Sister Collet, when did you deliver a message that nobody knew anything about?" Sister Joan demanded, following.

"This morning. I'd just said to Sister Williams that we'd have a quick look over the ward before I went off duty and left her in charge and she remembered that there was a note someone had given her on her way over to the main building. Just a scribble asking me to go over to the children's unit. I thought it might be urgent so I went right over, but nobody knew anything about it. Then I went back to the surgical ward. Sister Williams was making a cup of tea for one of the patients. I was quite cross about it because someone should've been on the ward but she's a nice girl so I didn't say anything. We started the ward round and found Mrs Lee. That's all, Sister."

She had lengthened her stride and was making for the staircase. Sister Joan stood, gazing after her thoughtfully. This wasn't all. It wasn't all by a long chalk but she hadn't the faintest idea how next to proceed.

She went back to the van where Padraic sat, chewing on an empty pipe, his eyes bleak.

"Here's the carrier bag," Sister Joan said, handing it up to him. "I've one more errand to do before we leave. I'm sorry to keep you waiting."

"Oh, I don't mind sitting here." He gave her a faint, forced smile. "There'll be plenty to see to once we get going. Death's a busy time, isn't it, Sister?"

"For the living, yes." Sister Joan nodded to him and hurried back across the forecourt.

"Would Sister Meecham be on the premises?" she asked the nurse at the reception desk.

"I think she's up in her office." The girl glanced up indifferently. "Go on up, Sister. It's on the top floor."

"I know roughly where it is. Thank you."

The nurse mumbled something and continued to flick over the pages of a magazine in front of her. Sister Joan doubted if it was a copy of the *Lancet*.

The office which housed the shiny new computer was a large, pleasant room with a couple of easy chairs, a flat-topped desk and a range of filing cabinets with pot plants on top of each one. A rather sentimental print depicting Florence Nightingale with her lamp and the ubiquitous soldier gazing up at her from the floor hung on one wall. Sister Meecham was checking what looked like a menu and looked up as Sister Joan tapped on the door.

"Yes? Oh, Sister Joan! Come in, won't you?"

"I hope I'm not disturbing you," Sister Joan said.

"No, not at all. I was just checking over the menus. We're supposed to give the patients a choice these days and it can be quite difficult to please everybody. Some of the patients seem to think they're staying in a five-star hotel! What can I do for you, Sister?"

"You'll have heard about Madge Lee's death earlier today."

"Yes. Yes, very sad but not entirely unexpected." Sister Meecham indicated a chair and rose. "Would you like a cup of coffee, Sister?"

"Nothing, thank you." Seating herself, Sister Joan looked up at the taller woman. "I was hoping to find out if the bottle of brandy that's usually here is still here."

She had scored a palpable hit. Sister Meecham turned a dull red and then paled.

"Brandy, Sister?" she said.

"That dark-brown liquid that gets you drunk," Sister Joan said.

"I do know what brandy is," Sister Meecham said. "I fail to see — "

"A bottle of brandy is kept up here for emergencies?" Sister Joan put it as tactfully as she could.

"As a matter of fact, yes. In the bottom drawer of that filing cabinet. It's unlocked and there's no secret about it," Sister Meecham said defensively.

"May I see it?"

"You may have a tot if you like, Sister!" Sophie Meecham bent down, tugged open the steel drawer, and stopped, her hand continuing to grope.

"It isn't here," she said flatly. "Sister, I swear that — someone must've nicked it. I don't understand — I heard something about Mrs Lee having got hold of a bottle of brandy and drunk most of it, but I received the distinct impression that it was brought in a carrier bag. Of course, Sister Collet and Sister Williams haven't yet written their reports on the incident."

"I think it is almost certain that the bottle of brandy came from inside the hospital," Sister Joan said. "I don't suppose there's any liquor kept on the wards?"

"No, of course not." Sophie Meecham slid home the drawer and stood up. "There is a small amount of liquor kept in the staff quarters, but the staff sign for it and the bill is totted up at the end of each month. They are not, of course, permitted to drink on duty. The brandy kept here is, as you say, purely for emergencies. I can hardly believe that a woman as drunk as Mrs Lee was said to be would leave the side ward, come up here and steal the brandy. How would she know it was here in the first place?"

"Somebody's taken it," Sister Joan said mildly.

"I think you'll find that Mister Lee brought in a bottle of brandy for his wife." Sophie Meecham smoothed down the skirt of her uniform. "Of course, it was the very last thing he should've left with her but the man's a Romany!"

"But not an idiot."

"Of course not, but he may have thought

that an extra drink might not harm her, or it may have been in the — oh, I really don't know, Sister!"

"How was the bottle sealed?"

"It had a screw top, Sister Joan, which was released by means of a spring-clip before being twisted loose. It was quite stiff."

"I see." Sister Joan tried to visualize a hungover Madge Lee lurching unseen up the stairs, entering the office, finding the liquor, unsealing the bottle, going back down the stairs and immediately drinking herself into a fatal convulsion. She found it impossible.

"I understand that a bottle was found in the side ward?" Sophie Meecham said.

"Yes. Caught in the bedcovers," Sister Joan said. "Madge Lee had drunk most of it and then dropped it when she had her seizure. Sister Collet and Sister Williams cleaned up the room between them. The bottle was washed out. The problem is that neither of them seems to have found the bottle top. If Padraic Lee had brought in a bottle of liquor which I don't believe he did, then surely he'd have brought in one with a top to it. If he'd done that then his wife would've grabbed the bottle when the nurses' backs were turned, unscrewed it and taken a couple of long swigs. Then she'd have let the bottle slip from her grasp and had a fatal convulsion. The top of the bottle wouldn't have walked off by itself."

"I fail to see what you're implying," Sophie Meecham said.

"That someone came up here, took the brandy bottle, undid it up here — you said yourself it was difficult to undo — and then they took the open bottle down to the side ward, handed it to Madge Lee who was just coming round from her binge, and — "

"But someone would've seen them surely!"

"Sister Williams came on duty an hour before Sister Collet went off duty. She was called away over to the children's unit and while she was gone Sister Williams made one of the patients a cup of tea. Someone could easily have slipped into the side ward then, and if the bottle was already undone they wouldn't have to waste time getting it open, would they?"

There was an instant's silence. Sophie Meecham stared at Sister Joan, her hands still smoothing her uniform. Then she said, "Haven't you got enough to do over at the convent without inventing mysteries for yourself to solve? First Mrs Cummings who died of a heart attack and now Madge Lee — both deaths logically accounted for by virtue of their medical history, but you must come along and ask a string of questions — upsetting my nurses, sowing completely unjustified doubts, playing at detective! Dr Geeson was quite satisfied in both cases with the cause of death, and willing to sign the death certificates. What is wrong with you, Sister?"

"I've got a naturally suspicious mind," Sister Joan said meekly.

"Well, you can keep your nasty little suspicions to yourself!" Two bright spots of colour in her cheeks made her almost pretty. "My nurses are compassionate, intelligent workers, dedicated professionals! We all of us work under constant stress, long hours, double spells of duty, low pay! We do our best for those in our care! God knows we do! Sometimes people die here. We're not able to stop every single patient from dying, you know! Even Dr Geeson can't do that, and he's a fine doctor. He's an excellent doctor! If I were to give him the merest hint of what you've been implying he'd complain to — to your bishop, I'm sure he would. And who would want to kill an elderly woman with heart trouble and a drunken gypsy woman? Who'd gain?"

"I'm sure you're going to tell me," Sister Joan said resignedly.

"Mrs Cummings left her property to your prioress, didn't she?" The scarlet came and went in Sophie Meecham's face. "And with Madge Lee dead her husband won't have to spend half his time pretending that everything's just fine! And yet I can't see those two joining forces to start committing murders all over the place. Now, excuse me for being rude, but I'd like you to get the hell out of here!"

"Of course." Sister Joan made for the door. "I'm sorry to have upset you, Sister Meecham. I do realize that as head ward sister you're naturally concerned for the reputation of your staff."

"And there's no motive for anyone to kill anyone else!"

"Oh, there's always a motive," Sister Joan said gently. "I'll see myself out."

Padraic wasn't in the van when she reached the forecourt. At a little distance his pickup was parked and a small group of men stood by it, Padraic in their midst.

"Sister Joan, my pals fixed up my truck!" He came towards her. "We'll go back together, and collect Edith and Tabitha on the way. I do thank you kindly for the lift here."

"You'll let me know if there's anything else I can do."

"I will indeed, Sister." He shook hands solemnly.

Already he was unconsciously assuming the dignified mantle of bereavement. Yet he'd loved his wife, or more likely loved the memory of the girl she'd been before the family weakness had claimed her.

She hadn't the smallest excuse for lingering any further. Two people had died of causes that were consistent with their medical histories. Dr Geeson was satisfied. The most that could be alleged was a certain inefficiency in hospital procedure and shortage of staff was the clear culprit there. She bit her lip, turned towards her van and halted as Sister Merryl emerged from the children's unit and came towards her.

"You here again, Sister? We'll have to charge you rent soon," she said cheerfully.

"I gave Padraic Lee a lift down when we received the news about his wife," Sister Joan said.

"The poor thing died, didn't she?" Sister Merryl looked vaguely sympathetic though the upward curving lines of her face made the expression sit uneasily on her features.

"Apparently she got hold of a bottle of brandy," Sister Joan said.

"Doesn't surprise me!" Sister Merryl clucked her tongue. "It's not like the old days at St Keyne's, I can tell you! Why, the things that go on these days would not have been tolerated under one of the old-style matrons."

"Like Sister Meecham's drinking," Sister Joan hazarded.

"Oh, we're not supposed to know about that," Sister Merryl said. "She keeps a bottle of brandy up in the office for emergencies. Well, we all know about that, of course, but I'd like a pound for every time Sister Meecham has to top it up when she's had a stint up there on duty!"

"I'm told that some doctors drink too."

"Men can hold it better," Sister Merryl said tolerantly. "Why, I've seen old Dr Meredith sail into the operating theatre three sheets to the wind and whip out an appendix! Steady as a rock he was, except when he was sober."

"He doesn't operate now, does he?" Sister Joan asked.

"He's semi-retired these days, comes into casualty mainly, and now and then pops along to the children's unit. He's got a nice friendly manner which is more than anyone can say for Dr Geeson, though he's very efficient."

"Two doctors doesn't sound sufficient even for a small hospital."

"Oh, we've a couple of interns." Sister Merryl sniffed loudly. "Think they know it all, but no real harm in them to be fair. And of course the local GPs take turns at coming in. But the real workers are the nurses! The hospital couldn't function without them. I include myself in that because I may only be part-time now but I'm one of the old school, and what I can do in ten minutes takes some of these young girls twenty! Addlepated some of them!"

"Sister Collet seems a little vague," Sister Joan said.

"Well, we all know why, Sister, don't we? It never does to mix private and professional business, does it? It means her mind is on something else half the time. Never knows exactly where she's left her keys; never sure exactly where she's supposed to be — she turned up at the children's unit this morning looking for Miss Fleetwood. Seemed to think she was wanted."

"How's the little girl — Amy Foster?"

"Still here." Sister Merryl clucked her tongue again. "Poor little mite! Never says a word. They did promise a place for her at the children's home but they're bursting at the seams as it is. And she goes absolutely rigid when someone suggests fostering again. She knows the word, you see, and remembers."

"There is something that troubles me a little." Sister Joan felt as if she was making her way through a thick fog with no clear views of anything. "There's a rumour that people have been a bit careless about the drug cupboards — forgetting to sign for what they take, leaving keys around, that kind of thing."

"Well, I'll not ask where that rumour started," Sister Merryl said.

Since she had just started it herself Sister Joan felt a definite sense of relief.

"I couldn't really credit it," she said.

"Sister, I don't blame you! Thirty grams of digoxin not signed for until Sister Collet remembered that she'd taken some to be made up in the dispensary. Of course, she rushed back to sign the register at once."

"Dix — what you said is quite a powerful drug, isn't it?"

"Powerful?" Sister Merryl rolled her eyes. "Let me tell you that the normal daily dosage for a heart condition is one milligram. One milligram, Sister! It has to be very, very gradually reduced too if the patient's condition is improving. Having thirty grams of the stuff wandering around a hospital doesn't bear thinking about!"

"I can imagine."

Her imagination was, she thought, really beginning to work overtime now.

"It wouldn't have happened in Matron's

time," Sister Merryl said wistfully. "I tell you, Sister, things are changing for the worse. They blame lack of funding but I blame lack of discipline!"

"I'm sure you're right," Sister Joan said.

She was still in the fog but she had the distinct impression that it would soon begin to clear. Before she could frame another question, Sister Merryl glanced at her fob watch and uttered a small shriek.

"I'm due at reception! Here's me going on about inefficiency and five minutes late already. Nice talking to you, Sister. 'Bye!"

6

"This is very bad news, Sister." Mother Dorothy spoke sombrely, her face tight with distress.

"Some people would call it a blessed release," Sister Joan said.

"Some might, but we are not among that number. Mrs Lee leaves a widower and two young daughters behind her. It's very sad indeed, and naturally you had to stay to do what lay within your power. You missed your afternoon cup of tea but I've no doubt that you never even thought of that."

Sister Joan, who had thought of it constantly on her way back to the convent, lowered her eyes modestly.

"When you have driven Sister Marie to the hospital in the morning you must go over to the Lees and find out if there's anything that we can do. Sister Perpetua will wish to attend the funeral since she had reason to be grateful to Padraic Lee for his gifts of fish. You'll find out what arrangements are being made?"

"Yes, Mother Prioress. There is one other thing — " Sister Joan hesitated, wondering how best to phrase it.

"Yes?"

"I just wondered if you knew what medication your godmother was on."

"As a matter of fact I do," Mother Dorothy said. "She was on something called digoxin, a milligram per day, but her doctor had begun to gradually decrease the dose since he thought her condition was improving. I wrote to inform him of my godmother's death and he wrote back in a most helpful manner."

"Was he surprised to learn she'd died of a heart attack?" Sister Joan asked.

"He said he would not have expected it, but that one can never tell with individual patients."

"Thank you, Mother." Sister Joan hesitated again, then said, "You were concerned about Mrs Cummings's sudden death. May I go on trying to find out what happened?"

"You think there's cause? If you do then surely the police — "

"Suspicion isn't proof," Sister Joan said. "I've nothing definite to take to the police. When I have then, of course, I'll approach them."

"Then be careful, Sister." The prioress frowned slightly as she turned away.

Careful not to break the law or careful not to fall a victim? Sister Joan gave one last longing thought to the cup of tea she hadn't had and went through to the chapel to catch up on a little praying.

The talk at recreation was all of Padraic's loss.

"For whatever her faults," Sister Perpetua said, "she never forfeited his affection. It must be a great blessing to retain the love of a decent man."

"Surely we have God's love whatever our sins?" Sister David said.

"But Divinity pours out affection without our having to do anything to earn it," Sister Katherine demurred. "Men are more fickle."

She spoke as if somewhere in her past something unspoken lay buried.

"We must send a nice wreath," Sister Martha said. "The dahlias are looking nice."

"I'll find out tomorrow what the funeral arrangements are when I've driven Sister Marie over to the hospital," Sister Joan promised.

"Sister Marie is being very brave," Sister David remarked. "Her cheek is very badly swollen yet she declares it doesn't hurt much at all."

"That's not bravery!" Sister Gabrielle said with a snort of amusement. "She's scared of having the tooth out, that's all. Sister Marie's no martyr!"

"If you'll excuse me, Sisters, I'd better slip down and tell her to be ready at eight thirty tomorrow morning and not to eat or drink anything after midnight tonight."

Sister Joan folded up the stocking she was mending and went out, stifling a chuckle as she heard Sister Gabrielle's tart, "And before you start praising Sister Joan for giving up part of recreation, Sister David, just think on that she can't stand darning anyway!"

The two lay sisters were in the kitchen, enjoying their own mild recreation, with Sister Teresa knitting and Sister Marie reading. They looked up as she came in.

"How's the tooth?" Sister Joan enquired.

"Not as painful as it was," Sister Marie said valiantly.

"It'll feel even better when it isn't there any longer," Sister Joan said. "Don't eat or drink anything after midnight and be ready at eight for me to drive you over to St Keyne's. I daresay you'll be home by tomorrow evening."

Sister Marie smiled wanly.

Alice who had been lying on her beanbag pretending she was the most well-trained dog in the world stood up and looked, tail hopefully wagging, towards the door.

"It's my turn to take her," Sister Marie began.

"I'll take her. I won't be long."

Sister Joan opened the back door and stepped out into the yard. It was already quite dark but a moon lit the archway beneath which one passed to the side of the great house. From her stall Lilith whinnied a greeting.

"Day after tomorrow, girl! I'll take you for a nice brisk canter then." Sister Joan took the main path that led between high shrubberies to the front drive.

The main gates stood open as usual and against the stone pillars a tall figure was leaning. Alice yelped and bounded to meet Luther who stood respectfully straight as he recognized Sister Joan.

"Good evening, Luther. It's late for you to be about, isn't it?" She paused, nodding at him amiably.

"There's weeping in the camp," Luther said. "There's the smell of dying and black clothes in the camp."

"For poor Madge Lee. You know your cousin's wife has died?"

"Old Hagar told me. I'm feared of the dying smell."

"There's nothing to fear about dying," Sister Joan said gently. "It comes to us all,

Luther. We simply step out of our bodies when the time comes. Then we move on into the light."

"How do you know when you've not been there?" Luther asked.

And how the hell do I know? Sister Joan thought. Am I saying all this out of compassion for a man who's lacking in his wits but without really believing it? Or do I believe it deep in my guts where all the most valid feelings have their seat?

"Do you remember being born, Luther?" she asked.

"No, Sister. Reckon I was too young," he said apologetically.

"Well, before you were born, when you were in Heaven waiting for a body, you were probably just as scared about leaving there and coming here," she said, throwing Darwin to the winds. "Dying is the same kind of thing."

"And we all get born at the right time, Sister?"

"Right!"

"But we don't all get dead at the right time," Luther said.

"Probably not." She frowned, recalling those who had died violently before they had fully begun to live, those who might have died before their due time with only vague suspicions and no real proof to speed the wheels of justice.

"Children ought to live a very long time," Luther said. "Nuns too!"

"Thank you, Luther. I'm sure we do our best," she said kindly.

"I heard tell one of the sisters is going to the hospital," Luther said. "She isn't going there to die, is she?"

"No, of course not!" She was startled by her own vehemence. "Sister Marie has a bad tooth that needs to come out."

"Tie a long thread round it and slam the door," Luther said helpfully.

"It'll take a bit more than that, but it's nothing to worry about, honestly," Sister Joan said. "She'll be home again by tomorrow night. You can come with me to pick her up if you like."

"I don't like hospitals," Luther said darkly. "They locked me up in one once just for looking at pretty ladies."

"We know you were only looking," Sister Joan said patiently. "The pretty ladies got scared when you used to follow them. You're not doing that again, are you?"

"No, Sister! It's not right to scare ladies," Luther said. "Anyway ladies are nice to me sometimes too. There was one gave me a sweet last night. I didn't eat it. I saved it for Sister Martha. It's wrapped up in silver paper."

He took it out of the pocket of his threadbare jacket and carefully pulled off the foil.

"A lady gave you this?"

Sister Joan stared down at the tablet, whitened by the cresting moon.

"Outside the pub," Luther said. "She gave one to Madge Lee too."

"Did you know the lady?" Sister Joan asked.

Luther shook his head and began wrapping up the tablet again.

"Tell you what!" She kept her voice light and casual. "Why not let me give Sister Martha the sweet? I'll tell her it's from you."

"I might lose it before tomorrow," Luther said.

"Yes, you might." Sister Joan held out her hand.

"Tell Sister Martha I'll come and help with the apple-picking tomorrow," Luther said, shambling off.

"Would you like to come to the chapel for a few minutes?" she invited. "You know the door's always open and nobody's there right now."

"God is," Luther said. "Best keep out of

His way when there's the smell of death about." He patted Alice clumsily on the head and went off across the moor.

Sister Joan called Alice to heel, promising her a longer walk very soon, and went back to the convent. It was easy enough to extract a treacle toffee from the small tin of toffees in the pantry and take it up to the recreation room for Sister Martha with Luther's compliments, but not until she was in her own cell after the grand silence had begun was she able to unwrap the original tablet and examine it more closely by the light of her candle.

There was no doubt about it. Sister Joan hadn't spent three years in art college without coming across LSD. She'd never tried it herself though she had smoked the occasional joint, feeling warm and sleepy with Jacob's arm around her. Some of the other students had had bad trips, trying to walk out of second-floor windows, becoming angry when those with cooler heads tried to stop them from playing chicken on the motorway. She had the idea that LSD was a bit old hat by now. Crack cocaine and Ecstasy were the drugs one read about in the papers. Madge Lee had been unusually belligerent outside the pub. If she'd taken the 'sweet' then her behaviour was explained. But who would stand outside a pub giving away tablets of LSD or anything else? She wrapped it up again and put it in the corner of her locker before she began the nightly ritual of removing her habit, splashing her face with cold water, cleaning her teeth, pulling on white nightgown and nightcap and blowing out her candle.

There were no helpful messages emerging from the subconscious to explode into vivid dreaming. There was only sleep with an uneasiness pervading it, a feeling in the brief seconds of wakefulness as she changed position that something was very wrong, very wrong indeed.

The sound of the clapper at five o'clock, mingled with Sister Teresa's strong young voice, calling, "Christ is risen!" jolted her awake.

She left the bed and was on her knees with the ease of long practice, her own voice answering as the announcement was made at her door, "Thanks be to God!"

It was not yet light but she washed and dressed without lighting her candle, each separate action performed now almost without any conscious thought, and finally lit her candle and cast a rueful glance at her bed as she left her cell.

"Sisters must try to compose themselves

to sleep in the position in which they will be laid in their shroud," her novice mistress had impressed upon her. "Then if death comes while you sleep you will be prepared."

If death had come for me last night, Sister Joan thought wryly, I'd have had to be disentangled from the bedclothes.

She picked up her candle and joined the silent procession of sisters as they padded along the corridor, down the main staircase and towards the chapel for the two-hour silent worship that preceded the daily mass.

Louisa Cummings had been taking diminishing doses of digoxin prescribed by her regular doctor when she had been transferred to St Keyne's for her hip-replacement operation. There had been a muddle in the computer and her operation had been delayed, cause for irritation but not surely for a fatal heart attack. That same night Ward Sister Meecham and the student nurse, Ceri Williams, had found her dead in bed, bedcovers smooth under her clenched hand. Sister Collet, the duty nurse, had been in the toilet and had heard nothing. Sister Merryl had told her that thirty grams of digoxin had been taken from the drugs cupboard and signed for later by a flustered Sister Collet. Then Madge Lee, having been offered and probably taken an LSD tablet, had turned violent and been taken off to the hospital where the next morning she'd managed to drink most of the contents of an opened bottle of brandy, have a convulsion and die at the precise time when Sister Collet had gone over to the children's unit on account of a message nobody admitted sending and Ceri Williams was brewing tea for a patient.

Ward Sister Sophie Meecham liked to relieve stress by an occasional tipple up in the office. She didn't welcome questions. Sister Tracy Collet was scatterbrained, never in the right place at the right time, sentimental enough to weep bitterly over a cheap heirloom ring. Sister Ceri Williams was inexperienced, apt to regard the senior staff with awe, while Sister Merryl, being of the old school, despised them all equally. Dr Geeson was virtually in charge since Dr Meredith was elderly and Dr Geeson liked his corpses neatly tidied away, no questions asked.

There was no motive for killing Louisa Cummings, no motive for killing Madge Lee, or to be more accurate, Sister Joan corrected herself, only Mother Dorothy and Padraic had even the shadows of motives and nobody could seriously suspect them for a moment. Was she, as Sophie Meecham had accused, simply looking for mysteries where none existed because she craved a little extra excitement in her life?

"Amen," said Sister Joan, belatedly joining in the closing prayer and realizing with a start that Father Stephens had emerged from the sacristy.

She concentrated on the mass with painful intensity, blocking out all extraneous thought, and went up to breakfast feeling marginally more spiritually refreshed.

Unlike Father Malone who enjoyed a bit of a gossip over the fruit, bread and coffee Father Stephens drank his coffee and ate his apple in silence, with only a few polite commonplaces exchanged with Mother Dorothy or Sister Hilaria. Sister Joan munched her own bread and fruit, denied herself coffee in favour of a mug of hot water — and serve me right for not worshipping with my whole heart and soul — and went up to tidy her cell and transfer the tablet in its silver wrapping into the depths of her pocket.

The brisk morning routine continued. By 8.30 she had brought the van round to the front, sternly discouraging the ebullient Alice from jumping in it, and was ready to receive Sister Marie who emerged from the kitchen with a scarf wrapped around her face and a distinctly nervous glint in her eyes.

"Right, Sister, let's get this show on the road!"

And if anybody said that to me when I was going to have a nasty extraction I'd punch them, she thought. Sister Marie nodded and crinkled the corners of her eyes in an effort to show that under the scarf she was smiling. Sister Marie was a sweetie and nothing had better happen to her while she was in St Keyne's, Sister Joan thought, and clashed the gears noisily as they drove off.

"I have to drive over to the Romany camp but I'll ring the hospital later and find out if you're ready to come home," she said cheerfully.

"Would you, Sister?" Sister Marie still sounded timorous.

"No, I'll do better than that!" Sister Joan made up her mind on the instant. "I'll wait until you've had the tooth out and make sure you're comfortable before I go over to the camp."

If there was any possibility of another 'accident' then the presence of a nun seated watchfully outside the operating theatre might prove a necessary check to evil intentions.

I must be getting paranoid about all this, she thought, waving to Brother Cuthbert who had just emerged from his hermitage.

Perhaps it was a slack morning or a new

efficiency was abroad but when they reached St Keyne's they had barely five minutes to wait before they were being ushered along to the operating theatre, where Sister Joan was secretly and intensely relieved to see that the dentist was there, flanked by Sister Warren and the elderly Dr Meredith.

"I decided to come along myself to check everything out," Mr Tregarron said, shaking hands briskly. "I don't like to leave my patients in the lurch so to speak! Feeling rather fragile, I shouldn't wonder, Sister!"

Sister Marie murmured something indistinguishable and cast a pleading look towards Sister Joan.

"I'll be right outside," Sister Joan said encouragingly.

"There's a small viewing section for students who turn up from time to time," Dr Meredith said. "You can watch everything from there if you like."

"Thank you, Doctor," Sister Joan said, with as much enthusiasm as she could muster. "I think that's very nice of you."

She gave Sister Marie another encouraging smile and a thumbs-up sign and went into the glassed-in box which afforded a bird's eye view of the theatre below. There was a long bench here and a pair of opera glasses, presumably for the use of any student who wanted a close-up view. Sister Joan decided not to take advantage of their presence and sat down, cheering herself up with the thought that if the scene became too gory she could always tell her beads with tightly shut eyes.

To her relief the entire procedure took less time than she had imagined and, as Mr Tregarron continually blocked her view she was able to sit placidly enough until the white-gowned figure on the long chair was sitting up and spitting into a basin.

"Everything went well?" She left the booth and buttonholed the dentist.

"Beautiful little job!" Mr Tregarron sounded as pleased as if he'd just seen a great work of art. "Came out clean as a whistle! There's still a nasty little pocket of infection there but antibiotics will take care of that."

"When can Sister Marie come home?"

"Give her a couple of hours to check the bleeding's stopped and then she can drive back with you," Dr Meredith said.

"Meanwhile she'll be — ?"

"In the recovery room in the main building," Sister Warren said. "I'm on duty there."

"See you in a couple of hours then." Sister Joan hesitated, then said, "You will be staying with her yourself?"

"Yes. We've not got too much on this morning. I'll take good care of her, Sister."

So there was no need to worry. Sister Joan went out to the van and drove back on to the moorland track with the inward decision that she was going to stop seeing mysteries round every corner.

An unusual quiet hung over the Romany camp. The children were, of course, at school but the dogs refrained from barking as she drew up and the few women gossiping by the river bank spoke softly instead of laughing and teasing one another. The windows of the Lee caravan were shuttered and Padraic himself sat on the steps, black crêpe round his arm, his expression downcast.

"Good morning, Padraic." Sister Joan adapted her own face and voice to solemnity. "Are the children at home?"

"They went to school." Padraic half rose, then sat down again. "They wanted to be with their friends and so they ought to be. This is a sad place for children now."

"Yes indeed." Sister Joan refrained from commenting that Edith and Tabitha weren't likely to mourn very long for a mother who had taken very little notice of them during her lifetime.

"The truth is that in a few days I'll feel the relief of it," Padraic said. "No more wondering where she is of an evening when the children are tucked up in bed and I'm not minded to beg a neighbour to keep an eye on them while I go out looking! No more lies, Sister. But right this moment I can only see her when she was a bit of a thing with hair down to her waist and such a pretty laugh! I miss her and she wasn't often here."

"Of course you miss her," Sister Joan said. "We all send our love and sympathy from the community. Sister Perpetua and I will represent the convent at the funeral so if you can let me know the time of it — ?"

"Day after tomorrow at eleven. Father Malone has offered to take the service. She was a Catholic, you know."

"No, I didn't know."

"Baptized and everything like the girls," he said with a touch of mournful pride. "I'm Catholic at Easter and Christmastime but Madge was Catholic to the bone though she never went near a church. It's a funny world, isn't it, Sister?"

"It is indeed." Sister Joan waited an instant, then said, "Your wife was sick you know. That was no lie. Alcoholism is a sickness. She never took any other drugs, did she?"

"What sort of drugs?" Padraic asked.

"Oh, Ecstasy or LSD or that kind of thing?"

"She never mixed anything with the alcohol. She had that much sense. Why d'ye ask?"

"I heard a rumour that some drugs were being given away or sold — I don't know which — outside the pub the night before last. If Madge was already — not very well, she might've tried one, perhaps?"

"Aye, possibly." Padraic looked at her keenly. "If she took something extra on top of the drink that might've made her noisy, made her smash the window, mightn't it?"

"Yes. Yes, it's very likely."

"But nobody in town would've given Madge anything like that," he said after a moment's cogitation. "They all knew Madge. Give her a place to sleep it off or some black coffee but not drugs, Sister!"

"Someone from out of town?"

"There's nobody from out of town selling drugs hereabouts," Padraic said. "There's not the money around in a little old place like this. They go to the big towns or to somewhere the colleges are. But I never took her any brandy in, Sister, so they'd best not start blaming me for that!"

"No, of course not, Padraic. I'd better get back to the hospital. Sister Marie had a wisdom tooth out earlier today and I'm due to drive her home again."

"Is she all right?" He rose, blinking away some dismal thought of his own. "I thought the dentist did teeth."

"This was a particularly nasty extraction so Mr Tregarron decided to send her to St Keyne's but it turned out to be fairly straightforward. Will you give my love to Edith and Tabitha?"

"I will surely, Sister. Eleven the day after tomorrow then? In the parish church."

"Sister Perpetua and I will be there. Oh, is Luther in camp?"

"Not seen him since yesterday," Padraic said. "He took off last night when we were keening for my Madge."

"Right then, God bless."

Evidently death had scared Luther away. She would've liked to ask him more about the lady who had given Madge and himself the foil-wrapped tablets.

She drove back to the hospital, parked the van in the forecourt and saw a tall figure emerging from the main building.

"Detective Sergeant Mill, how are you? Did your wife like her anniversary gift?" Mentioning his wife was a kind of defence mechanism. It reminded her that he was married, even if not entirely happily, and that she was a fully professed religious. Otherwise the spark of affection that glowed between them might blaze into something more.

"She put it in the china cabinet. You're not involved in this, are you, Sister?"

"Involved in what?"

She was suddenly aware that there were two police cars drawn up before the main building.

"A little girl's gone missing from the children's unit," he said. "Seeing you I assumed that — "

"Sister Marie had a wisdom tooth out this morning. I'm here to take her home again. Which little girl? How?"

"A four year old called Amy Foster."

"The one who was abused by her foster parents? I met her briefly. When did she go?"

"Sometime in the past hour as far as we can tell. The children have their lunch at twelve and afterwards those who aren't confined to bed go into the garden at the back of the unit if they want to play or they can stay inside with a book. Amy Foster never played with the other children. She used to go into the garden and just sit there, as far as I can tell. Just sit under a bush or a tree and pull up the grass around her. Sometimes she'd bang herself against the tree or scrape her hands along the wall, poor mite! Anyway she went out into the garden today and nobody's seen her since. They searched for ten minutes and then very sensibly called us."

"Could she have wandered into the road?"

"Not from the garden. It's completely enclosed with a fairly high wall around it. The main door of the unit isn't locked but it's far too heavy for a child to open and the handle's too high anyway. Anyway the nurse on duty was at the desk the entire time and says that nobody passed her. The back door leads into the garden and the side door's kept locked except when the delivery man comes."

"Perhaps she's hiding somewhere inside the unit?"

"It doesn't look like it." His dark, winged brows were drawn together into a frown. "It isn't an enormous complex after all — doesn't cater for more than fifteen or twenty children. It looks as if someone snatched her."

"Dear God, but I do hope not!" Sister Joan had paled. "One hears such terrible things. What about the foster parents? The ones who originally ill-treated her?"

"Both on remand in gaol," he said briefly. "The case hasn't come to trial yet and when it does I've my fingers crossed that they'll both go down for a long stretch. No, unless the child grew wings and soared over the wall there's no way she left that garden under her own steam. Look, maybe we could have a coffee or something later? Seems ages since we sat down and solved something together. At the moment I'm pretty tied up."

"There are one or two matters on which I'd appreciate your advice," Sister Joan said.

"Right!" He shot her a glance. "Right then! Take Sister Marie home and — today's no good. I'm going to be tied up here and tomorrow is the chief constable's annual visit. How about the day after? Or are these matters urgent?"

"No, the day after tomorrow will be fine. It isn't exactly official business but I'm sure Mother Prioress will give me permission to have a coffee in town."

"Two thirty at the Swallow Café? If I can't make it I'll let you know in good time. Excuse me now!"

He disappeared rapidly in the direction of the children's unit. Sister Collet, passing him on her way out, paused irresolutely as she saw Sister Joan and then hurried up to her.

"You've heard?" Under the little starched cap her face was white and strained. "I can't believe it's happened you know! She had her lunch with the other children — Amy Foster, I mean. She ate it very nicely too. Sister Williams and I were very pleased. Then we took those who wanted to go outside into the garden and Sister Williams went off duty and I was on the front desk."

"Nobody was supervising the children in the garden?"

"Sister Meecham was supposed to come over but she was held up and didn't get here until twenty minutes later. The children were within calling distance and I couldn't leave the desk. There were only half a dozen outside anyway and there were the eight inside who aren't ambulatory and might've needed something! I told the detective sergeant that it was nobody's fault! We're short staffed and we spend our time running, just running, from one section of the hospital to another. It's a nightmare, Sister!"

"I'm sure you'll find the little girl," Sister Joan said with more optimism than she felt. "You can't blame yourself, Sister."

"But I was on duty! Sophie Meecham was supposed to join me but she was checking the drugs unit. If she'd been able to get over here on time this might not have happened. The children are none of them terribly sick so she reckoned there wasn't any particular urgency."

"I have to go and collect Sister Marie," Sister Joan said. "If I were you, Sister Collet, I'd sit down quietly with a cup of tea and jot down all the things that happened from the time you gave the children their lunch. Something might have occurred that you hardly noticed at the time but it might prove to be significant later."

"I'll do that! Sophie Meecham had better do it too! If she paid more heed to what was going on around here instead of — oh, never mind! Thank you, Sister!"

Tracy Collet took to her heels and rushed away again. Sister Joan looked after her with a thoughtful expression, then made her own way to the recovery room where she was relieved to find Sister Marie, still with her cheek swollen but with some of the usual sparkle back in her eyes.

"What's going on, Sister?" She spoke somewhat indistinctly. "There are police here so Sister Warren says."

"Some administrative muddle," Sister Joan said, exchanging a brief glance with the attendant nurse. "You'd better cover your mouth with your scarf in case you get a draught in your face. Any special instructions for Sister Perpetua?"

"A mild painkiller every couple of hours until the aching stops and nothing very hot or very cold to drink for the next twenty-four hours," Sister Warren said.

"Fine! I'll tell our infirmarian. Have you got everything?"

"I think so." Sister Marie rose, pulling her scarf across her face and shaking hands politely with Sister Warren. "Thank you for keeping me company. God bless."

Going out to the van again Sister Joan chattered trivialities until Sister Marie was safely ensconced in the passenger seat. Then she spoke briskly, "Would you excuse me for a couple of minutes, Sister? I have something to check on." She couldn't possibly drive back to the convent without asking if any trace had been found of that small, sad little girl.

Constable Petrie was on the reception desk, making notes and looking grave.

"No sign of her?" Sister Joan pushed open the heavy swing door and went up to him.

"Nothing so far, Sister." His pleasant face was weary. "This is just the kind of thing we all dread happening. She's vanished into thin air. Nobody's seen anything or heard anything. Those children should never have been left unattended in the garden. The trouble is that they're just toddlers and they didn't see anything they can tell us about even if there was anything to see. We'll have to widen the area we're searching now and that means bringing in extra men if they can be spared from anywhere."

"Surely there's some trace of her," Sister Joan insisted.

"Nothing. As far as we can tell she went off and sat by the wall. She was picking some flowers. We found a bunch on the grass near where she'd been. Looks as if she dropped it."

"What kind of flowers?" Sister Joan asked.

"Wild ones," Constable Petrie said. "Buttercups and some heather and a couple of dandelions and some trailing fern stuff. Odd that; so far we haven't seen a single wild flower in that garden. It's all grass and lilac bushes and a big bed of carnations."

7

"This isn't just a muddle or something, is it?" Sister Marie said, as they drove back to the convent. "Something serious must've happened for the police to be at the hospital."

"A little girl from the children's unit is missing," Sister Joan said, deciding there was no point in keeping the matter quiet any longer. "She wasn't exactly physically sick but withdrawn and traumatized after ill-treatment. Anyway she's probably hiding somewhere but they very wisely called the police immediately."

"Oh, I hope they find her," Sister Marie said softly. "Will they be asking for your help, Sister?"

"I think the police will handle this very well by themselves," Sister Joan said tersely.

At the convent she deposited Sister Marie in the capable hands of Sister Perpetua and went to find Mother Dorothy who looked up from the essay she was marking with a wry smile.

"Sister Bernadette has a novel way of expressing herself," she said. "She writes in her latest essay that our vows of chastity, obedience and compassion might be regarded as the big Cs. Rather like a pop group she adds. What did you wish to see me about, Sister?"

"Sister Marie had the tooth out and is in the infirmary now, resting."

"Good. One doesn't wish to encourage hypochondria among the community by fussing about minor ailments but in this life nothing is certain. You went over to see Padraic Lee?"

"Yes, Mother Dorothy. The funeral is at eleven the day after tomorrow. Father Malone will be taking the service."

"God rest her soul!" Crossing herself the prioress said, "I was not aware that Mrs Lee was a Catholic. That was a failure on our part, Sister. How is Padraic taking it?"

"He mourns for the woman she was when he married her."

"And if the husband can think of her with tenderness how much more will Our Blessed Lord show compassion! I think that I will attend the funeral myself, Sister, and take Sister Perpetua with me. Since only two of the community habitually attend outside funerals that means you will have to give up your own place."

"Yes, Mother Prioress." Sister Joan added

honestly, “It’s no great sacrifice because I don’t like funerals very much and I never had much patience with Madge Lee.”

“Compassion, Sister! We are Daughters of Compassion after all! You may drive us down to the church. I have no doubt that Father Malone will offer us both lunch so you may pick us up later on. Is that all?”

“Mother Prioress, you were not easy in your mind about your godmother’s sudden death.”

“That’s true. However, during the time that has elapsed nothing of particular note has come to light, has it?”

“There are certainly irregularities at St Keyne’s,” Sister Joan said carefully. “I don’t know whether or not this is malicious or sheer inefficiency or a mixture of both. I do feel that it might be a good idea to consult Detective Sergeant Mill about it. If he agrees that something requires investigating he has the authority to do it.”

“Which means you wish to call in at the police station while Sister Perpetua and I are at Madge Lee’s funeral?”

“What I think doesn’t really warrant a formal statement yet,” Sister Joan said. “If I might have permission to have a quiet word outside official channels — ?”

“The latitude I allow you astonishes me

sometimes," Mother Dorothy said. "Very well, Sister. You may speak to the detective sergeant in some public place. I rely on you not to waste his time with baseless suspicions. Until then you had better go and help your sisters wherever help is needed, and in your spare moments read through these notes on which I'm basing our current discussions on the seven deadly sins, since you have been notable for your absences from our little gatherings."

Sister Joan took the file of neatly typed notes meekly, made her farewell salutation and withdrew. Her absences from the discussions hadn't been of her own choosing, she thought crossly. She seemed to spend hours recently driving up and down between hospital, Romany camp and convent. It wasn't like Mother Prioress to be so manifestly unfair, a sure sign that she too felt an inward unease that refused to depart.

She was halfway to her cell when she remembered and scooted back down the staircase, almost cannoning into the prioress as the latter emerged from her parlour.

"Sister Joan! Nuns don't run unless it's a matter of life and death! Is it?" Mother Dorothy demanded.

"No, Mother. I merely forgot to tell

you that a little girl has disappeared from St Keyne's," Sister Joan said breathlessly. "The police are looking for her."

"Thank you, Sister. I'll ring the station myself later to find out what happened. You had better spend this evening's recreation period getting your spiritual diary up to date with particular reference to your slapdash habits. *Dominus vobiscum*."

"*Et cum spiritu sancto*," Sister Joan said gloomily.

At recreation which followed supper she excused herself and slipped away up to the library where she could catch up on her spiritual reading and writing, never an occupation which cheered her up very much because her own jottings struck her as materialistic and banal in the extreme and Mother Dorothy's careful arguments laid out with clarity in her notes merely served to remind her that she had a long way to go. When the bell went for the final service of the day she slipped down and took her usual place, noting that Sister Marie had evidently been bundled off to bed and that Sister Mary Concepta looked frailer than ever. There was every likelihood that she would have to go into the hospital soon for another heart check-up, itself an excellent reason to find out exactly what was going on there.

"You will be sorry to hear that a four-year-old girl was apparently taken from St Keyne's Hospital earlier today." Making the announcement the prioress sounded gravely troubled. Evidently her call to the police station had brought her scant comfort.

"Since we are about to enter into the grand silence there can be no discussion of this until tomorrow," Mother Dorothy was continuing, "and it is in the highest degree unlikely that the child is on convent property. Nevertheless I have assured Constable Petrie that in the morning we will search the house and grounds thoroughly if the little girl hasn't been found. We will say an extra decade of the rosary and offer it to the police authorities that they may be successful in their search and bring it to a happy conclusion. Let us pray. Hail Mary, full of grace — "

A happy conclusion meant finding Amy alive, Sister Joan reflected, her beads sliding between finger and thumb. How often were missing children found safe and sound?

At breakfast the next morning Father Malone gently lamented the insecurity of modern life.

"When I was a little lad in Ireland didn't we run out into the fields and play safely until bedtime and now little ones aren't safe anywhere? I must confess to you, Sisters, that I've no compassion at all on those who steal children! None at all!"

"Neither did our Blessed Lord," Sister David said.

"Mind you, we don't know for certain that she was kidnapped," Sister Teresa ventured.

"She could hardly have climbed a wall all by herself," Mother Dorothy frowned. "She was with other children in the walled garden behind the children's unit when she disappeared, all of them apparently unsupervised for a few minutes. I rang the police first thing this morning straight after mass but so far there's no information. We intend to search the house and enclosure on our own account this morning, though I'm positive she's not here."

"We'd've heard her running around," Sister Katherine said.

They were all thinking of finding a live child, to be pulled from some hidey-hole and scolded and hugged. Not even Mother Dorothy was allowing herself to consider what must be only too likely.

"Yes, of course you would!" Father Malone had evidently grasped the darker possibility since he spoke too quickly and heartily, setting his cup down on the long table as he said, "Well, I must be getting back. There's to be an incident room set up at the station in case anybody has any news. God bless, Sisters!"

"Who's to search where?" Sister Perpetua asked. "I must tell you now that Sister Marie's still feeling poorly after her operation and I can't have my old ladies running round the place getting upset and overexcited."

"Sister Marie will stay by the telephone in case word comes from the police," Mother Dorothy said. "Sister Gabrielle and Sister Mary Concepta will join Sister Hilaria and Sister Bernadette in the chapel to pray for the safety of the little girl; Sister David and I will search the house upstairs and downstairs; the rest of you will search the grounds and outbuildings. Sister Joan, make the postulancy your field of operations if you please, and take Alice with you."

The postulancy had once been a small dower house at the far end of the sunken tennis court. Since the Daughters of Compassion had taken over the property it had served as a postulancy where Sister Hilaria could train the one or two novices who applied each year to join the Order in this part of Cornwall. Sister Joan never made her way along the path past the enclosure gardens and the convent cemetery without imagining long ago moonlit evenings when some daring beau might have prevailed on a daughter of the Tarquin family to stroll with him, arms entwined, nor went down across the weed-marred court with its rusting posts without picturing the girls in white dresses and young men in flannels who had once played there and were long gone, many of them killed in both World Wars.

She called Alice and set off, walking slowly, conscientiously parting the bushes, with the sinking feeling that this was all a waste of time. Whoever had taken Amy would hardly have trekked up five miles from town to deposit her on convent land. People who stole children generally had an escape route planned — a nearby house or flat, a car, someone who would cover for them if they were questioned.

She walked across the old tennis court and let herself in at the front door of the two-storey cottage where Sister Hilaria and Sister Bernadette must surely rattle around in a building converted to house six. Inside and out, walls and ceilings were whitewashed, white-slatted blinds and long white curtains protected the small windows. A passage with a narrow staircase directly ahead gave on to a small kitchen where tea and soup could be brewed, a room conserved as a library where books suitable for the innocent eyes of novices were neatly ranged on the shelves, a parlour for Sister Hilaria which was as bleak and bare as all the other rooms. On the other side of the passage, a long room furnished with desks and benches served as study with, behind it, another long room where novice mistress and charge held their recreation. Sister Joan, looking at the table on which a Scrabble set, and several dogeared jigsaws were stacked made up her mind to suggest that a couple of new games might be provided out of Louisa Cummings's legacy. She went up the stairs, looking into each of the six cells, only two now occupied, and looked also in the two tiny bathrooms at the end of the passage. The postulancy hummed with silence.

Outside Alice barked loudly. Sister Joan ran down the stairs in a manner that would have certainly excited Mother Dorothy's wrath had she been present, opened the front door and saw Sister Meecham fending off Alice with a shoulder bag.

"She won't hurt you!" Sister Joan called the dog sharply to heel, hiding her surprise when Alice actually obeyed. "She's still in training. It's Sister Meecham, isn't it?"

"Sophie Meecham, yes."

The other stood still, looking vaguely sheepish.

"May I help you?" Sister Joan felt the inadequacy of the question.

"I came for a walk," Sophie Meecham said. "To get away from things for a bit. It must be very peaceful here in the convent."

"Not always. We don't shut out the world entirely, you know," Sister Joan said gently.

"I suppose not." The other hesitated, then said abruptly, "But Catholics can make confession, can't they? Get things off their chest? And the priest can't say anything, not even if they admit to a murder?"

"No, the seal of the confessional is very strict." Sister Joan waited a moment, then said, "Was there something about a murder that troubles you? I'm not a priest but — "

"No, of course not," Sophie Meecham said. "No, I was just thinking of the worst thing anybody could possibly do and still be able to confess it. I suppose the priest sets punishment?"

"Penance; but that generally means setting right the wrong done as far as possible and saying a certain number of prayers. It's not exactly punishment, more a balancing up the ledger. Is there any news of the little girl? Of Amy?"

"Not as far as I know," Sophie Meecham

said. "No, the police set up an incident room and they're going round the town, asking people."

"Sister Collet must be feeling very upset," Sister Joan said. "She was on duty in the children's unit, wasn't she?"

"On the reception desk, yes."

"And she was on ward duty when Mrs Cummings died."

"Yes."

"She's a good nurse?"

The other's cheeks flamed suddenly. Sophie Meecham said in a voice that vibrated with suppressed anger, "She doesn't do her work conscientiously! Always woolgathering! Very pleasant and she does care about the patients but that's not enough! You can't mix private and public. It doesn't work. It never works!"

"Sister Meecham, can't you tell me what's worrying you?" Sister Joan asked.

"Are you under the seal of the confessional?" the other demanded.

"Well, no, not exactly! I couldn't promise not to pass on what you had to say, but I'd use the greatest discretion."

"I don't have anything to tell you," Sister Meecham said, and walked away rapidly.

Sister Joan stared after the retreating figure, biting her lip, wanting to run after her, shake information out of her, but it would have been quite useless. She went back inside the postulancy, double-checked the rooms, locked up and continued her search of the grounds with the increasing conviction that she'd do better to sit down and think through recent events instead of running around like a headless chicken.

"Anything?"

Sister Katherine joined her as she emerged from the shrubbery walk.

"Not a sign of anyone or anything," Sister Joan said.

"We've been just about everywhere," Sister Katherine said. "There's nothing at all. I'm not even sure what we're looking for. A child wouldn't stay hidden all night so near without someone hearing, and I can't face — the other thing."

"That she might be dead?" Sister Joan felt a fleeting pity as the other nun's pale face paled further and her slim fingers involuntarily clenched. Sister Katherine was wise never to leave the enclosure because her gentleness was ill equipped to deal with the reality of the world beyond.

"Sister, why don't you go back to the main house and make tea for everybody?" she said. "I'm sure Mother Dorothy will approve. Looking for someone who's disappeared is never very nice even when it's highly unlikely that you'll find anything."

"Thank you, Sister."

Sister Katherine glided away, clearly relieved. Sister Joan shook her head mentally and walked through into the acre of land which comprised the enclosure garden. A wall ran round it and a further wall blocked off a triangular piece of ground used as the convent cemetery. In the main garden, root vegetables, beans and cabbages mingled with the now feathery fronds of asparagus, bramble bushes, herbs, trees heavy with apples and pears. Sister Martha sold the surplus in the market, having provided sufficient for the entire community.

She was there now, peering up into the trees as if she hoped to find a small girl seated on the branches.

"No luck, Sister?" Sister Joan joined her.

"I think this is a waste of time," Sister Martha said frankly, lowering her gaze. "I honestly don't believe that we'll find anyone here. But it makes us feel useful, I suppose. I'm praying the weather holds so that I can get in the Conference pears before the squirrels beat me to it. Luther was supposed to come and help me today and he's usually very reliable but he hasn't turned up. Too excited by all the goings on in town, I suppose."

"I'll lend you a hand if you like, Sister," Sister Joan offered. "There's nothing in the postulancy either."

"There's a fruit skip over there." Sister Martha looked pleased to be doing something practical. "Sister Teresa wants to pickle some of the pears this year. That will make a nice change when we have cheese. Sister David says the Romans were very fond of pickled fruit."

"They ate dormice too," Sister Joan reminded her. "Better tell those squirrels of yours to watch out!"

Sister Martha laughed, then abruptly sobered, her small face troubled.

"Is it wrong to joke at a time like this?" she asked anxiously. "The truth is that I don't want to think about that poor little girl! That's cowardly of me, I know, but Father Malone was saying this morning that she has no parents and that the people she was with before abused her. Poor little thing! I can't bear to think about it, Sister, and I know Sister Katherine feels the same way. You've just missed a couple of ripe ones, Sister!"

"Sorry!" Sister Joan scrambled up the ladder again.

In the back of her mind something was stirring. Something that Sister Martha had said. It tied up with something else casually heard, but she couldn't remember either of the remarks. Words thrown away casually clung to the edges of her memory but never came fully into focus.

"I hope Luther's all right," Sister Martha was saying. "One never knows how he might react when anything out of the ordinary happens. Yet he's generally so reliable."

"There's Madge Lee's funeral tomorrow morning," Sister Joan said.

"And Luther's afraid of death. Can you imagine what that must be like?"

"Very easily," Sister Joan said soberly.

"I think it's splendid of you to be able to put yourself into another person's mind and understand how they think," Sister Martha said earnestly. "It's no wonder people confide in you, Sister!"

"Not always." Sister Joan thought of Sophie Meecham, shoulders tight as she marched away.

They gathered in the kitchen for the unofficial cup of tea, each one coming in and answering enquiring looks with a silent shake of the head. Sister Gabrielle plodded in, her hawk face seamed and browned, her stick tapping impatiently.

"If I pray any longer," she announced, "it's going to sound like nagging! Is that tea? Nothing like a good cup of tea to get the mind working clearly. Sister Hilaria has gone over to the postulancy with Bernadette for something to drink there. Water, no doubt. I'm not made of such stern stuff!"

"Would you like your tea here or in the Infirmary?" Sister Teresa asked.

"Here, of course!" Sister Gabrielle looked with some satisfaction round the large, shiny kitchen. "I really fail to see why once we reach a certain age we get shunted into the infirmary like naughty children. Someone get me a chair though. My knees are cracking like fireworks. Sister Mary Concepta, do sit down and stop fidgeting! I'm sure our combined prayers will have achieved some result!"

She lowered herself into the hastily provided chair with a grunt and sipped her tea.

The prioress came in with Sister David at her heels. Looking at her, Sister Joan found herself wondering what would have to happen short of an earthquake to throw Mother Dorothy into a panic. Probably not even an earthquake! The only sign of agitation her superior displayed was an added edge to her voice, a sharper gleam from the eyes behind the round spectacles.

She said, "A telephone call has come from the police — from Constable Petrie. So far they have not found the child but they have found some smears of dried blood on the wall of the garden behind the children's unit. I'm afraid that is a most disquieting discovery but we must continue to pray and to hope. I take it that none of you found anything?"

She looked about the semicircle of faces.

"Nothing at all," Sister Perpetua said.

"Well, it was what might be termed a long shot." The prioress used the idiom with delicate emphasis. "There is nothing more of a practical nature we can do except keep our eyes and ears open for any unusual event. And, of course, it goes without saying that we shall continue to pray for the little girl's safety. To my mind that is the most practical course of action we can take."

"Amen," Sister Gabrielle said.

"There is one further matter." Mother Dorothy frowned slightly. "Nobody seems to have seen Luther for the past forty-eight hours. Padraic rang earlier to ask if his cousin had turned up here to help Sister Martha as he promised. Nobody has seen Luther?"

"Not since the other evening," Sister Joan said. "He was hanging round the main gate. The mourning for Madge Lee had upset him. He's probably gone to ground until the funeral is over."

In the depths of her pocket the foil-wrapped tablet felt as heavy as a stone. She wished that it was possible to have her chat with Detective Sergeant Mill sooner than the time arranged, but he would have his time fully occupied with the hunt for Amy.

"You can't think there's any connection!" Sister Martha exclaimed suddenly, her face flaming. "Poor Luther is one of the gentlest creatures alive. He'd never hurt a child!"

"Amy had the habit of hurting herself," Sister Joan said. "She frequently banged her head against the nearest solid object or scratched at her arms and legs. Abused children often feel worthless and guilty and try to punish themselves I understand."

"Poor little mite!" Sister Katherine had winced. "Surely she should've been watched more carefully then, not left unsupervised in the garden?"

"I believe that they are short-staffed in St Keyne's," Mother Dorothy said, "and the changeover to being Trust maintained hasn't gone altogether smoothly. We can't expect immediate perfection in any organization."

"Time's getting on." Mother Dorothy spoke briskly. "We'll return to our normal routine for the rest of the day. Sister Martha, can you supply a nice bouquet of flowers for Madge Lee?"

"Yes, Mother Dorothy."

The routine of the convent resumed its even rhythm. Sister Teresa started to prepare the simple lunch of soup, a salad sandwich and a piece of fruit which varied only on Christmas Day when there was poached salmon with a mustard cream dressing. Sister Joan helped put out the plates and cut bread and count apples into a large wooden bowl while her mind continued to be teased by something spoken that she could no longer hear clearly.

If she went on trying to remember she never would remember! She carried the food upstairs to the graciously proportioned room that had been a drawing-room but was now divided into two, with double doors opening into the back section which was used as a room in which the nightly recreation could be held.

Lunch was a silent meal, unlike breakfast where talking was allowed or supper during which one of the sisters read from a devotional book. Sister Joan let her gaze move slowly over her companions. Sister Gabrielle had stomped her way upstairs, but Sister Mary Concepta had stayed in the infirmary with Sister Marie and Sister Teresa, being the lay sister, ate as she always did after she had served the others. Odd, Sister Joan thought, how women dressed exactly alike and performing the same actions, could still look different. All the rules and routine in the world couldn't stamp out one's own individual personality. Mother Dorothy ate neatly and swiftly, only occasionally raising her head to let the light from the wide landing gleam on her spectacles. Sister Hilaria seemed not to notice she was eating at all. She dipped her spoon into the watercress soup, lifted it, and held it poised in the air for a moment as if she wasn't certain what it was doing there before conveying it to her mouth, while at her side Sister Bernadette ate with the hearty appetite of a young woman who enjoys food and has no dark or secret side.

I'm woolgathering! Sister Joan thought impatiently. We all have our dark and secret side. The world itself has another face and the moon a side it never shows.

In the bustling hospital, where nurses struggled to get to their duties on time, fighting stress and tiredness, someone was taking advantage of that. Drugs were being taken from a unit to which a great many people could gain access without much trouble, and then the drugs taken were entered belatedly in the register. A nurse on duty went to the toilet while an elderly woman died of a heart attack that shouldn't have occurred, and the same nurse sat at a reception desk while one of the children in her charge vanished into thin air, leaving smears of blood behind. Someone gave Madge Lee and Luther foil-wrapped tablets and now Madge Lee was dead, killed by one bottle of brandy that had turned up mysteriously minus its cap at the same time Sister Meecham's secret tipple had disappeared from the office. And Sister Collet had wept bitterly when she had received a legacy of a modest ring.

The names revolved in her mind endlessly like a litany. Sophie Meecham, Tracy Collet, Ceri Williams, Sister Merryl, Sister Warren, Sister Croft, Dr Meredith, Dr Geeson — a name was missing and she didn't know which one it was nor which face fitted it. Someone else linked with — what?

"Let us say grace." Mother Dorothy had folded her napkin and rose, folding her narrow hands.

Sister Joan bowed her head and crossed herself. On her mind the faces were imprinted, some smiling and full face, others in profile, one walking away, growing smaller and smaller until she receded into nothing, like Amy.

Like Amy . . . like Amy Foster. Foster. Sister Foster was on men's surgical giving a drink of tea to a patient on the night Louisa Cummings was killed. Sister Foster would do anything for a man. Someone had said that casually when she'd made enquiries. Foster. It wasn't an unusual name but she hadn't come across it very often in Cornwall. Was there a connection of some kind? An instinct deeper than logic told her that there was.

"Sister Joan, you seemed somewhat absent-minded during lunch," Mother Dorothy said.

"Mother?" Sister Joan hastily assumed an alert expression.

"You picked up a fork with which to eat your soup," Mother Dorothy said dryly. "I can appreciate your anxiety. We are all anxious about the child but since there's nothing further we can do in a practical sense then please concentrate your attention on the duties you have here. A wandering mind is a slothful mind, Sister, and since our little discussion this afternoon is to be on the subject of sloth then you may care to jot down your thoughts on it after you've mucked out the stable."

"Yes, Mother Dorothy," Sister Joan said, and set her soul in patience to await the morrow.

It came on laggard feet, crawling through the hours that stretched themselves across the intervening time.

Father Stephens came to offer the mass, his movements as graceful as if he watched himself in a mirror, his voice teasing out the sensuousness of the words. Definitely a candidate for a bishopric, Sister Joan thought, then found within herself a tiny pocket of compassion for a young priest with ambition who finds himself as assistant to a much loved and respected old pastor.

Mother Dorothy excused herself during breakfast and went off to telephone the police, returning as Father Stephens was just leaving to inform the community that nothing further had been discovered.

By 10.30 Sister Joan was helping both the prioress and Sister Perpetua into the van and Sister Martha bustled up with a sheaf of dahlias in varying shades of bronze and gold.

"Will you please find out if anyone has seen Luther?" she begged. "I'm becoming quite seriously concerned about him."

"Yes, of course, Sister. Anything we hear we'll relay on our return." Mother Dorothy nodded approval at the sheaf.

As they drove through the gates on to the bumpy track she said, "Sister Joan, you will not need to pick us up after the service and lunch with Father Malone. Father Stephens informed me this morning that he will bring us both back to the convent, so you are free to use the extra time to make what enquiries you deem necessary."

"About the little girl?" Sister Perpetua asked.

"That and other matters, Sister. There are certain irregularities in the procedures at St Keyne's which require to be addressed."

"If something's going on down there," Sister Perpetua returned with energy, "I'd like it stopped before Sister Mary Concepta has to have another check up!"

Brother Cuthbert emerged from his stone hermitage and waved to them, his freckled young face anxious as he loped towards the van.

"Good morning, Mother Prioress. Sisters. Is there any news of the little girl who's missing? There were police searching the moors until quite late last night. I went along with them for part of the time until Detective Sergeant Mill decided we might be walking over valuable evidence and not see it in the dark."

"No word as yet, Brother Cuthbert," Mother Dorothy said.

"I have been praying about it," Brother

Cuthbert said. "My own feeling is that some lady who has no children of her own saw Amy Foster and decided to take her home. Unwise but not malicious, don't you think? Are you going to the funeral service for Padraic Lee's wife?"

"To the requiem," Sister Joan said.

"She was a Catholic, of course! I'd forgotten. I must make haste then."

"You'd better come with us," Sister Joan said. "Otherwise you'll be late."

"That's very kind of you, Sister." His cheerful face had lengthened slightly. "The truth is that I'm more at ease working on engines than riding in them, but needs must — "

"When Sister Joan drives," Sister Perpetua said dryly. "Lock up and jump in."

"Oh, I never bother to lock up," the young monk said, opening the door and clambering up beside Sister Perpetua. "It would be dreadful if someone needed shelter and I was out and they couldn't get in. Anyway I've nothing worth the stealing. Do you think Luther will be at the funeral? I understand he's not been seen for a couple of days."

"Probably not, but I'm sure he will turn up sooner or later. He always does," Sister Joan said.

"He fears death," Brother Cuthbert said in

a wondering tone. "Now I can't pretend that I would welcome death if it came too soon because the world is such a marvellous place that I want to enjoy it for as long as possible, but I daresay there are even greater delights in store for us when we are finally called."

"You're always so optimistic," Sister Joan said.

Usually his cheerfully placid nature soothed and cheered her but this morning she had too much on her mind. There were too many loose ends to be tied up, too many answers waiting for questions she hadn't yet formulated in her own mind.

"I know," Brother Cuthbert said apologetically. "It irritates people terribly at times but it's habitual with me, I'm afraid."

"God preserve us from long-faced saints!" Mother Dorothy said, quoting St Teresa. "You go right on being cheerful, Brother Cuthbert. You may drop us here, Sister, on the corner. We can walk the last few yards to the church. Your time is your own now until tea this afternoon. I trust you'll make full use of it."

"I will, Mother," Sister Joan said, and held in her impatience as the three climbed down from the van.

First stop the hospital, she thought, and drove off the moment the doors were shut.

8

The hospital presented its normal aspect of half-organized bustle. There were two police constables in the forecourt, neither of them known to her, which meant that men from other local forces had been drafted in. Both of them glanced incuriously towards Sister Joan but made no move to question her as she climbed down from the vehicle and went into the main building.

Ceri Williams was on the reception desk. She looked tired, her usually rosy face slightly drawn as she greeted Sister Joan.

"You've not heard anything, I suppose? About Amy, I mean?"

"Not a thing," Sister Joan said. "I'm here to make a flying visit round the wards. Is it all right if I go up?"

"Yes, of course. I'm going off duty in a few minutes," Ceri Williams said. "Was there anything you wanted to ask me?"

"I'm not really here to ask questions," Sister Joan said. "I daresay the police have grilled everybody thoroughly."

"Those of us who were on the premises," Ceri Williams said. "I felt ever so sorry for

Sister Collet. She was at the reception desk in the children's unit. I suppose she should have checked in the wards to see the children but those who weren't out in the garden were either in their beds or resting in the playroom so she figured there wasn't much need. I'd just gone off duty and I had looked in on all the children, including the ones in the garden."

"Did you see Amy?"

"She was sitting by the back wall," Sister Williams said, screwing up her eyes as she recreated the scene mentally. "She never would play with the other children. Miss Fleetwood fears she may be traumatized so severely that she will never be entirely normal. Isn't that just awful!"

"I hope Shirley Fleetwood's wrong," Sister Joan said. "Thank you, Sister. Maybe I'll see you later."

She went up the staircase, turning in the direction of the men's surgical ward.

"Sister Joan, is there any news?"

Sister Warren, something nearer human weakness in her resolute expression, looked up from the desk as Sister Joan went in. Of the four occupants of the ward two were reading the newspapers, a third drinking a cup of coffee, the fourth sufficiently lively to send a long low wolf whistle in Sister Joan's direction. Sister Joan flapped her hand at him in mock reproof and spoke to Sister Warren.

"I'm actually looking for Sister Foster. She was on duty in this ward on the night Mrs Cummings died."

"We get moved around so much that we're seldom in the same place more than once or twice a month," Sister Warren said. "The duty roster's in the office. I think Sister Meecham's there."

"Thanks. I'll take a look." Sister Joan turned to go as the other detained her, lowering her voice.

"You'll have heard about the little girl, of course. The height of inefficiency if you want my opinion. At the very least Sister Collet deserves a severe reprimand. Sister Meecham is altogether too lenient with the staff and of course complaints to the manager do absolutely no good at all. That wretched individual is hardly ever here!"

"I've not heard anything," Sister Joan said. "Thank you."

There seemed to be precious little friendship among the nurses, she reflected, as she made her way to the office. Sisters Warren and Merryl had scant sympathy with the modern way of doing things and the other nurses seemed to be in a constant state of agitation which had very little to do with patient care.

The office door was partly open, the room itself empty. Sister Joan went in and looked round at the filing cabinets, the shiny computer, the flat-topped desk on which some X-ray photographs were ranged. The duty roster for the month was on the wall. Sister Foster was off duty until the evening.

"What are you doing here, Sister?"

Dr Geeson had paused at the door and was staring at her.

"Sister Meecham isn't here," Sister Joan evaded.

"Unauthorized persons really cannot be allowed to wander round the hospital," he said.

"No, of course not." Sister Joan regarded him gravely.

"You wished to see Sister Meecham?"

"I saw her yesterday. She came by the convent."

"I've no idea where she is." He spoke coldly, obviously waiting for her to leave. If he dared, Sister Joan thought with a prickle of amusement, he'd give me a good hard shove through the door.

"Thank you anyway, Doctor." She nodded pleasantly and went out again.

Sister Foster wasn't on duty which, with

any luck, meant she was in the residents' unit. Sister Joan went down the stairs again, left the main building and crossed the forecourt. The door of the residents' unit was unlocked and she pushed it ajar and went in. The common room where she had spoken to Tracy Collet was deserted. She stood uncertainly in the entrance hall as a slim figure descended the narrow staircase.

"Sister Prince?"

"Yes — and you're — ?"

"Sister Joan from the convent. Are you just going on duty?"

"To casualty," Carol Prince said. "Did you want to see somebody?"

"Does Sister Foster live in this unit?"

"Betty Foster? Yes. Not that she spends many nights in her own bed," the other said with a disparaging air. "Number four. Go on up."

She scooted past, intent on getting to casualty on time.

Number Four was on the upper storey, a neat white card printed with the name. She lifted her hand and tapped.

There was an appreciable pause before the door opened. A tallish young woman, hair pulled back into a ponytail, held it open, one eyebrow slightly raised as she contemplated the smaller woman before her.

"Are you collecting for something?" she enquired.

"Sister Foster? No, I'm not collecting for anything. My name is Sister Joan and I'd be grateful if I might have a few words."

"I'm off duty." Betty Foster sounded distinctly unwelcoming.

"It's about Amy," Sister Joan said.

Betty Foster opened the door wider, turned her back and walked across the room within, hips swaying under her silky housecoat. She wore no make-up but it was easy to tell that when she was dressed and painted she would look extremely attractive. Filled with the promise of sexuality, Sister Joan thought, watching the other light a cigarette and blow a perfect smoke ring before she turned, leaning against the chest of drawers and nodding towards a chair.

"You can sit down if you like," she said reluctantly. "The police have already asked some questions. I wasn't on duty yesterday anyway. I've had a bit of a cold so I took a couple of days owing to me. I wasn't here anyway."

"You went out when you had a cold?" Sister Joan commented mildly, seating herself.

"A gentleman friend offered to run me over to Penzance. We had a very nice lunch. He rang the police and confirmed what I said. So I really can't help you any further. You're the nun who helps out the police now and then, aren't you?"

"Now and then. Strictly in an amateur capacity. I've no official standing."

"Well, I *can't* add anything to what I've already said," Betty Foster said.

"You didn't see Amy yesterday then? But you do work in the children's unit sometimes?"

"We all take turns in every department. What of it?"

"Did it worry you that Amy was damaging herself? Banging her head and scratching her arms and legs?"

"I suppose." Betty Foster turned abruptly and stubbed out the cigarette in a saucer. There was a sudden tension in the set of her shoulders.

"It would certainly worry me if my daughter was in such a state," Sister Joan said.

"Yes, but — " Betty Foster swung back to face her. "How did you know? Has someone guessed? I haven't said one word! Not to the police, not to anybody! How did you find out?"

"Actually I didn't," Sister Joan confessed. "I simply thought that Foster wasn't a local name and someone mentioned that you were — rather susceptible to the opposite sex, so I made a random guess and it paid off. Did you take the job here because of Amy?"

"No, of course not! Amy wasn't here when I took up my post two years back."

"You're not from round here originally?"

"Essex. I did my nurse's training in London, in Battersea. I had to drop out for a year when Amy was born. She was put in a children's home. I never agreed to permanent adoption. She was to be fostered until I'd got enough together to get a little flat and have her with me. I never gave her away."

"The father wouldn't help?"

"I don't want anything off him," Betty Foster said. "Anyway he's always denied that Amy was his."

"So you applied for a job at St Keyne's so that you could be near Amy. Did you go and see her?"

"No. She doesn't know anything about me. Nobody does. It was just the worst luck that she was brought to St Keyne's when her foster parents ill-treated her."

"You must've been unhappy about that. About her being ill-treated, I mean?"

"If they hadn't been put in gaol I'd've killed them!" Betty Foster said. "It's not her fault that she was born, poor thing! She's ready for nursery school now, so if I can get a flat and only work days she could be with me. I've been saving up and some of my gentlemen friends have been very generous."

"And I take it the rest of the staff aren't aware of your — extracurricular activities?"

"They know I have gentlemen friends," Betty Foster said, "but they don't know about Amy. At least — no, why would they know? Who'd tell?"

"What about the social worker? Shirley Fleetwood?"

"Shirley Fleetwood doesn't see what's under her nose," Betty Foster said scornfully. "I mean, my name's in Amy's file but I didn't notify my change of address when I left London, so she never made the connection. I send money for Amy regularly from a London bank. Not much but I'm saving up for the future for us."

"With the help of your gentlemen friends?"

"Nothing wrong with that!" Betty Foster gave a high, hard little laugh. "Get what you can while the juices are flowing and then get out, that's my motto!"

"It takes all sorts," Sister Joan said, heroically concealing her own opinion.

"And now she's been taken." Betty Foster

sat down abruptly on the end of the unmade bed. "It's like a nightmare! Just as I was seeing my way clear to having her with me someone takes her!"

"Have you told the police that you're her natural mother?"

"Nothing to do with them!" was the sulky response. "I wasn't on duty and so my friend told them and, as he doesn't know about Amy and I wasn't on duty anyway, the police constable never asked me any more questions. But it's upset me more than I care to say."

She was almost certainly speaking the truth, Sister Joan reflected. Despite her cheap sexiness, her surface hardness, she had cared enough about her child to get a job in the same area where the child was being fostered and she had never agreed to give up Amy for permanent adoption.

"When Amy is found will you apply to the courts for custody?" she asked.

"I'll have a nice little place for the two of us and her name down for nursery school," Betty Foster said. "They can't keep her from me, can they?"

"I shouldn't think so. Amy doesn't know that you're her mother?"

"Not a thing." The hard young mouth quivered suddenly. "I don't mind telling you, Sister, that I was quite upset when I heard what'd happened to her. And since she's been in the children's unit I've tried to keep an eye open for her. She keeps trying to hurt herself it seems, but she never gets the chance when I'm on duty."

"When you apply to the courts," Sister Joan said, rising, "mention my name. It may help if it's clear that you have a respectable friend."

"Instead of one of my gentlemen you mean?" Betty Foster laughed again and then, as abruptly, spoke with sudden passion. "There won't be any gentlemen after I get Amy back. I will get her back, won't I? She isn't — you know?"

"I am praying not," Sister Joan said soberly. "Thank you for talking to me."

She came away from the residents' unit in a thoughtful frame of mind, veering away from the van and taking the entry that ran down the side of the children's unit. The solitary policeman at the front door nodded to her without interest. Nuns weren't, it seemed, automatic suspects when a child was kidnapped. She walked on, turning the corner and finding herself on a patch of waste ground, doubtless earmarked for some further extension when hospital funds permitted, with the garden wall stretching along her right-hand side. It was a five foot wall, certainly too smooth and high for a child of four to climb. Sister Joan who was herself five feet two inches had to stand on tiptoe in order to look over into the fringe of bushes and the weeping willow that decorated the lawn. There was no way she could have leaned over and lifted up Amy unless she stood on a stepladder.

"Having a look round, Sister?"

Detective Sergeant Mill stood behind her, his voice making her jump.

"There's no way that Amy could've climbed over this wall by herself," she said.

"The smear of blood we found was near the top on the inner side, as if she scraped her knee against the stone as she was being hauled up. If my guess is right you've been over to see Sister Foster."

"You know about that?"

"Give us credit for a bit of whatever made Sherlock Holmes successful!" he protested.

"She doesn't know that you know?"

"Not yet. When the child disappeared the first thing we did was obtain her file from Social Services. Shirley Fleetwood was very helpful about that. There's always the remote possibility that the mother decided to take her without going to the courts to establish full parental rights, and Betty Foster seems remarkably indifferent to the fact that her little girl's gone missing."

"That's just a front. She's probably scared that her job here might be in jeopardy if anyone knew. Since they know already apparently it isn't."

"She seems to be a good nurse from the little we've asked. Compassionate and ready for a bit of a laugh with the patients."

"Especially the male ones," Sister Joan said, and laughed herself.

"Weren't we due to meet later?" He regarded her questioningly.

"After lunch. Mother Dorothy gave me leave."

"I'll treat you to a bite of lunch instead. Don't worry, I'll square it with Mother Dorothy. The Swallow Café?"

"I rather fancy a pub lunch," Sister Joan said.

"You never cease to astonish me," he said gravely. "Which pub?"

"The one where Madge Lee broke the window."

"The Crown and Anchor. Come on, I'll drive you there."

When they reached the public house with its window pane newly replaced and a blackboard outside advertising everything with chips, Detective Sergeant Mill gave her another questioning glance.

"Why the urge for alcohol?" he enquired.

"I'll have a coffee and a toasted cheese sandwich," she said firmly. "I thought we might keep our eyes and ears open, find out who's been giving away drugs?"

"Drugs at lunch time? Bit of a long shot!"

"Well, we might strike lucky," she argued. "Sometimes just being in the right place at the right time can set something in motion."

"Something other than gossip about a respectable police sergeant taking a very pretty woman out for lunch?"

"A nun," she corrected primly. "And not so pretty either."

"You're not standing where I'm standing," he retorted with a grin.

Even friends sometimes flirted together, she reminded herself, hastily alighting from the car before he had time to walk round and assist her. It was a way of reminding themselves that if they wished to leave the safe platonic level they could do so. In her case that didn't, of course, apply.

The pub interior was quiet, cosy and warm. It reminded her of the way pubs used to be when she'd been eighteen years old and freshly hatched from the local sixth form.

Twenty years ago! She stifled something that might have been a sigh and said brightly, "Let's order and then we can chat up the landlord."

There was no need for them to open any conversation however. The landlord came round from the bar, hand outstretched, saying, "Jim Trecorne. Any news about the little girl who was snatched?"

"Nothing so far," Detective Sergeant Mill said. "Sister Joan is helping me with a few enquiries on another matter. Madge Lee — "

"I was fearful sorry about that." The landlord shook his head. "I feel badly about it seeing as it was me refused to serve her. She'd a skinful already when she came in, and with Padraic being a mate of mine I figured he'd not thank me for giving her more. Next thing I know there was a bloody big stone through my window, begging your pardon, Sister! But I never knew Madge to be noisy or violent before."

"Did you notice anyone giving her drugs?" Sister Joan asked.

"Drugs! I won't have anything like that in my pub," Jim Trecorne said firmly. "I've a clean licence and I mean to keep it that way."

"Outside your pub." Sister Joan delved

into her pocket and produced the foil-wrapped tablet. "A woman gave this one to Luther — you know Luther? And she gave one to Madge Lee before she, Madge that is, came in and tried to get a drink here. I think it may be LSD."

"I'll get it analysed," Detective Sergeant Mill said.

"I didn't see anyone selling or giving anything," Jim Trecorne said, furrowing his brow. "I'd've had something to say about that! I can ask Jean if you like. She was helping on the bar that night."

"And while you're about it a coffee, a ploughman's, a toasted cheese sandwich and some of your best cider, please," Detective Sergeant Mill added.

"Right away!" Jim Trecorne went off briskly.

"You ought to have reported this before," Detective Sergeant Mill murmured.

"I couldn't. You were tied up with the search for Amy Foster and Mother Dorothy does have to give her permission before I can leave the convent or even telephone," Sister Joan said indignantly. "Anyway poor Madge Lee had died from drinking most of a bottle of brandy she managed to get hold of in the hospital. I suppose there could be an autopsy even now but it would upset Padraic terribly."

"Madge Lee was cremated about ten minutes ago," the detective said without emphasis.

"Oh, my Lord!" Sister Joan looked at him in consternation. "I didn't think — oh, I'm most terribly sorry, Alan! I should have insisted on seeing you or telephoning you but they were absolutely certain that she died of acute alcohol poisoning. She'd been treated for it for years."

"If we can find someone who actually saw her swallowing the tablet and if this tablet proves to be LSD then the drug may have been a contributory factor," he said. "The drug certainly wouldn't have helped her."

"And if she'd started to hallucinate then she might've become unusually violent," Sister Joan said. "Luther gave me this. He said a lady had given him a sweet and he'd saved it for Sister Martha."

"And you recognized it as an LSD tablet?" His dark eyebrows rose.

"I've seen them before," she said briefly.

"And tried them?"

"I'm not that daft!"

"Glad to hear it, but not having been acquainted with you during your misspent youth I'm pleased to be reassured on the point."

His smile told her she would hear no more about her blunder in delaying telling him about the incident.

Jim Trecorne returned with their drinks accompanied by a plump woman in a flowered overall who set the ploughman's and the toasted cheese sandwich before them.

"Jean says she saw someone giving out tablets," the landlord said.

"When?" Detective Sergeant Mill looked at the woman.

"Two — three nights ago, the night that Madge Lee broke the window and cut her hand on the flying glass," Jean said. "Big soft Luther was hanging about and she gave him one. She gave one to Madge too."

"Did you see Madge swallow it?" Detective Sergeant Mill asked.

"I did as a matter of fact," Jean said. "She was already quite drunk though we wouldn't serve her here and I told her not to go eating anything she didn't know anything about. She just pulled off the silver paper and swallowed it like an aspirin. I was going to tell the woman to sheer off but she'd already gone so I came inside. Five minutes later Madge rolled in demanding a gin and tonic, and Mr Trecorne here refused to serve her and advised her to go home. That was when she broke the window."

"The woman who gave out the tablets — did you know her?"

Jean considered and shook her head.

"Never got a good look at her," she said. "She was standing in the shadow and she moved off when I went over to Madge. She had red hair though. I saw it from the back as she went under the street lamp. Bright ginger hair. Curly and shoulder length."

"Thank you. That was very helpful," Detective Sergeant Mill said.

"It wasn't the tablet killed Madge, was it?" Jean asked worriedly.

"Almost certainly not. If you happen to see the red-haired woman again will you give me a ring?"

"Yes, of course," Jean nodded, and went back to her kitchen quarters.

"She should've told me about it," Jim Trecorne lingered to say, "but with all the fuss when Madge smashed the window I daresay she forgot. Enjoy your meal."

"Try a bit of ham with your cheese sandwich," Detective Sergeant Mill suggested, lifting a forkful from his untouched plate.

"No thanks. You know we're vegetarian and anyway I gave up pork when I was at art college, so the temptations receded."

She had spoken unwarily. His glance was keen as he said, "The Jewish boyfriend? You must've been smitten!"

"It was a long time ago. Alan, about the LSD, could it have come from the hospital?"

"I've no idea. I didn't think they used LSD these days. Drugs going missing from St Keyne's, are they?"

"Sister Collet signed for thirty grams of digoxin just before Mrs Louisa Cummings died."

"Digoxin being?"

"It's used in very minute doses to slow down the heart in certain cases of heart disease. Mrs Cummings was on it when she was transferred to St Keyne's for her hip replacement. Her normal dosage was being gradually weakened because her heart condition had stabilized. Mother Dorothy rang her GP and got that information. Mrs Cummings left a diary behind and mentioned in it that her tablets were different. I kept the diary in the library in case the entry was important but it looks as if the tablets were different simply because the dosage was being decreased. Nothing sinister there."

"Mrs Cummings died of a heart attack, surely?"

"Yes, but Mother Dorothy wasn't very happy about it."

"And asked you to ferret around?"

"Well, not precisely," Sister Joan hesitated. "She just had a feeling that her godmother wasn't so sick that she'd have a fatal heart attack just because her operation was delayed for a few hours. Anyway I did ask a few questions and it all seemed quite straightforward except for a couple of odd things."

"Which you're going to tell me about when you've taken another bite of your sandwich."

Obediently she swallowed a mouthful of the crisp toast and succulently melting cheese.

"Ward Sister Meecham was due to make her general rounds of the wards at twelve. Sister Collet was on the women's surgical ward and she'd checked the patients a couple of hours before."

"Medically checked them?" he asked.

"No, just glanced to make sure they were comfortable. At that hour nearly all the patients are asleep anyway, I gather, and there were no seriously ill ladies on the ward. Anyway when Sophie Meecham came round at twelve with the student nurse, Ceri Williams, they found Mrs Cummings had died. Dr Geeson was called and in view of her history of heart problems was quite ready to sign the death certificate."

"But you and Mother Dorothy weren't happy." He speared a pickled onion, looked at it consideringly and pushed it off his fork again.

"Louisa Cummings was a fairly tough old lady," Sister Joan said. "She wasn't the sort to have a massive heart attack just because her operation had been postponed. I know that's terribly unscientific but there was something else. Sister Collet told me that Mrs Cummings's hand was clenched in a last spasm but the sheet beneath it was smooth. It stuck in her mind."

"Hardly evidence," Detective Sergeant Mill pointed out.

"No, of course not. Anyway she was cremated and that's a fairly final thing."

"Was she a wealthy woman?"

"She left everything to Mother Dorothy," Sister Joan said uncomfortably. "And if you're going to say anything — !"

"I'm not." He slanted her a grin. "I wouldn't dare suspect Mother Dorothy! I take it she didn't know about the legacy?"

"She was astonished but Louisa Cummings had no children and no surviving blood relatives so everything goes to our Order. There's a house in Devon which can be either sold or rented out and Mother Dorothy is sharing the money with our mother house in

London and giving generously to the hospital and the children's home. Oh, and she gave Sister Collet Mrs Cummings's engagement ring. I was having it valued when you came in to buy the anniversary present for your wife."

"Was Sister Collet pleased with the bequest?"

"She burst into tears," Sister Joan said, remembering. "She's a nervy, slapdash kind of person, always running to catch herself up."

"And she was on duty when Madge Lee died."

"She was on duty when Madge Lee was brought in the previous night. She was just going off duty, about to make the ward round and hand over to Ceri Williams when she got a message to go over to the children's unit. When she got there nobody knew anything about any message and when she got back and did the ward round she found Madge dead with a bottle of brandy, most of it drunk, tangled in the bedclothes. The bottle came from the office where Sister Meecham keeps it. She enjoys a tipple now and then. Someone had opened it and taken it into the side ward where Madge was drying out. Ceri Williams helped clean the side ward after Dr Geeson had been called, the body taken down to the mortuary, and Constable Petrie informed, and she can't recall seeing a bottle top. Sister Collet took the bottle itself to be washed out."

"And Madge Lee was in no condition to get out of the side ward, find her way up to the office, open a bottle of brandy and carry it back to the side ward where she got back into bed and drank most of the contents."

"And Padraic would never have taken in anything alcoholic for his wife."

"How did the message from the children's unit reach Sister Collet?"

"On a piece of paper. Just a scribble. She probably screwed it up and threw it in the trash bin. Sister Ceri Williams was making a drink for one of the patients so she wouldn't have seen anybody go into the side ward. It opens on to the corridor outside the main ward."

"You haven't given me very much to go on." He drummed softly with his fingers on the tabletop. "Louisa Cummings dies of a heart attack — not expected but not impossible either since she was seventy-five and had been taking medication for a heart condition for some considerable time. I agree the removal of a quantity of — digoxin? — from the drugs unit which wasn't signed for until later looks suspicious but it could have been needed urgently for another patient and Sister Collet, being in a hurry, rushed back later to sign the register. And Madge Lee might've procured a bottle of brandy from somewhere else and concealed it in the side ward at any time during the night. She wasn't unconscious, was she?"

"She was sleeping on and off," Sister Joan said.

"And alcoholics can be very resourceful. I'm not trying to damn your theories but — what connection was there between Louisa Cummings and Madge Lee? None. To the best of our knowledge they never even met. What motive did anyone have for doing away with either of them? None. Mrs Cummings's property goes to your Order and Madge Lee had nothing to leave. She drank heavily but she wasn't an unpleasant or violent individual. She had no enemies and Padraic, who had every reason to regard her as a millstone round his neck, remained deeply attached to her. I'd agree with you that procedures at St Keyne's need tightening up but I can't see evidence of deliberate malicious intent, except in the case of little Amy Foster. Someone's snatched her and the longer the search goes on the less optimistic I become."

"I seem to have been wasting your time then. It was the last thing I ever wanted to do," Sister Joan said, with a grimace.

"Hold your horses! I'm playing Devil's advocate here." He laid his hand briefly on her arm. "Sister Joan, hard evidence is for the courts but every investigation has to start somewhere and very often it starts with a gut feeling that something's wrong. I trust your instincts, so I'm not brushing aside anything you've told me. I'll get this tablet analysed and the description, such as it is, of the red-haired woman put out. And I'll keep a close eye on events at St Keyne's as far as I can. Right now the first priority has to be that little girl."

"Yes, of course. There's Luther too."

"Luther? What's he been up to?"

"Nothing as far as I know. He just hasn't been around for the last couple of days. He doesn't like funerals and wakes and mourning so he's very likely gone to ground until everything's back to normal but Sister Martha's concerned."

"Luther will turn up again in his own good time." Detective Sergeant Mill broke off as his mobile phone beeped. "Excuse me, Sister."

He listened, his face betraying nothing, said curtly, "Right! On my way!"

"Someone's found Amy?" Sister Joan asked, half hoping, half fearing.

"Sister Tracy Collet's been found dead," he said. "Will you come with me to the hospital now?"

"Of course." She was already on her feet.

"I'll just pay the bill." He went over to the bar and rejoined her as she went out to the car.

"What's happened?" she asked as they drove back down the main street and up the hill.

"That was Sister Meecham. She went over to the residents' unit when Sister Collet didn't turn up in the ward. She found her dead. Looks like an overdose of sleeping tablets. Self-administered probably."

"You won't just accept that, will you?"

"Right now I'm not about to accept anything at face value. Here we are! We'll go straight there before anyone starts cleaning up the scene."

Sophie Meecham was at the door of the unit. She looked white and grim, and there was a strong scent of eau-de-cologne on her breath as she greeted them with a hurried, "This way, Detective Sergeant Mill. Dr Geeson is with her now."

Sister Joan's presence she ignored and the look she bestowed on the detective held a certain cloudiness as she turned and led the way up the stairs. Following, Sister Joan guessed that the shock of the discovery had sent Sister Meecham straight to the nearest bottle of alcohol before she had telephoned the police and then rinsed out her mouth with eau-de-cologne.

Constable Petrie was at the open door of one of the rooms on the first storey, standing aside as his sergeant appeared.

"In there, sir. Sister Meecham rang the station and I rang you and came here at once."

"Quite right. Dr Geeson, good afternoon."

"It's no use." The doctor straightened up from the bed. "She's been dead about three-quarters of an hour, I'd say. Thank you, Sister Meecham. That will be all."

"For the moment," Detective Sergeant Mill said.

His easy assumption of authority was impressive. Dr Geeson frowned at him.

"It looks absolutely straightforward," he said. "The glass is here and she clearly dissolved the tablets in water and drank the lot. There's a bottle of sleeping pills on her bedside table. I've not touched it but I'm certain you'll find only her prints on both glass and bottle."

"I'll need to speak to you later, Dr

Geeson," Detective Sergeant Mill said. "Also to other members of the staff. Petrie, is the police surgeon on his way?"

"Yes, sir." Petrie came smartly to attention.

"Thank you then, Doctor."

Dr Geeson nodded, glanced towards the recumbent figure and went out.

Tracy Collet lay on her back, eyes half open, an expression of surprise still etched on her features. She was in uniform, apart from her shoes which stood ready to be slipped on near the dressing-table. The room looked messy, with clothes strewn across the backs of the two chairs, a crumpled magazine on the floor, a scent of fading flowers pervading the air.

"Look!" Sister Joan pointed towards the small built-in wardrobe against one corner.

The wardrobe door was closed but something curly and red hung on the handle. It was a curiously pathetic object, hanging there, divorced from the head it had been intended to adorn.

Sister Joan and Detective Sergeant Mill looked at each other. Then he said quietly, "My apologies. Your instincts were as usual right, Sister. It looks as if the goings on around here require the most careful investigation."

9

Sister Joan took a step back, belatedly crossing herself in the presence of the dead. She realized suddenly that Detective Sergeant Mill had broken the news of Sister Collet's death without any preliminaries as if she herself was a colleague and not a religious, and she herself had responded more like an investigator than a nun. The thought troubled her obscurely as he said, "Why would Tracy Collet commit suicide, do you think?"

"If she's been supplying banned drugs locally and Madge Lee died indirectly as a result of that her conscience must surely have troubled her," Sister Joan said.

"No signs of a struggle." He looked round the untidy room.

"She was due to go on duty, wasn't she?" Sister Joan said. "Perhaps this wasn't a genuine suicide attempt. She may have counted on someone coming to find her."

"No note. Of course she may have intended the wig as a kind of confession. What do you think, Sister?"

"I can't believe she killed herself," Sister Joan said slowly. "I didn't know her very well but she struck me as an easy-going young woman, not too particular about timetables, but worried. Worried, Alan, not conscience stricken."

"The police surgeon's here, sir," Constable Petrie stepped in to say.

"Right. We'll have the fingerprint boys here too," Detective Sergeant Mill said. "Then I want the room sealed. I shall also want access to the office files and the drugs unit. Sister, don't touch that!"

He had spoken too late. Sister Joan had lifted the red wig off the wardrobe door and was regarding it thoughtfully.

"It's too large," she said.

"What?"

Both policemen looked at her.

"For Sister Collet's head," Sister Joan said. "She has — had — quite delicate features with a small head and fine hair. This wig would have slipped down round her face and looked ridiculous."

"You've an accurate eye, Sister," Constable Petrie said admiringly.

The police surgeon stepped in, nodding brusquely before moving to the body. Sister Joan excused herself and slipped out of the room and down the stairs.

Hospitals, she reflected, were places where death regularly occurred and made no special stir, but this was different. She could sense the shock and disbelief of the members of staff huddled in the common room below, the trying to come to terms with the fact that one of their own had died suddenly. Over by the children's unit the solitary policeman looked more alert than he had done before. She wondered what link — for surely there was a link — bound three deaths and the disappearances of a child and a simple-minded man. There would be a culprit and the link would be discovered, but at this moment she wanted to jump in the van and head back to the convent, to close the chapel door against the harsh realities of the world.

"There'll be a post-mortem," Detective Sergeant Mill said, joining her. "Sister, have you got to go straight back to the convent?"

"No." She spoke reluctantly.

"Then have a bit of compassion on an overworked, undermanned police force and hang around for an hour," he said. "I need to ask a few questions of those on duty and your presence would be a bonus."

The praying would have to wait. She bit back a sigh and said, "I'll help in any way I can of course. I take it that you want me to sit by and observe?"

"I've told Constable Petrie to round up

as many of the staff as he can in the main building common room. Just observe, Sister. That's all."

"Right." She began to walk with him across the forecourt to the reception area. At the desk Mr Johns, the part-time porter, was talking to a constable.

"Sister Joan, good afternoon." Mr Johns greeted her sombrely. "This is a very sad state of affairs, isn't it? My wife will be sorry to hear about it."

"Very sad indeed, Mr Johns," she agreed.

"I only heard about it when I came on duty half an hour ago. Mind you, I got here a bit early today and it's lucky that I did. Ceri Williams was on the desk this morning and she was terribly upset. We all are. She was a nice person was Sister Collet."

"Where's Sister Williams now?" Detective Sergeant Mill asked.

"With the rest of the staff, sir, up in the common room," the constable said. "They're in a hurry to get it over with because there are patients to attend. This is the list of those who were on the premises this morning. Shall I let the others get back to their work?"

"Take their names and addresses and we'll talk to them later if it's necessary."

"Right, sir!" The constable disappeared up the stairs.

"We'll take a good look at the drugs unit first — " Detective Sergeant Mill broke off as Dr Geeson hove into view.

The frostiness always apparent in the doctor's manner was positively glacial as he joined them.

"May I ask how the hospital is expected to continue to function under these conditions?" he enquired. "I am left with a mere handful of volunteers who are incapable of doing anything more than putting on a plaster or making tea. Surely an obvious suicide doesn't demand this kind of close investigation?"

"The sooner we start the sooner we finish," Detective Sergeant Mill said. "Do you have the key of the drugs unit?"

"I've just been there," Dr Geeson said. "There is a quantity of what you would term LSD tablets missing and not signed for."

"You still use the drug?"

"Its use these days is very rare," Dr Geeson said. "I certainly never prescribe it. However, at one time, for certain psychologically disturbed patients it was used in small amounts in an effort to free the subconscious from trauma. Most hospitals still have a tiny amount in stock. We had quite a lot and I did suggest to Sister Meecham that it ought to be disposed of. She evidently didn't take my advice. I've also noted that Sister Collet signed somewhat belatedly for thirty grams of digoxin. That's a very large amount to be withdrawn at any one time. If you wish to look for yourselves here's the key. The other key hangs in the office — "

"So any member of staff could take it at any time," Sister Joan said.

"There's absolutely no reason why any of them should," Dr Geeson said. "Contrary to what you seem inclined to believe medical staff are not all drug users or drug pushers. The manager here is not a doctor but an excellent business administrator who keeps the financial side of things running at a smooth economic level and reports regularly to the board of trustees. His actual physical presence is seldom required and he has the good sense to let us get on with our jobs without interference."

"Did you see Sister Collet this morning?" Detective Sergeant Mill asked.

"She went off night duty at seven, I believe," he said, considering. "She was due to take over again from Sister Meecham at one o'clock and when half an hour went by without her putting in an appearance Sister Meecham first rang the residents' unit and then, having received no answer, she went across to find out what had happened for herself. When she found Sister Collet she immediately rang the police station and then informed me. I went over at once but she was dead. Any attempt at resuscitation would have been fruitless. I did not, of course, touch or move anything in the room."

"What was your opinion of Sister Collet?"

"Mid-twenties, inclined to be absent-minded, sympathetic towards the patients but apt to regard them in a more personal manner than is considered desirable. Beyond that I can't say. I don't socialize very often."

"And you can think of no reason why she should've taken large amounts of digoxin and LSD?"

"She signed for them," Dr Geeson pointed out. "I have no idea whether or not she was the one who took them. For my own part I would never use LSD, and the digoxin which I do use for those heart-disease cases that require it, I use in minute quantities and also sign for it. If there's nothing else I have ward rounds to make and only a skeleton staff to assist me."

"Thank you, Doctor." Detective Sergeant Mill had taken the key. "Please carry on."

Dr Geeson stalked past them, with no more than a slight grunt of acknowledgement.

"That's the type who yanks out appendixes

for laughs," Detective Sergeant Mill said, looking after him.

"Dressed in a little brief authority," Sister Joan said wryly. "Are we going to the drugs unit now?"

"Wouldn't do any good," he said, "since my knowledge of drugs is strictly limited. I'll have our police surgeon look and decide if anything strikes him as out of the way. I'll catch you up, Sister."

She went on up the stairs.

In the common room she found a small group gathered together. Together but curiously silent, she thought, arriving in the doorway and surveying them swiftly. Ward Sister Meecham sat a little apart as if to emphasize her seniority, her eyes slightly puffy as if she'd just finished crying. In another chair, Sister Merryl was drinking a cup of tea. Jan Warren, Betty Foster and Ceri Williams sat together on a long couch, each clearly occupied with her own thoughts. Dr Meredith stood by the window shoulders hunched, gazing out as if he wanted nothing to do with any of it.

"Sister Joan, has anything happened?" Sister Merryl asked, putting down her cup and half rising. "Dr Meredith and I are due in casualty and we really haven't the time to spare waiting here. Poor Tracy Collet killed herself, didn't she?"

"It looks like that," Sister Joan said cautiously.

"Poor girl!" Sister Merryl clucked her tongue sympathetically. "I knew that something was wrong. She was always a bit inclined to draw inside herself, you know, but recently she obviously had something on her mind. It was very clear to me!"

"Did you ask her about it?" Sister Joan enquired.

"Oh no, Sister, I wouldn't pry!" Sister Merryl said, sounding slightly shocked. "Tracy always did keep herself to herself, you know. But this last couple of months she seemed more withdrawn than usual. You said yourself, Dr Meredith, that she seemed not to have her mind on her work!"

"She wasn't concentrating," the doctor said, not turning from the window.

"I found her crying in the sluice room one day," Jan Warren volunteered. "I asked her what was wrong and she as good as told me to mind my own business."

Detective Sergeant Mill came in. There was an immediate change in the atmosphere, a tightening up that was almost physical.

"Dr Meredith, I understand that you came on duty at nine this morning." The detective began without preamble. "Did you see Sister Collet at all?"

"The last time I saw her was very briefly yesterday," Dr Meredith said. "I was on the way to my car and she was just going on duty. We didn't speak."

"And this morning?"

"Dr Meredith and I have been in casualty all morning," Sister Merryl put in. "We neither of us saw her."

"When did you last see her, Sister — Merryl?" He consulted a list in his hand.

"Yesterday," Sister Merryl said. "I came up here for a cup of tea just before I went off duty. She looked in, said hello and went off again. Then I went home."

"You don't live in the residents' unit?"

"I've my own flat in town," she said. "I got back there, had a bite to eat, fed my cat, and did a bit of ironing. Then I had an early night. This morning I came on duty but I didn't see her at all."

"Thank you, Dr Meredith. Sister Merryl."

"Is that all?" Sister Merryl looked disappointed as she hauled herself to her feet. "I was just saying to Sister Joan that something was worrying Sister Collet, had been for some time."

"But she didn't tell you what it was?"

"I didn't wish to intrude," she said primly.

"Then we needn't detain you any longer for the moment. Thank you again."

They went out together, Sister Merryl two paces behind the doctor.

"Old cow!" Sister Warren said under her breath.

"Sister, that will do!" Sister Meecham roused herself from her own abstraction.

"You don't like Sister Merryl?" Detective Sergeant Mill looked at Jan Warren.

"She's one of the old school," Jan Warren said. "Not that they don't have their uses but they are forever harking back to the old days and how wonderful it was when Matron ruled supreme. She's a bit jealous of the younger nurses."

"Can you add something to what we know already?" he asked.

"I was in the children's unit," she said. "I saw Sister Collet once or twice yesterday. Not to speak to, just on her way to or from somewhere. I think it's better not to get too friendly with the rest of staff because it can interfere with one's work. Is there any word about Amy Foster?"

"Enquiries are continuing," Detective Sergeant Mill said.

"And we expect to make an arrest soon!" Betty Foster had risen abruptly. "Why are we making all this fuss about Tracy Collet when a small girl's missing? She might be dead — murdered by now!"

"We're all sorry about Amy," Ceri Williams said, "but there's nothing we can do."

"I suppose not." She sat down again abruptly, leaning her head on her hand.

"It wasn't your fault that Amy went missing," Jan Warren said. "Sister Collet was on duty."

"Did either of you see Sister Collet this morning? Sister Foster? Sister Warren?" Detective Sergeant Mill looked from one to the other.

They shook their heads.

"And you were waiting for her to arrive so that you could go off duty?" He glanced at Sister Meecham.

"I thought she might've overslept," Sister Meecham said. "I rang — there's a telephone over in the lobby there but nobody answered so I slipped across to knock on her door. There was no answer and when I tried the knob the door opened. I thought at first she was asleep. I ran downstairs and phoned the police station at once, of course."

"Can any of you think of any reason why she would choose to kill herself?"

"She didn't check up properly on the patients on the night Mrs Cummings died,"

Sister Meecham said hesitantly. "She was apt to be careless about the little things and I had warned her before to keep her mind on her work. And then she was absent from the main building when Madge Lee died."

"That wasn't her fault," Ceri Williams said quickly. "There was a scribbled note on the desk asking her to go across to the children's unit. When she got there she couldn't find anyone who'd sent for her. I was alone on the ward and I should've looked in on Mrs Lee but it's impossible to be in two places at once."

"And then she was on the desk in the children's unit when Amy Foster vanished," Sister Warren said.

"I think it preyed on her mind." Sister Meecham twisted her fingers together in her lap. "She was a sensitive girl. Quiet and sensitive."

"You may be right." Detective Sergeant Mill looked at them in turn. "Can you think of anything else, Sister Joan?"

"I wondered why Sister Collet put too much sugar in the cocoa," Sister Joan said.

"What?" Somewhat nonplussed, he stared at her.

"Someone mentioned that among other absent-minded things she did, Sister Collet put too much sugar in the cocoa. Whose cocoa?"

"I believe I can explain that," Sister Meecham said. "About three months back an old tramp was brought in. We thought at first he was drunk but Dr Meredith recognized the man as a diabetic. He'd known him slightly for years. A notice to that effect was being put up over his bed and I was in the office typing it out. Meanwhile Sister Collet came on duty and seeing that he was waking up she made him a cup of cocoa and put in two large spoonfuls of sugar. By the time I came down with the notice he'd slipped into a fatal coma. It wasn't anyone's fault but Sister Collet was very upset about it."

"Do you have the tramp's name?" Detective Sergeant Mill prepared to make a note.

"Nobody knew it," Sister Meecham said. "He was buried as a John Doe."

"Cremated, Sister Meecham," Sister Warren said.

"He was a derelict, no known relatives or friends, no fixed abode," Ceri Williams said. Her eyes had brimmed with tears again. "Sister Collet and I were so sorry for him, and we all told her not to blame herself. He might've died anyway."

"Well, that seems to be it then." Detective Sergeant Mill closed his notebook. "There will be an inquest in due course when the results of the autopsy are known."

"There's to be an autopsy?" Sister Meecham stood up very slowly.

"On Sister Collet, yes of course. Our police surgeon is conducting it at this moment."

"But surely there's no need!" Her voice had risen. "She killed herself. Dr Geeson said it was obviously an overdose of sleeping tablets. You've heard that she was worried about the mistakes she'd been making. Why have an autopsy?"

"Because it's the law," Detective Sergeant Mill said flatly. "There seems to be a rooted objection to carrying out the correct procedures in this establishment. I must warn you that an enquiry may well be ordered by the coroner. That's all for now."

Sister Joan, glancing back as she followed him into the corridor, saw that Sister Meecham had never ceased to twist her fingers, making ugly little cracking noises.

"You didn't mention the red wig," she said, when they were in the open again.

"I'm saving that for the right moment," he told her. "What d'ye think, Sister? Something very nasty in the woodpile, don't you believe?"

"Yes." She nodded soberly as they paced across the forecourt. "Sister Collet seems to have made more than her fair share of mistakes recently. Maybe she was sick or on the edge of a breakdown or something?"

"The wig would definitely have been too big for her. I checked that."

"She might've found it," Sister Joan said doubtfully. "Or someone else might have hung it on the wardrobe door to tie her in with the drugs?"

"I incline to the second theory though I'm damned if I can fit the whole thing together," he said irritably.

"An old tramp whom Dr Meredith knew slightly and recognized to be a diabetic is taken into casualty and while Sister Meecham is typing out his medical details Sister Collet gives him a cup of sweet cocoa and sends him into a diabetic coma. A couple of months later Louisa Cummings dies of a heart attack while Sister Collet is on duty. A few days a go Madge Lee gets hold of or is given a bottle of brandy, drinks most of it and dies. Again Sister Collet is on duty. And Sister Collet was on duty when Amy Foster vanished from the garden. Could there have been something besides brandy in that bottle?"

"Anything's possible but as we've had three cremations the chances of finding out are pretty slim."

"Nothing does fit together," Sister Joan

said. "There aren't any motives for these deaths, and all of them could have been natural."

"Do you believe that?" He looked at her sharply.

"No, I don't," she said decidedly. "Somewhere there's a link. We haven't found it yet, that's all."

"I'm going down to the mortuary," he said abruptly. "Will you come with me?"

"No, but I'll wait outside while you find out how the autopsy's going."

"You'd never make a detective on the Force," he said, turning towards a side door.

"I hope not!" she said thankfully.

"I won't be long." He pushed open the door and went down a flight of stone steps.

Death wasn't a beautiful thing, Sister Joan thought. Life was beautiful and what came after death was, please God, beautiful too, but the act of dying, the ritual that often surrounded an unexpected demise struck her as obscene. Tracy Collet had been a young attractive woman with a gentle manner and now she was blood and bone and flesh, being cut and probed by a man who had no personal interest in her at all.

She walked a little way, shivering despite the sunshine that illuminated the sombre tones of stone and brick.

Detective Sergeant Mill reappeared, closing the heavy door behind him, his dark face unreadable.

"They're making steady progress," he said without emotion.

"Meaning?"

"Meaning they've found a quantity of digoxin in the stomach contents."

"Then she took it for herself?"

"She certainly signed for it. Apparently digoxin slows down the heart and is valuable in cases of rapid heart palpitation. Give too much and the heart simply stops."

"The empty bottle in her room?"

"Traces of digoxin in it and in the glass she drank from."

"Suicide then?" Sister Joan's blue eyes blazed. "No, I don't believe it! People don't kill themselves because they make a couple of mistakes. I know the old tramp died but Sister Collet didn't even know he was a diabetic. I don't believe it."

"She was nearly four months pregnant," Detective Sergeant Mill said.

"Pregnant!"

Sister Joan stopped and stared at him, the colour ebbing and flowing in her face. "Dear Lord, but of course she was! I ought to have realized that."

"I don't see how."

"She was absent-minded. Pregnant women never have much on their minds except the coming baby so my sister-in-law tells me. And on the night that Louisa Cummings died Sister Collet wasn't well. She had to visit the toilet more than once. And she was over emotional too! She cried bitterly when I gave her the ring. Of course she was pregnant, and trying to hide the fact from her colleagues."

"That might be a reason for suicide," he suggested.

"Not for Tracy Collet," Sister Joan said.

"She wasn't married."

Sister Joan looked at him and found herself smiling slightly.

"Single mothers are two a penny these days," she said. "I've not yet heard of anyone killing herself because she was pregnant and unmarried. But it isn't only that. Tracy Collet was a nurse, Alan! Whatever their level of efficiency or their personalities I'd say that every nursing sister at St Keyne's cares about life. Tracy Collet had that life growing inside her and she would never have harmed it in any way."

"No signs of force," he pointed out.

"Then perhaps she was tricked into drinking the concoction. She hadn't been feeling good; she was under a strain. Someone offers to give her something that will ensure she gets a few hours uninterrupted sleep?"

"That means it could be almost anybody who was on or off duty. Difficult!"

"I don't believe that the hospital has more than one murderer running round," Sister Joan said. "The same person who gave Tracy Collet that lethal cocktail had everything to do with the deaths of Mrs Cummings and Madge Lee and perhaps the old tramp too."

"We're talking serial murder here," he said.

"It's not impossible," she argued.

"Not impossible but rare. That's what makes serial killers so fascinating. They seem to live by a different code of values than the rest of us. Most murders turn out to be very personal affairs for very mundane reasons — money, sex, you know."

"And there's a pattern to them. I know that too. I mean that the murderer had a bad relationship with a blonde so he finds every blonde he can and kills her and he doesn't stop because the blonde who caused the original damage is out of his reach or he hasn't got the nerve to do anything to her. I've read about it."

"Not in the convent library surely?"

"I was thirty years old before I entered the religious life," she reminded him. "Before that I did open the occasional book."

"Then we have to find the similarities between the victims. Something they had in common. Let's assume that tramp was killed, though personally I doubt it."

"He was a diabetic, known but not by name to Dr Meredith, picked up after he'd collapsed in the street and taken to casualty," Sister Joan mused aloud. "Sophie Meecham went over to the office to type up his medical record and meanwhile Tracy Collet gave him a nice sweet cup of cocoa. Maybe that was just a mistake, an innocent error. Nobody had any reason to kill him."

"He doesn't seem to have had much of a life anyway," Detective Sergeant Mill said. "Mrs Cummings? Mother Dorothy inherited her property."

"Mother Dorothy hadn't the least idea that she was due to inherit anything and she was nowhere near St Keyne's when her godmother died!"

"Hold your horses, Sister!" He sent her an amused grin. "I was about to eliminate her as a possible suspect. Nobody else stood to gain from Louisa Cummings's death. Her operation had been postponed because there was a blip in the computer."

"Could that have been deliberate?"

He shook his head.

"Possible but highly unlikely. The computer was only recently installed and they're still trying to get the hang of it. Anyway the hip replacement was only postponed for a few hours. It meant an extra night on the ward for her, that's all, and she was irritated and not upset by the delay, yet during the night she suffers a fatal heart attack."

"And Sister Collet doesn't check out the patients properly because she's in the toilet being sick. Alan, there's a door right by the end bed that Mrs Cummings was in. It leads down to the kitchen. Someone could've come up that way and given Mrs Cummings a massive dose of digoxin while Sister Collet was in the toilet."

"Mrs Cummings was already on digoxin."

"On steadily decreasing doses. In her diary she mentions that the tablets are different. If someone stepped up the dose suddenly — not that we'll ever know because she was cremated."

"Madge Lee?"

"No way in the world did Madge Lee get out of the bed in the side ward, go up to the office, find Sister Meecham's bottle of brandy, open it, carry it down to the side ward and after climbing back into bed drink most of the contents and die of acute alcoholic poisoning!"

"Then someone undid that bottle and took it to her while Sister Collet was going over to the children's unit and Sister Williams was making a hot drink for another patient. Tracy Collet again."

"Nobody had anything to gain from Madge's death."

"Padraic? Now don't bridle up, Sister! I'm very well aware that Padraic can do no wrong in the eyes of your community because he regularly supplies you with excellent fish that simply leap out of private fishing streams and land at his feet begging to be taken to the convent! But Madge was a liability to him. I'm playing Devil's advocate here."

"Don't waste your time," Sister Joan advised. "Padraic went on loving his wife despite everything. She wasn't normally violent, remember."

"The red-haired woman gave her an LSD tablet outside the pub. Combined with alcohol that made her unusually aggressive. So she was brought here and the next morning just as she's recovering from her binge someone pours neat brandy down her throat."

"We don't know it was neat brandy," Sister Joan objected. "There was an awful lot of digoxin missing from the drugs unit."

"And again Madge was cremated." He grimaced.

"And now Sister Collet has died." Her face was troubled as she looked up at him. "She apparently committed suicide but I don't believe that. I really can't believe that. She was given that drink by somebody, probably told it was a sleeping draught. Digoxin slows the heart so she'd just have died peacefully."

"It was Tracy Collet who signed for the digoxin. Wouldn't she have known?"

"She may have signed for it but she signed the register later on so perhaps someone else took the stuff and then asked her to sign the register — you know, saying that they'd been under pressure and neglected to do so. And she wouldn't have known that she'd been given the drug in her drink because she'd never suffered from heart trouble."

"And again there was no reason for anybody to kill her, and you're pretty certain she wouldn't have committed suicide."

"I'm absolutely certain," Sister Joan said. "Alan, I think I'd like to sit down by myself and look at the various members of the hospital staff. Do we have any details on them?"

"Constable Petrie got these details from

the office files. He made photocopies for you." He took a thin sheaf of papers from his pocket and gave them to her.

"The first chance I get," she promised. "I have to get back now. You'll let us know as soon as there's any news about Amy?"

"She remains my main concern," he said gravely. "I can do something for the living if Amy is still alive. Every hour that goes by makes it less likely."

They had reached the van. Sister Joan unlocked the door and hoisted herself behind the wheel.

"Thank you for the lunch," she said.

"It was a pleasure, Sister."

"The baby." Fastening her seatbelt she glanced at him, a shadow in her face. "Was it a boy or a girl? Could they tell?"

"It would've been a girl."

"God bless her!" she said softly. "There's another reason why Sister Collet might not have committed suicide. She'd have known the child was developed sufficiently even for its sex to be defined, so she wouldn't have killed herself."

"Had it occurred to you that if Tracy Collet was our murderer she might've had a last-minute fit of conscience and decided to make away with herself?"

"Tracy Collet was a nice person."

"Many killers have been extremely nice people apart from their unfortunate propensity to commit the odd murder."

"You're a cynic!"

"And you're a sentimentalist! Drive carefully, Sister."

She nodded and drove off slowly, avoiding the rash of cars parked across the forecourt.

Someone was walking in through the open gates. She slowed politely but Dr Geeson didn't pay her any attention. He was strolling with his head up and his hands deep in the pockets of his white coat, and he was whistling cheerfully as he came.

10

"It was a most affecting and interesting ceremony," Mother Dorothy said. "The church was almost full and Father Malone preached a most sympathetic sermon."

She had joined the community at recreation though usually she employed the time in catching up on her paperwork.

"He never mentioned alcoholism once," Sister Perpetua said.

"No, he talked about her love for her husband and about the two children she left behind. Edith and Tabitha are growing up into very nice girls now, Sister Joan. I think you may take some of the credit for that since you taught them when we had our little local school."

"Thank you, Mother, but they weren't with me for very long. Padraic deserves the credit," Sister Joan said.

"He has taken the death hard though he is bearing up very well," Mother Dorothy said. "After the cremation we had lunch with Father Malone and then we drove back with him, stopping on the way home at the Romany camp to tender our condolences once again."

"They were having a kind of wake," Sister Perpetua said. "Bonfires blazing and all her possessions being burned along with the wood. There was some singing and a bit of dancing too. Of course, we only stayed for a moment but it looked quite jolly." She sounded rather wistful.

"So how has the day gone with the rest of you?" Mother Dorothy looked round the semicircle. "Sister David?"

"I helped Sister Martha with the fruit picking," Sister David said earnestly. "It made a pleasant change from being in the library most of the day."

"It would've been better still if Luther had turned up," Sister Martha said. "He's so much taller than Sister David and me. I don't suppose anyone's heard anything?"

There was a general shaking of heads. Sister Gabrielle said, "You should've asked me to help you. I'm quite tall."

"You're also eighty-nine in a couple of weeks," Sister Perpetua said. "If you think you're going to get permission to shin up ladders you may think again, Sister!"

"You haven't heard anything of Luther, Sister Joan?" Sister Mary Concepta looked at her hopefully.

"Nothing," Sister Joan said. "He hasn't

been reported yet as a missing person as far as I know. People have every right to go off where they choose without informing anyone."

"But Luther isn't exactly — well, he's a bit slow-witted, isn't he?" Sister David said.

"Indeed he is not!" Little Sister Martha looked as fierce as her sweet-natured features would permit. "He never received any encouragement, that's all. He has as much sense as anybody when he cares to show it!"

"Sisters, this is recreation not recrimination," Mother Dorothy said.

"I didn't mean to be rude about Luther," Sister David said, flushing. "I'm sure you know more of his qualities than I do, Sister Martha."

"You said the church was full for Mrs Lee's funeral," Sister Katherine said in her gentle way. "That must've been a great comfort for Padraic."

"And quite a few wreaths on the coffin," Sister Perpetua said. "Yours looked lovely, Sister Martha. There were carnations from the children, and a bouquet of red roses from Padraic and dahlias and asters and a bunch of wild flowers that looked very pretty. And the men wore black armbands in the old manner. They add a touch of dignity I always think."

"Funerals should be dignified," Sister Gabrielle said. "Weddings too. I've no patience with those people who want to get married while they're leaping hand in hand out of a hot-air balloon or diving into a dolphin pool!"

A ripple of laughter ran round the semicircle. Mother Dorothy, glancing at Sister Joan, said, "You're very quiet, Sister. Did anything particular happen today that you feel you can talk about?"

"One of the nurses at the hospital has died," Sister Joan said, putting down her knitting. "Sister Collet. You recall the name, Mother?"

"She was in charge of the ward when my godmother died. I had a very sweet note from her thanking me for the ring. Sister, you ought to have told me immediately you came in!"

"I beg pardon, Mother, but you'd just returned with Father Malone and I thought it best to wait," Sister Joan said. "Anyway I felt I needed a couple of quiet hours in the chapel."

"What happened?"

"She was found in her room at the residents' unit around lunchtime. She hadn't gone back on duty and the chief ward sister went across thinking she'd overslept. The police were called."

"You were at the hospital?" Mother Dorothy asked.

"No, Mother. I was discussing the disappearance of little Amy Foster among other matters with Detective Sergeant Mill as you gave me leave to do when the message came. A post-mortem was begun almost immediately."

"But surely — !" The prioress broke off and frowned. "Sister, of what did Sister Collet die? Or don't they know yet?"

"She drank a glass of water in which a number of lethal tablets had been crushed," Sister Joan said.

There were murmurings of dismay and several crosses were hastily drawn upon the air.

"This is dreadful news," Mother Dorothy said quietly. "So many terrible things seemed to have occurred recently at that hospital. I assume that Detective Sergeant Mill has asked for the benefit of your expertise?"

"Subject to your consent," Sister Joan said meekly.

"Which is, of course, given. We must always endeavour to carry out our civic duties as well as our religious ones. Will you require permission to go into town again in the near future?"

"It may be necessary, Mother."

"Then by all means do so when it becomes necessary. The sooner this matter is cleared up the better. I do pray that Sister Collet didn't drink that lethal dose deliberately."

"I'm positive she didn't," Sister Joan said firmly.

"Another sad accident perhaps?" Mother Dorothy shook her head slightly.

"I realize this isn't a topic for general discussion," Sister Gabrielle said, "but I'd like to make it clear that we can't have Sister Mary Concepta going into St Keyne's for a check up until we can be sure she'll be coming out again!"

"Hear, hear!" Sister Perpetua clapped her hands softly, avoiding Mother Dorothy's frown.

"I'm feeling quite well at the moment," Sister Mary Concepta said, "but if I was to be taken ill and die I hope that I'd accept it gracefully. Age does make one less useful after all."

"You weren't put on earth to be useful, Mary Concepta," Sister Gabrielle scowled. "You were put here to render my old age a series of fidgety crises!"

The bell marking the end of the hour-long recreation period sounded. Pieces of knitting and sewing were hastily folded up and the sisters rose, folding their hands within their wide sleeves, falling into line for the nightly walk to the chapel where a further hour's worship would round off the day.

"Two hours' meditation and a mass every morning, two hours' religious discussion and study in the afternoon and another hour at night!" Detective Sergeant Mill had exclaimed once when she had attempted to describe the unvarying daily routine. "When do you get time to work?"

"That is our main work," she had answered, stifling a laugh at the horror on his face.

"You must have knees of iron!" he had commented.

"Some of us creak a bit," she'd admitted. "Sister Gabrielle has leave to sit when she feels extremely uncomfortable, but she seldom avails herself of the privilege. It's a question of pride with her."

"It's a question of masochism," he'd retorted. "Don't you show a little compassion to yourselves as well as to everybody else? No, don't tell me! My agnostic soul would rebel against details of hair shirts, etcetera!"

"Hair shirts are out of fashion this century," Sister Joan had retorted with a smile.

She hadn't mentioned the weekly discipline

that all sisters imposed upon themselves. It was after all only a symbolic act designed to remind the flesh that it must be subject to the spirit. He would have regarded it as medieval and unmeaningful. There were some things on which nun and policeman would never see eye to eye.

There were other matters concerning Sister Collet which she hadn't yet confided to Mother Dorothy and she was grateful for the tact that prevented her superior from demanding full information as it unfolded. When Mother Dorothy gave permission for her to assist the police she left it to Sister Joan as to what and when everything could be revealed.

In the chapel she bowed her head and prayed silently for all those who seemed to have become part of an apparently random series of events. Yet even as she prayed stray images broke free and floated to the surface of her mind.

Sister Collet giving a cup of sweet cocoa to an old tramp, a bunch of wild flowers — two bunches of wild flowers, but she was weary and couldn't remember where the second one fitted in. Ward Sister Sophie Meecham's hands twisting and turning in her lap; Dr Geeson cheerfully whistling as he strolled through the hospital gates; drugs signed for by the person who might not have taken them; a curly red wig that didn't fit a particular head.

Kneeling for the blessing as the grand silence began she found it an effort to get up again. At this moment she needed her bed and no dreaming to disturb her slumber, she decided, meeting Mother Dorothy's sharply questioning eyes with a reassuring nod and a half smile.

If she dreamed at all she didn't recall it when she woke up the next morning to Sister Teresa's cheerful, "Christ is risen!"

Sister Teresa and Sister Marie had been up since 4.30, she reminded herself, sliding to her knees to make the appropriate response. She herself felt energetic and quick-witted despite the fact that the sky outside her small window was still hung with fading stars. She accomplished her toilet swiftly and went down to the chapel feeling as if she could cope with the new day that lay ahead.

Kneeling in her usual place she felt something prickly against the material of her habit. A swift glance downwards showed her the cause. Tucked under the kneeling hassock was a large bunch of holly, its berries still green. She reached down cautiously and pushed it further out of sight, repressing a yelp as one of the leaves stuck into the side of her hand.

Though the door which connected the chapel wing to the main building was locked at night the outer door of the chapel was left unlocked. Mother Dorothy had always insisted that it was better to risk a burglary than to deny someone the opportunity to seek spiritual comfort in the chapel, and remained blithely indifferent to the fact that the only people likely to be wandering about on the moor in the middle of the night were almost certainly up to no good in the first place.

The holly pricked at her mind as it had pricked her hand. She set herself to concentrating entirely on her meditations, but the philosophical sayings of St Thomas Aquinas were too frequently interrupted by stray sentences spoken at random by faces she had scarcely known six weeks before but which were now becoming familiar.

Ward Sister Sophie Meecham, outwardly the calm, efficient nurse who in earlier times might confidently be expected to rise to the post of matron. Even without that title the job was a stressful one. Sophie Meecham ruled her staff with a loose rein and herself resorted to an occasional swig from the brandy bottle in the office. Sister

Collet was — had been — tender hearted, slapdash and emotional, rushing into the drugs unit to sign for the digoxin she — or someone else — had taken. Sister Merryl was of the old school, together with Sister Warren regarding the new ways as suspect. She suspected that Dr Geeson with his hard eyes and immaculate hair would be in favour of anything that spared him from having to establish a personal rapport with a patient. But people weren't so simple and uncomplicated, she reminded herself.

After breakfast she excused herself, caught the eye of Mother Dorothy who nodded as if to reinforce the permission she had previously given and went back to the chapel. Sister David would be arriving at any moment to dust the chapel and change the water in the vase at the foot of the Lady Altar and check that the silver candlesticks still gleamed. As sacristan she took her duties as seriously as she took everything else.

The bunch of holly was still under the hassock. It was tied with a length of thin string. She lifted it out cautiously, avoiding the prickles and carried it up to the library.

Settled at a table under one of the skylights, the bunch of holly at her feet, she drew out the thin sheaf of typed information that Detective Sergeant Mill had given her. In the end justice relied on solid facts. They were here, life histories neatly compressed into a few sentences.

> Dr Enoch Meredith. Aged 59. Born Swansea. Educated Charterhouse. Medical degree from Bart's, London. Qualified as surgeon in 1962. Settled in Cornwall 1963. Married Alicia Fenton, 1970. No children. Wife died 1987. Left general practice full-time in 1988. In 1990 became part-time consultant at St Keyne's.

There was nothing there to suggest the murderer. A childless widower, growing bored during retirement and choosing to get back into harness. Possibly slightly jealous of a younger doctor who was now in a senior position?

> Dr Russell Geeson. Aged 34. Born London. Educated Harrow and Cambridge. Medical degree from Cambridge, 1985. 1990 left post as resident surgeon at Battersea General Hospital and moved to St Keyne's as resident surgeon.

Sister Joan leaned her chin on her hand and grimaced. Not much there to go on beyond the fact that an obviously capable and ambitious doctor had moved from a large city hospital to a smaller rural establishment. Perhaps he preferred to be a big fish in a small pond.

> Ward Sister Sophie Meecham. Aged 34. Born London. Educated Fulham Comprehensive. Basic nursing training in Battersea General Hospital. Qualified 1985. Ward Sister at Battersea General Hospital until her transfer to St Keyne's in 1990. Promoted to chief ward sister 1991. Unmarried.

So which one had followed the other? Had Dr Geeson advised Sophie Meecham to follow his example or had she opted for a rural post? Perhaps the friendship between them had stopped Dr Geeson from remonstrating with Sister Meecham about her tippling. Was there any friendship between them outside their professional relationship? Thinking of Sophie Meecham's thin figure and undistinguished features Sister Joan begged leave to doubt it.

> Sister Maud Merryl. Aged 47. Born in Paignton. Educated at Paignton High School. Basic nursing training

at St Columba's General Hospital, Torquay. Joined St Keyne's in 1971. Unmarried.

Sister Jan Warren. Aged 36. Born in Canterbury. Educated Canterbury High School. Basic nursing training at Dartford General Hospital. Nursing Sister at Dartford Trust Hospital. Married David Wickley 1983. Widowed 1986. Resumed maiden name and joined staff at St Keyne's in 1988. No children.

So the coldly efficient Jan Warren had a past sorrow in her life. Sister Joan felt a pang of compassion, suddenly seeing Sister Warren's hard exterior as a shield against unwanted feeling.

Sister Elizabeth Foster. Aged 29. Born Battersea. Educated Battersea Comprehensive School. Basic nursing training at Battersea, 1991. Gave birth to female child, Amy Foster. Father not named. Appointed as ward sister at St Keyne's in 1993.

Sister Joan read over the sparse entries once again. The picture that was forming in her mind was growing clearer. She was certain that Detective Sergeant Mill had already arrived at the same conclusions. She frowned slightly and read through the rest of the file.

Ward Sister Tracy Collet. Aged 25. Born in Wrexham. Educated at Wrexham High School for Girls. Basic nursing course at St Faith's Hospital, Birmingham. Appointed as ward sister at St Keyne's in 1993. Single. No living relatives. Died 1995, September. Cause of death digoxin poisoning. Pregnant three and a half months.

Ward Sister Ann Croft. Aged 24. Born Penzance. Educated Merchant Taylors School. Basic training at St Keyne's Hospital. Engaged to James McKensie, motor mechanic.

Ward Sister Ceri Williams. Aged 23. Born Wrexham. Educated privately. Basic nursing course now being taken at St Keyne's. Two years completed with credits. Single.

Howard Johns. Aged 62. Male orderly and porter. Retired 1994. Returned to

St Keyne's where he had worked for thirty-five years as part-time orderly.

It was all there, she supposed, and yet it wasn't. The list of facts established links between various members of the staff but it didn't tell you anything about the actual people. It didn't explain anything about their interior lives, the fears that crushed them, the hopes that buoyed them up.

She drew a piece of paper towards her, picked up a pencil and began to make her own jottings. If you want to find the murderer first study the victim, she mused.

John Doe. Aged sixties? Tramp. Diabetic. Died 1995 after drinking a cup of sweet cocoa supplied by Sister Collet. His medical notes being typed up at the time by Sister Meecham. Cause of death, diabetic coma.

Louisa Cummings, widow. Aged 75. Died 1995 of heart attack. Was being treated for a mild heart condition and awaiting a hip-replacement operation. Sister Collet on duty at the time. Death discovered by Sisters Meecham and Williams. Left her property to Mother Dorothy, her goddaughter.

Madge Lee, thirties. Alcoholic. Took LSD tablet from red-haired woman outside public house and became violent. Cut her hand on broken glass and died the next morning having drunk most of a bottle of brandy. Cause of death acute alcoholic poisoning. Personal possessions burned in accordance with Romany custom.

Sister Tracy Collet. Drank glass of water in which large number of digoxin tablets had been dissolved shortly before being due on duty. No suicide note found. Red wig hanging on wardrobe door was too large for her. Wearing her uniform minus shoes. Signed for thirty grams of digoxin. Query — was this just before Louisa Cummings died? Pregnant.

Amy Foster. Aged 4. Daughter of Sister Elizabeth Foster. Born in Battersea. Fostered from birth. Abused by foster parents and brought to St Keyne's Children's Unit. Habit of injuring herself. Disappeared from garden when Sister Collet was on duty.

Something was still missing. Some motive bound these together. Sister Joan winced as she realized that she had included Amy's name in the list of the deceased. She picked up the pencil again and carefully drew a line above the name to separate it from the others.

"I beg your pardon, Sister Joan!" Sister David had come in and paused, irresolute. "I didn't mean to disturb you."

"You're not disturbing me, Sister. I'm at an impasse." Sister Joan leaned back in her chair, letting the pencil drop from her fingers.

"I know we're not supposed to ask questions," Sister David said, "but are you helping the police with another murder investigation?"

"At the moment I'm not helping anybody," Sister Joan said wryly. "I'm not even certain that a murder or murders have been committed. Look at this list, Sister, and tell me if anything springs to mind."

Sister David adjusted her spectacles on her snub nose and peered at Sister Joan's handwriting.

"They all seemed to have been very sad people," she observed after a moment. "I mean nobody will really miss them very much, will they? Not even poor Madge Lee. Padraic won't admit it but she wasn't the best sort of wife for him, was she? Oh, you've been over to the old chapel! After everything that happened I'm surprised you have the courage. I wouldn't!"[1]

"I've not been near the old chapel," Sister Joan said.

"That's the only place where that particular genus of holly grows," Sister David said. "I was reading about the flora and fauna of this area and I recall reading that and meaning to mention it to you."

"I didn't pick the holly," Sister Joan said.

"Oh, sorry!" Sister David looked confused. "Seeing it there by your feet I assumed that you'd picked it for some reason."

"Sister David, did anyone ever tell you that you're a genius?" Sister Joan bent and picked up the green, prickly bunch, her blue eyes suddenly sparkling.

"Not recently," Sister David said, with an unexpected flash of humour.

"Well, you are! You've just set me back on track! I'll see you later."

"I'm glad I could be of some help," Sister David said blankly, as her fellow religious hastened out of the library and down the narrow stairs.

The main telephone was in the passage

---

[1] See *Vow of Adoration*

outside the infirmary. Sister Joan glanced into the room and saw that both Sister Gabrielle and Sister Mary Concepta were absent. Through the open window she could hear Sister Marie's cheerful, "I really do feel quite fit again, Sisters, but if you wish to sit in the garden for a little while I'll gladly keep you company."

She lifted the receiver and dialled the police station.

"Detective Sergeant Mill just stepped out," Constable Petrie informed her. "Do you want me to find him?"

"Ask him to meet me in about three-quarters of an hour by the old Presbyterian chapel near the Peter house," Sister Joan said crisply.

Then she was hurrying out to the stable to saddle Lilith.

The moorland track ran past the Romany camp and the stone hermitage, curved round the walls of the convent enclosure, joined up again to run in a fairly straight line towards what was still called the 'new estate' though it had stood for years and been extended considerably since Sister Joan's own arrival in Cornwall. A narrower track, too rough and stony for the van rayed out on to the heights of the moor. On the heights stood the house owned by the local antique dealer and the side road that took one down into the town arrowing from the far side of the building, but the ground before the house was a medley of tiny fields with crumbling drystone walls and great billowing stretches of purple heather.

The chapel was crumbling into decay along with the walls, its roof half gone, its windows retaining only shards of broken glass. The door hung on its hinges and ivy and bramble fought for supremacy.

Sister Joan reined in Lilith who, eager for a gallop had carried her like Pegasus over the uneven ground, and dismounted, pausing only to loop the reins over the stump of a nearby tree. She had tied the holly to the saddle-bag and now untied it, holding it with care as she approached the tumbledown chapel.

Inside dust and bird droppings lay thickly on the cracked stone floor. The few remaining pews were starred and chipped by time, swollen with damp in many places. There was no sense of worship here, only a pervading atmosphere of neglect and despondency.

Not looking to left or right, she walked up the aisle and laid the holly on what had once been a communion table but was now cracked and stained.

"I received your message," she said clearly.

"I think that it's time we talked, don't you?"

The last syllables of her words echoed back queerly. The back of her neck prickled as if she had just stroked it with the holly as she heard a harsh grating sound.

In the corner a mesh of iron was being slowly raised. She heard footsteps on iron rungs and then a long drawn out breath of relief.

"It was very clever of you to send me the holly, Luther," she said, half turning. "How did you know where I knelt?"

"I come into the chapel now and then," Luther said, stepping closer to her. "I like to watch."

"From where?" Sister Joan asked in surprise.

"I go up the stairs behind the statue of Our Lady Mary and sit there," Luther said. "Sister David knows I sit there but God can't see me."

"You brought the holly over during the night?"

He nodded solemnly.

"This holly only grows in this spot," he said. "I knew you'd know that, being so clever as you are, and come here."

"Sister David was the clever one," Sister Joan admitted. "Did you put a bunch of wild flowers on the coffin in the church too?"

"Madge was there but they'd closed the lid," Luther said. "I put the flowers with the others after dark. I didn't touch nothing."

"I'm sure you didn't," Sister Joan said. "It was you who dropped the wild flowers at the garden in the hospital, wasn't it?"

"I picked 'em for Sister Marie," he said proudly. "She's very nice is Sister Marie. Not as nice as Sister Martha but getting that way. I took the flowers to the hospital, but I got confused. I get a bit confused near hospitals. I was scared to go in the big door and ask where Sister Marie was so I went round the backs of all those buildings and had a look round."

"Luther, I've asked Detective Sergeant Mill to meet me here," Sister Joan said. "You know Detective Sergeant Mill, don't you? Luther, what did you do with Amy?"

"The little girl was crying," Luther said. "All by herself and crying. I leaned down and pulled her up over the wall, but she scraped her knee on the stone and she cried more. I was going to give her a flower but I dropped them over the wall and then I heard someone coming out into the garden so I ran."

"Where's Amy now?" Sister Joan repeated.

"The little girl's cold," Luther said. "It's

cold down in the old crypt. I got into the big house there and took a couple of blankets. Only for a lend of them! And I took some milk and some biscuits but the little girl's getting hungry. I don't know what to do now, Sister."

"Go down and get Amy." Sister Joan kept her tone calm and conversational. "That sounds like Detective Sergeant Mill now."

She gave him what she trusted looked like a reassuring smile and went out to the open again just as the police car parked on the slope above and two figures scrambled out.

"What's happened, Sister?" Detective Sergeant Mill was first to reach her with Shirley Fleetwood not far behind. "I was discussing Amy's disappearance with Miss Fleetwood when Petrie relayed your message so she came along too. Have you found Amy? This chapel was searched."

"Not well enough apparently. There's a crypt underneath and Luther took her down there."

"Is she all right?"

It was Shirley Fleetwood who spoke, her professional façade momentarily submerged by a more compassionate, caring person.

"Here they are," Detective Sergeant Mill said.

Luther came slowly out of the old chapel,

a small and decidedly grubby little girl held against his shoulder.

"You won't go hitting her again, will you?" he said.

"Nobody's going to hurt anyone," Shirley Fleetwood said. "I promise you."

Amy was passed over rather like a limp little parcel, but as Luther stepped back she lifted her head, waved her hand vigorously and called in a piercing treble, "'Bye, Luther! Thank you!"

"That's all right, little girl!" Luther's face split into a wide grin. "You be good now and Luther will come and see you one day."

"This is the first time I've ever heard her speak," Shirley Fleetwood said in a low voice.

"What happens now? You're not going to charge Luther with anything, are you?" Sister Joan said anxiously.

"She seems unharmed if a trifle smelly." Shirley Fleetwood wrinkled up her nose.

"If you're satisfied then I see no reason to press charges," Detective Sergeant Mill said. "I'll have a good long talk with Luther though. In today's climate of political correctness his actions could be misinterpreted."

"You said something about hitting her again." Shirley Fleetwood looked at Luther. "I've never struck a child in my life."

"Not you," Luther said. "The other one."

"Which other one?" Sister Joan said quickly.

"In the garden." Luther grimaced in an effort to remember. "She hit the little girl."

"Amy's been hitting herself," Sister Joan said quickly.

"Not in the garden." Luther looked obstinate. "In the garden the other one bent down and hit her. I looked over the wall and I saw but the other one didn't see me. She went away again. I ducked down quickly behind the wall and shut my eyes tight until she'd gone. Then I leaned over and picked up the little girl and I dropped the flowers I'd picked for Sister Marie."

"The other one, the one who hit her," Sister Joan spoke tensely, "did you know her?"

"No. Not her name." Luther shook his head.

"Had you seen her before?"

"She gave me a sweet," Luther said. "She had red hair."

11

"I have to get Amy back," Shirley Fleetwood said. She spoke automatically as if she was pulling the warm cloak of her own authority about her shoulders to challenge the cold wind of shock.

"Wait a moment!" Detective Sergeant Mill checked her as she turned to the police car. "Look, you can't take her to St Keyne's, not now we know that someone was actually hitting the child, making out that she'd done it herself."

"The woman with red hair." Shirley Fleetwood nodded, then shook her head. "The woman you were telling me about who wore a red wig and was giving drugs to Luther and Mrs Lee? It really is rather a lot to take in at one gulp!"

"Someone at the hospital has been quietly shortening a few lives," he said. "We don't know why or even how any proof will now come to light, but from what Luther just told us I'd lay odds that Amy is the next intended accident. A child who abuses herself can become a child who falls out of a window or swallows some noxious substance."

"But why would anyone want to do that to a little girl?" Shirley Fleetwood began, then made a wry grimace. "That was stupid!" she said frankly. "God knows there are plenty of people willing to hurt children. But would someone who hurts a child also do harm to a variety of older people, none of whom has anything in common?"

"They were all patients at St Keyne's," Sister Joan said.

"I'll take Amy home with me," Shirley Fleetwood said after a moment's thought, "but I shall require official sanction for that."

"You have it." Detective Sergeant Mill spoke briskly. "Miss Fleetwood, are you due for a couple of days off?"

"As a matter of fact yes, but I wasn't going to take them until we had word about Amy."

"Were you planning on going away when you did take time off?"

"Only to my mother's in Plymouth," Shirley Fleetwood said.

"I suggest that you take Amy there for a couple of days." He was making rapid notes in a small notebook. "Sister Joan, may we drive over to the convent for an hour or two?"

"Yes, of course, but I don't — " Sister

Joan stopped, feeling for once completely at a loss.

"Luther, there won't be any charges brought against you," Detective Sergeant Mill said, his tone one of quiet reassurance. "You'd better go and set your cousin's mind at rest. Padraic's worried about you."

"I'm scared to show myself," Luther confided, "in case the red-haired woman finds me."

"I doubt if she has any interest in you," Shirley Fleetwood said.

"She gave him an LSD tablet, didn't she? Outside the pub. She gave one to Luther and one to Madge Lee," Sister Joan said suddenly.

"One LSD tablet never killed anybody," Shirley Fleetwood said.

"Not directly, but if someone had a bad trip they might well injure themselves in some way. Madge Lee cut her hand on the broken glass and was taken to the hospital. The next morning she was dead. Even one tablet might send someone like Luther into a state that requires hospitalization," Detective Sergeant Mill picked up her thought.

"And in hospital you're so vulnerable," Sister Joan said.

"Go on over to Brother Cuthbert and

ask him if you can stay at his place for a couple of nights. Wait! I'll give you a note for him."

The detective was writing busily again. Shirley Fleetwood said, "This child needs a change of clothing and a hot meal!"

"Off you go, Luther!" Detective Sergeant Mill passed him the note. "Brother Cuthbert won't mind, will he? I merely asked him to let Luther stay out of sight for a day or two. Let's get to the convent."

"You start and I'll follow on Lilith," Sister Joan said.

The pony, hearing her name, whickered and pricked up her ears.

"I'll give you a hand up," Detective Sergeant Mill offered, unlooping the rein.

Using his cupped hands as leverage, Sister Joan swung herself into the saddle.

"Nice legs!" Detective Sergeant Mill said *sotto voce*, a schoolboy grin curving his mouth.

"I forgot to put on my jeans under my habit." Sister Joan's rosy cheeks were scarlet.

"Well, don't let it worry you," he said dryly. "Greater sins have been committed. See you later, Sister!"

He slapped Lilith lightly on the rump and went back to the car where Shirley Fleetwood was settling Amy. Luther had already taken off, his long legs covering the rough ground at speed.

Even so, by the time she trotted round to the stable, Sister Perpetua was already waiting in the yard.

"Sister Joan, what in the world is going on?" she exclaimed. "That missing child has turned up here with a social worker and Mother Dorothy is declaring that we are now a place of safety for those in danger of — I don't know what!"

"Miss Fleetwood and Amy will be leaving quietly as soon as it gets dark if I read Detective Sergeant Mill's intentions correctly," Sister Joan said. "I believe he has it in mind to trap a killer."

"Whatever happened to silent contemplation?" Sister Perpetua, looking hugely pleased at the prospect of an extra couple of souls to feed and fuss over, vanished kitchenwards.

"Mother Dorothy wants you in the parlour," Sister Marie said, coming out. "I'll stable Lilith and give her a rubdown for you."

"Thank you, Sister." Sister Joan delayed only just long enough to rinse her hands at the sink and hastened to the parlour where she found the prioress dispensing coffee to Detective Sergeant Mill and Shirley Fleetwood.

"*Dominus vobiscum.*" Mother Dorothy indicated a stool.

"*Et cum spiritu sancto.*" Kneeling briefly and then seating herself Sister Joan discerned a faint elevation of Miss Fleetwood's eyebrows. No doubt she was amused at the medieval quality of the greeting.

"Detective Sergeant Mill has explained briefly what seems to have been happening," Mother Dorothy said in her precise fashion. "We must give thanks to Our Blessed Lord that no harm came to the little girl."

"Luther was the one who hid her away," Shirley Fleetwood said.

"Luther was the instrument," Mother Dorothy said. Her faint smile stated that she was distinctly unfazed by free-thinking social workers.

"Where is Amy?" Sister Joan enquired.

"Upstairs, getting a bath and lots of mothering from Sister Teresa," Mother Dorothy said. "We shall keep her here until after dark and then Constable Petrie will drive her and Miss Fleetwood over to Miss Fleetwood's mother in Plymouth."

"You want to give the impression they're still here," Sister Joan said.

"I wish there was some other way to do this," Mother Dorothy said. "Deceit is not a tool one cares to use."

"The end justifies the means," Detective Sergeant Mill said. "Isn't that what the Jesuits say?"

"It's a constant source of amazement to me," Mother Dorothy said, "how among numerous exceedingly wise precepts formulated by St Ignatius Loyola that phrase has become a kind of sixteenth-century soundbite, capable of manifold misinterpretation. And we are not Jesuit nuns, Detective Sergeant Mill. Our watchword is Compassion."

"Compassion." Sister Joan echoed the word, her body suddenly tensing.

An old tramp suffering from diabetes, an old lady waiting for a hip-replacement operation, an alcoholic gypsy woman, a young woman expecting an illegitimate baby, a child who was already traumatized by previous abuse, a simple-minded man — all objects of compassion. A deadly compassion.

"Sister?" Mother Dorothy was looking at her.

"Nothing, Mother Dorothy. You were saying the end justifies the means, Detective Sergeant Mill. Meaning?"

"So far we have four deaths." He ticked them off briskly. "Old John Doe whose death might well have been an accident since Sister Tracy Collet apparently had no idea he was a diabetic. Louisa Cummings who might have died of a heart attack while Sister Collet was in the toilet. Madge Lee who smuggled in or was given sufficient alcohol to finally kill her while Sister Collet was over in the children's unit. So far Sister Collet seems to be the chief suspect."

"Her death might've been a suicide," Shirley Fleetwood said.

"Possible but unlikely. She was a compassionate young woman, not terribly efficient and obviously susceptible to some man or other but not the type to harm anyone else or to harm herself when she was carrying a healthy child. Someone was hoping we'd tie her in to the previous deaths and draw the obvious conclusions, but the red wig was a touch too spectacular. Whoever hung it on the wardrobe door must've done so after Sister Collet had died. It strikes me as highly unlikely that someone would come in, hang up the wig without explanation and go away again leaving Tracy Collet to commit suicide. The fact is that whoever put the wig there failed to check whether or not it would've fitted Sister Collet's head. Instead of pinning all the peculiar incidents on Tracy Collet and giving us every reason to conclude she had killed herself under the stress of conscience or fear of being found out that wig merely proved that somebody else was involved. The trouble is that we have a great many suspects."

"It had to be someone who was in the vicinity at the time all the deaths occurred," Shirley Fleetwood said.

"And that's bloody difficult to prove — excuse me, Mother Dorothy! Sister. That hospital is badly run. Slackly run. The manager is hardly ever there; keys to the drugs unit are far too available to the members of staff; because of short-staffing and over-work they're constantly on the move between the various wards."

"Sister Collet signed for the missing digoxin," Sister Joan reminded him.

"If she'd taken it herself surely she'd've signed for it at the time. Then its being missing wouldn't have caused any comment when the cupboards were checked," Shirley Fleetwood said.

"She signed for it later when Sister Meecham noticed the digoxin had gone. Ward Sister Meecham ought to have enquired why so much had been taken and what it had been used for," Detective Sergeant Mill said.

"Sophie Meecham drinks more than is wise," Shirley Fleetwood said. "She's by no means an alcoholic or even a heavy drinker but it's an open secret that she finds the work stressful and pops up to the office for a quick nip every now and then."

"Perhaps Sister Collet knew or guessed who'd taken the drug and wished to protect them," Mother Dorothy said, her tone unexpectedly lively.

Detective Sergeant Mill glanced at her and grinned. "You'd make a good detective, Mother Prioress," he said.

"Thank you, but one of our community involved with police work is more than sufficient," Mother Dorothy said crisply.

"She was protecting Dr Geeson," Sister Joan said.

"Why?" Detective Sergeant Mill rapped out the words.

"Because he's the father of the child she was expecting," Sister Joan said.

"You've reasons for saying that?"

"Dr Geeson was shocked at first when the existence of the unborn baby was discovered but later on I saw him as I was driving out through the hospital gates. He was smiling and whistling. I suppose he'd realized that her death had let him off the hook."

"That's not exactly proof," Shirley Fleetwood said.

"Sister Betty Foster was rather cutting about Sister Collet's inefficiency when I talked to her," Sister Joan said slowly. "The rest of the staff seem to have liked her and to have excused her slapdash ways but Betty Foster had a more critical attitude. There's another thing too: Betty Foster said she didn't come to work in this area because her daughter was here. I think that she did but that may have been only part of the reason. She refused to name the father of her child but she and Dr Geeson came from the same area of London and trained at the same hospital. It's possible that she hoped for him to acknowledge Amy or give her some financial help but when she got here he was having an affair with Sister Collet. Sister Foster may well have been jealous of her, though she really hadn't any cause. When I gave Tracy Collet your godmother's ring, Mother Dorothy, she burst into tears and was most distressed. I think she knew she could never expect an engagement ring from Dr Geeson, and she was upset about it, especially if she'd signed for the digoxin under the impression he'd taken it."

"Why would he take the drug anyway?" Detective Sergeant Mill enquired.

"I don't think he did," Sister Joan said earnestly. "I think that Sister Collet believed him capable of it. Maybe she'd seen him round that area or something, so when Sister Meecham mentioned a large quantity of digoxin was missing Tracy Collet signed for it, perhaps hoping to hold the fact over Dr Geeson's head and force him to marry her, but I don't think her plan worked because he hadn't taken it in the first place."

"But she might still have made things awkward for him," Shirley Fleetwood said.

"Which gives him a motive for getting rid of her. Oh dear! this is all most unpleasant," Mother Dorothy said in a low voice.

"But no motive for getting rid of anybody else," Detective Sergeant Mill pointed out.

"A most immoral young man nevertheless." She pursed her lips.

"Not sufficient compassion," Sister Joan said.

"None at all if he seduced two young nurses and then refused to take responsibility for the results," Mother Dorothy said critically.

"Do we know when the digoxin was taken?" Sister Joan enquired.

"I checked up on that," he said. "About three months back. Sister Collet signed for the drug a couple of hours after Sister Meecham had checked the drugs unit and noticed a large quantity was missing."

"Then Tracy Collet would have been suspecting that she was pregnant," Shirley

Fleetwood said. "She might've been protecting Dr Geeson because she was still in love with him and figured he'd be so grateful that he'd marry her."

"They died very quietly, very peacefully," Sister Joan said.

"Meaning?" Detective Sergeant Mill looked at her.

"It was something someone said but I can't recall who. That old tramp slipped into a diabetic coma and passed away after Sister Collet gave him a cup of sugary cocoa. Mrs Cummings died of a so-called heart attack without making a sound. I know that Tracy Collet was being nauseous and went at least twice to the bathroom but there were other patients in that ward. There ought to have been some noise because one of her hands was clenched in a last spasm but the sheet beneath it was smooth."

"You mean someone stood and watched her die?"

"Having slipped up the back stairs from the ground-floor kitchen. Any sound that Louisa Cummings made could be stifled very easily and the sheet smoothed neatly before the killer slipped away again. Nurses automatically smooth sheets and plump up pillows, don't they?"

"And we've only Sister Collet's word that

she went to the bathroom at all," Shirley Fleetwood said.

"Which brings us back to suicide?" Mother Dorothy looked round at them.

"Sister David said something very interesting," Sister Joan said. "Luther left a bunch of holly that only grows near the old chapel so that I'd guess where to find him. I took it up to the library while I was making some notes and Sister David assumed that I'd picked the holly because it was at my feet. Don't you see?"

"Not until you cast light upon our darkness," Detective Sergeant Mill said dryly.

"Madge Lee was found dead with an open bottle of brandy containing only the dregs of the contents caught up in the bedclothes. What if she hadn't drunk any of the brandy at all? What if something had been given her earlier on — would they give her black coffee to sober her up? She starts to slip into a coma and then someone puts the brandy in the side ward. It would be assumed that she'd died of alcoholic poisoning. There wouldn't be an inquest. But the brandy was just planted to cause everybody to jump to the wrong conclusion."

"Digoxin in the black coffee?" Detective Sergeant Mill had his notebook out again.

"With digoxin you'd die fairly fast depending on the strength of the dose," Shirley Fleetwood said. "Perhaps an involuntary spasm as the heartbeat grew slower and slower. A peaceful death."

"And we know that Tracy Collet died of an overdose of digoxin," Detective Sergeant Mill said.

"Would she have drunk a glassful of some unidentified substance knowing that a lot of digoxin was missing?" Shirley Fleetwood said.

"If she trusted whoever gave it to her," Sister Joan mused.

"Dr Geeson?"

"I don't believe so, Mother Prioress. She must've been aware by then that she couldn't trust Dr Geeson to do anything halfway decent. She was depressed and unhappy and her work was going badly and she didn't know what to do. Then someone knocks on the door and offers her a headache remedy — ?"

"Surely not, Sister!" Shirley Fleetwood broke in impatiently. "Tracy Collet might have been depressed and inefficient but no nurse drinks an unknown substance as trustingly as that."

"Love potions," Mother Dorothy said.

"I beg your pardon, Mother Prioress?"

Detective Sergeant Mill stared at her.

"I was thinking of love potions," Mother Dorothy said. "Long ago when I was a girl at school a very charming man used to come twice weekly to teach piano. Most members of the fifth remove were infatuated with him though I cannot for the life of me recall that he ever did anything to encourage us. However one of the girls had smuggled in a magazine, one of those romantic but quite innocent publications telling you how to snare your man and keep your husband and make dusters out of tablecloths. They printed an old recipe which was said to work wonders if you drank it and then breathed in the general direction of the man of your choice."

"Mother Dorothy, you didn't!" Sister Joan gazed fascinated at her superior.

"I'm afraid I did. At fifteen one can be quite incredibly silly." Mother Dorothy sounded tolerant of her former youthful self. "It occurred to me that Sister Collet — may her soul rest in peace — must have been emotionally rather immature, very caring and eager to do the right thing but unable to hide her feelings. She may well have confided in someone that she was in love and the man wasn't interested, something like that."

"Then she'd have confided in another

woman," Detective Sergeant Mill said.

"There is another possibility." Shirley Fleetwood was frowning slightly. "She was pregnant. Perhaps she had hoped to get a proposal of marriage out of the father and hadn't told him about the child because, being a nice young woman, she didn't want to stoop to blackmail. She must've been at her wits' end not knowing whether to go ahead and have the baby or have an abortion and time was running out. No doctor enjoys having to perform a late termination. Anyway she could hardly have it done at St Keyne's, could she? She would have to go elsewhere, get time off. Perhaps she confided in whoever it was and they promised to get something that would bring about an abortion. It's possible."

"I fear so." Mother Dorothy looked sad.

The luncheon gong sounded in the recesses of the building.

"May I offer you some luncheon?" Mother Dorothy asked. "Sister Joan, since there is still important business to decide we shall eat here in the parlour. Go and get a tray from Sister Teresa if you will."

"Certainly, Mother."

Sister Joan couldn't repress a slight chuckle once she was outside the parlour. Since lunch invariably consisted of soup, a salad sandwich, a piece of fruit and a glass of water she suspected that Detective Sergeant Mill would've preferred to repair to the nearest pub.

"I'll help you carry in the food, Sister. The little girl is fast asleep by the by. She seems none the worse for what happened to her apart from a nasty bruise on her face."

"That bruise will be the last one she'll ever have," Sister Joan said, adding, "Please God."

"Amen!" Sister Teresa looked doubtfully at the water jug and reached up for a bottle of lemonade.

Sister Joan found herself biting her lip in perplexity as she followed Sister Teresa down the passage, both carrying laden trays.

The deaths had been peaceful ones, she thought, but Amy's case was different. Luther had seen the red-haired woman hitting Amy. That was what had impelled him to take the little girl away. It might be possible to parade people before Luther so that he could make an identification but even if he succeeded would it ever stand up in court?

"It looks splendid!" Detective Sergeant Mill said as the trays were deposited on the large, flat-topped desk. His tone was one of politely concealed dismay.

"Thank you, Sister Teresa." Mother Dorothy

dismissed the lay sister with a smiling nod.

The tomato soup was thick and warming. They ate and drank in silence, Mother Dorothy having murmured a shortened form of grace to which Sister Joan and Shirley Fleetwood said an amen while Detective Sergeant Mill merely nodded his head briskly.

Luncheons were silent meals and this one was no exception. Shirley Fleetwood started to say something at one point, met Mother Dorothy's cool gaze, and let her voice trail away.

"For what we have received may the Lord make us truly thankful. Amen."

Mother Dorothy crossed herself and gestured to Sister Joan to take away the empty dishes.

In the kitchen Sister Marie was washing up. "Amy's awake," she volunteered. "Sister Teresa found a tin of alphabet soup so she's heated that up for her. We none of us are sure what's going on. When I was having my tooth done I felt absolutely secure there but now I'm not so certain that I ought to have done."

"You were perfectly safe, Sister," Sister Joan said. "I sat in the observation booth while the operation was going on. Anyway, if anything had happened to you then you'd've been sorely missed and we'd all have made a great fuss."

"That's the lovely thing about the religious life!" Sister Marie exclaimed. "No matter how old and frail you get, no matter what the circumstances of your birth, you're equal with your sisters, always held safely in their affection. Nobody is ever regarded as useless, are they?"

"Sister Marie, you're a treasure!" Sister Joan clapped her hands together, narrowly avoiding the temptation of bestowing a forbidden, impulsive hug on the younger nun.

"I don't think so," Sister Marie said modestly.

Sister Joan was already on her way back to the parlour.

"Sister! Must you rush about everywhere?" Mother Dorothy complained mildly as she entered.

"I beg your pardon, Mother." Sister Joan hastily knelt, kissed the floor and rose with her blue eyes sparkling. "I believe I have the motive for all these events!"

"Which is?" Detective Sergeant Mill looked at her.

"I think they were all mercy killings," Sister Joan said. "Not exactly euthanasia but murders committed out of a twisted kind of compassion. The old tramp was a diabetic, and had no home or family, not even a proper name by which other people knew him; Louisa Cummings was a childless widow with no blood relatives, with a heart condition and the prospect of an operation which might or might not be successful; Madge Lee was alcoholic and a constant embarrassment to her husband even though Padraic's so loyal to her; Sister Collet was expecting a child which she may have felt forced to abort and her work was definitely suffering."

"And Amy is illegitimate and has already been abused. Unless very great care is taken she may grow up damaged," Shirley Fleetwood said.

"And Luther is simple-minded and can't cope with a real job."

"You think that Luther's an intended victim?" Mother Dorothy looked uneasy.

"He was given an LSD tablet and thought it was a sweet. If he'd taken it he might well have ended up in hospital like Madge Lee."

"So our murderer must work within the hospital itself. She or he requires the hospital in order to carry out the eliminations decided upon." Detective Sergeant Mill leaned his chin on his hand and raised a thoughtful eyebrow. "Of course. Deaths in hospital are not often questioned, are they? Drugs are used and death certificates signed without too much bother, and the fact that the place isn't run as efficiently as it might be only gives an added help to the killer."

"You have a plan?" Mother Dorothy gave him her full attention.

"I've been turning over various possibilities in my mind," he said. "What we need to do is lure our quarry away from the security of the hospital complex. I had thought of letting it be known that Amy and Luther were here in the convent. However, for that I'd need your express permission, Mother Dorothy."

"You have it," the prioress said slowly.

"It might prove very traumatic for the rest of the community," Sister Joan put in.

"We shall assemble in the chapel," Mother Dorothy said.

"And if the murderer does turn up?" Shirley Fleetwood looked sceptical.

"We shall be praying for them," Mother Dorothy said.

12

There was an unreal quality to the day, Sister Joan thought. Detective Sergeant Mill had driven off to consult with his fellow officers at the police station; Shirley had rung her mother to announce that she'd be arriving later that night; Mother Dorothy had gathered the other members of the community together to give them a careful account of what was happening. There was an atmosphere of slightly tremulous expectation as if a storm was brewing.

"Mother Dorothy, may I drive down into town?" she asked, waylaying her superior as they emerged from chapel.

"Something troubles you, Sister?" Mother Dorothy looked at her sharply.

"Yes, but I don't quite know what it is," Sister Joan said frankly. "I know that everything seems to be in hand but something's nagging at me and even praying about it doesn't help."

"Very well." Mother Dorothy frowned but answered readily enough. "I too am uneasy. It seems to me that someone as ruthless and clever as this person we seem to be dealing with must be is unlikely to walk so easily into a trap. Try to get back in time for supper."

"Thank you, Mother Dorothy."

Driving down into town, turning up the hill that led from the bustling main street to the hospital she tried to analyse the uneasiness that held her in its grip.

Always before when she had been involved in helping on a case there had been an unexpected climax, an event that had sent the adrenalin rushing to her veins, spiced a quiet existence with sudden peril. But now the trap had been set and all that was required was to wait for someone to walk into it. And it wasn't going to work. She didn't know how she could be so sure of that but she was sure.

At the hospital there were no watchful policemen. Amy had been found so there was no further need of them. The late afternoon sun was still warm but the first faint tinge of evening softened the outlines of the hospital units.

She parked the van and got out, resolving to follow her instincts since she had no clear plan of action. What was it that Detective Sergeant Mill had said?

"Dr Geeson isn't on duty so I contacted Dr Meredith and told him that Amy was safe and would be staying with the sisters for a couple of days. I asked him to inform the various members of staff concerned separately. I explained that certain things were still being kept under wraps. He seemed surprised at the request but agreed. Now we shall wait and see."

A police car driven by Constable Petrie would whisk Amy and Shirley Fleetwood to Plymouth as soon as darkness had fallen, avoiding the town. Everything was set up.

"Is Luther supposed to be here with us too?" Mother Dorothy had enquired.

"Yes. Dr Meredith has been given to understand that Luther can identify the person who took Amy. We haven't, of course, let it be known that it was Luther himself who took her."

"So many untruths," Mother Dorothy had murmured, shaking her veiled head slightly.

"In police work they're often necessary."

"I wasn't criticizing you, Detective Sergeant Mill," she had said. "I was merely regretting the necessity for them."

Betty Foster was emerging from the main building, her face lighting into a smile as she saw Sister Joan.

"Have you heard, Sister?" Her voice was slightly breathless. "They've found Amy and she's unharmed! Dr Meredith told me on the quiet earlier this afternoon. He must've guessed that I'm her mother or else why tell me? Apparently the police want the news kept quiet because until whoever took her is arrested she might still be at risk."

"Then I hope you haven't gone blurting it out all over the hospital," Sister Joan said severely.

"No, of course not!" Betty Foster looked indignant. "I care a great deal for Amy, Sister, even though I mightn't show it. I've had to bite my tongue sometimes when I've heard some of the others say how dreadful it must be for a child to have no mother. I've wanted to shout out that I'm her mother even if she doesn't know it yet. I thought it better to keep quiet about it."

"And telling a nun doesn't count," Sister Joan said dryly.

"But I've not said a word to anyone else," Betty Foster said. "I've been hugging myself inside for the last couple of hours. I've been making plans too, Sister. I'm going to apply to the court for full custody of Amy. I don't want her fostered any longer or stuck in a children's home. I'm in a position to care for her myself now."

"Thanks to your gentlemen friends," Sister Joan said.

"Don't knock it until you've tried it,

Sister!" Betty Foster looked suddenly charming and impertinent.

"I won't!" Sister Joan said, laughing as she turned and walked on.

"Has something happened? I heard you laughing!" Ceri Williams looked up from the reception desk as Sister Joan went in.

"The news about Amy. Didn't Dr Meredith tell you?"

Ceri Williams looked at her blankly.

"He hasn't said anything," she said. "Is she all right?"

"We found her with Luther. They're both fine. Dr Meredith was asked to tell the staff quietly since the police are still keeping the matter under wraps. Keep it to yourself."

"I will," Ceri Williams said solemnly. "I daresay Dr Meredith thought that a student nurse wasn't important enough to be trusted with a secret. I don't really know him very well at all, him only being part-time. What happened? Why was Luther with her?"

"It's a long story," Sister Joan said, wondering how to avoid a direct lie. "If Dr Meredith had managed to get hold of you he'd've told you that Luther can identify the person who took Amy and so they're both in a very, very safe place."

"The convent. Convents have always been sanctuaries, haven't they? Oh, I'm so pleased that it turned out well," Ceri Williams said softly.

"I've all my fingers crossed," Sister Joan said, beginning to ascend the staircase to the upper floor.

Outside the staff sitting-room she met Dr Geeson.

"Here again, Sister?" He looked at her coldly.

"Like an avenging angel!" Sister Joan said lightly. "May I ask you a question, Doctor?"

"I have a few minutes to spare." He glanced at his watch and turned back into the sitting-room.

"I take it that Tracy Collet's funeral will take place soon?" Sister Joan said, following.

"I've no idea. Presumably the almoner will know."

"I would've thought that you might have been interested in the funeral arrangements or are you simply too relieved that she and her child are dead to bother any longer?"

"You're making an unwarrantable assumption, Sister." His fingers had involuntarily clenched.

"I don't think so," Sister Joan said calmly. "You and Betty Foster were both at Battersea, weren't you? Then you came here and so did she shortly after her daughter was born.

You do know that Amy is her child, don't you?"

"I had suspected that she might be," he said.

"You knew it," Sister Joan said with equal coldness. "Having seduced her and refused to take any responsibility for the coming child you transferred to this hospital and she followed you here, not merely because her little girl was being fostered in the same area but because you were here and she hoped that the affair might start up again. But you'd embarked on another affair with Tracy Collet though you weren't aware that she too was pregnant. So that was another responsibility you could reject."

"Your imagination has taken wings, Sister." He looked faintly amused. "You haven't the least proof of any of this. So, Sister Foster and I were at Battersea together? So were other doctors and nurses. Coming from the same place doesn't necessarily create a bond."

"Betty Foster knows the father of her child," Sister Joan said. "She's a decent young woman and she didn't choose to make trouble for you. Neither did Tracy Collet. She tried to persuade herself that you cared enough about her to marry her, but you didn't, did you? The truth is that you care for nobody. It may make you an efficient doctor but it doesn't make you an admirable one. Only the father of Tracy Collet's child would've been so relieved by her death that he strolled through the gate whistling!"

"I trust you don't intend to make this matter public," Dr Geeson said. "The laws of libel and slander apply also to nuns."

"Oh, I daresay there are others know about it without my having to say a word," Sister Joan said coldly.

"If you'll excuse me I have patients to attend." He looked at his watch again. "You may find this difficult to understand from the sentimental fog in which you dwell but there are some people who actually prefer a highly trained doctor with a scientific mind to a muddled old fool from Wrexham. Good day, Sister."

"Wrexham," Sister Joan said under her breath, watching him stride out. "Wrexham?"

In her mind a fact she had barely noted was surfacing. Two of the staff of St Keyne's had come from Wrexham. Well, it was a large town but, all the same, people who had trained in the same place even if not at the same time might well exchange notes when they found themselves in the same smallish hospital far from home. Turning, she almost ran back along the corridor and down the stairs. There was nobody at the main reception desk as she sped across the forecourt towards the residents' unit. The door of the unit was open and to her relief Dr Meredith was seated in the common room, sipping a small whisky. He looked up tiredly as she came in.

"Why didn't you tell Ceri Williams about Amy's being found and kept in a safe place?" she demanded.

"It was somewhat difficult to contact all those whom the detective sergeant wished to inform," he said.

"No, that wasn't the whole reason," Sister Joan said. "You come from Wrexham and Ceri Williams comes from Wrexham too. Did you know her before she came here as a student nurse?"

"I settled in Cornwall in 1963. Ceri Williams is twenty-three."

"Had you heard of her? Did you know the family?"

"My late wife was a cousin of Gwyneth Williams who was Ceri's grandmother." He set down the glass carefully. "We went back to Wrexham every year to see family and friends. I knew of Ceri. We met her once or twice when she was a child."

"And then she came here to train as a nurse. You must've taken some interest in that. Did you recommend her?"

"No." He spoke flatly, definitely. "I was not asked for my opinion but I was worried when Ceri Williams arrived here."

"Why? Doctor, you must tell me!"

"There was a younger sister." He spoke slowly and reluctantly. "Nesta Williams was a Down's Syndrome child, eight years Ceri's junior. She was found with a plastic bag over her head. Verdict: accident. I was uneasy about it. When my late wife and I visited the family after Nesta's birth we spoke briefly to Ceri. I believe we said something trite about having a special sister and Ceri looked up and said, "They don't live long, do they? It's better for them not to live long'. She might've been echoing something she'd heard an adult say but there was something most unchildlike in her eyes. Later on we heard the little girl had died. My wife was quite ill by then and I'd my hands full but I did worry about it. No proof of course."

"And then years later she turned up here as a student nurse?"

"Two years ago. She didn't really remember me. And she's an excellent student, most caring and compassionate. I decided my original worries were groundless."

"When the old tramp died three months

back, were you in casualty that day? Was Ceri Williams?"

"I was there when he was brought in. I knew him slightly. He never would tell me his name — a slight degree of paranoia there, but I had treated him for diabetes. I told Ward Sister Meecham to type a note to that effect when he was moved from casualty on to the general ward. Then I went off duty. Sister Collet had just come on duty."

"Isn't there a time overlap as one member of staff goes off duty and another comes on? From whom did Sister Collet take over?"

"From Ceri Williams," he said. "She was making hot drinks for the patients when I went off duty."

"So she could have sugared the cocoa and then simply left it to Sister Collet to hand it to him. Did you make full enquiries?"

"He died in a diabetic coma," he repeated.

"But you didn't ask who actually put the sugar in the cocoa? The dregs of the cup weren't analysed?"

"There was no reason for them to be. Sister Joan, there was no proof of malice against anybody. To have begun asking a series of leading questions may well have placed a black mark against a student nurse at the beginning of her career."

"Did you know that Tracy Collet had

signed for a quantity of digoxin just before the tramp was brought in?"

"At that time, no."

"And nobody would miss an old tramp who wouldn't even tell his name."

"There was no proof," he said.

"On the night Louisa Cummings died," Sister Joan persisted, "Ward Sister Meecham made the ward rounds at midnight with Ceri Williams. Where was Ceri Williams earlier in the evening?"

"I don't know. I wasn't on duty."

"So while Sister Collet was in the toilet being sick she could've slipped up the back stairs, poured the dose of digoxin down the old lady's throat or forced in a couple of tablets, smoothed the sheet and gone away again ready to accompany Sister Meecham on her ward rounds."

"That's a possible hypothesis," he said, "but there was no proof, no reason to suspect the death wasn't a natural one."

"And Madge Lee? Sister Collet was summoned to the children's unit by a scribbled note. Couldn't Ceri Williams have scribbled the note herself? Sister Collet said that Sister Williams was making a hot drink for a patient? Was she making black coffee for Madge Lee? Dr Meredith, she could've dissolved more digoxin tablets in that black coffee! Then all she had to do was put the opened bottle of brandy in Madge's hand and go back to the main ward. It was assumed that Madge had somehow or other got hold of the brandy herself, drunk most of it and died of alcoholic poisoning. Dr Meredith, didn't that thought occur to you?"

"It wasn't my business." His hand shook as she faced him. "I'm not a well man, Sister! I've not been well since my dear wife died! It wasn't my business!"

"But you didn't tell Ceri Williams that Amy had been found. Why not?"

"The little girl used to bang her head and scratch her arms and legs," he said. "Nobody actually caught her doing it. Of course, children can be secretive. I recall Sister Merryl saying that the child ought to be more carefully watched and Ceri Williams said, 'Poor little soul, what future has she got?' There was an expression in her eyes that reminded me of the day my wife and I went to see her newborn sister. I thought it best not to tell her."

"But I did tell her!" Dismay flooded Sister Joan's whole being as she stared at him.

"That's not important now," he began.

"Not important!" She whirled about and made for the door. "I have to get back and stop her!"

She was running to the van and the elderly doctor was lumbering behind her, no longer arguing but climbing into the passenger seat.

"She'll be on her way still. We can intercept her," Sister Joan said, starting the vehicle with a jerk. "Dear God, when Sister Collet died of an overdose of digoxin why didn't you do something, say something?"

He made no answer, but sat hunched up beside her.

The van speeded down the hill and along the main street and turned on to the moorland track.

"There she is!" Sister Joan slowed abruptly, her eyes on the figure ahead.

Ceri Williams was running, her plump figure moving with astonishing speed.

"She's making for the old schoolhouse. She must've guessed that Luther would be there!" Sister Joan pressed down on the accelerator and swung the van in a wide circle to cut the flying figure off.

"She'll do no harm now," Dr Meredith said. There was a strange, sad note in his voice.

The figure had stopped abruptly, holding one hand to its side, sinking down into the bracken like a rag doll thrown down by a bored child.

"I saw you arriving," Dr Meredith said in a tired, defeated tone. "I knew Ceri was on the reception desk, that she'd fall into your trap. I slipped a very large amount of sleeping powder into a cup of coffee and took it across to her. I expected it to work more swiftly but she is obviously in a heightened state of excitement and terror which delayed the effect."

"What effect?" Sister Joan clashed the gears as she drew to a halt and jumped down.

"The inevitable one." Dr Meredith was following her more slowly. "Digoxin isn't the only dangerous drug we keep in the hospital. I signed for this yesterday because I had an idea that I might be forced to use it."

"Then you — ?"

"I never killed anybody before." He had reached the figure lying in the bracken and was looking down with an expression on his face that stopped Sister Joan in her tracks. "It works very quickly at the end. I couldn't let the poor child go to trial. She would never have endured that, being questioned, having her good intentions misinterpreted. She had the very best intentions, you know. Last night we had a chat and she admitted to me that she'd slipped across to give Sister Collet something for her constant nausea. Sister

Collet was a very trusting young woman. Ceri told me how sorry she felt for her, being pregnant and knowing her work was suffering and she was becoming careless."

"There's more." Sister Joan was on her knees, frantically feeling for a pulse. "There has to be more!"

"Her mother's name was Ceri too," Dr Meredith said. "She was a lovely woman. My own dear wife never wanted children, wasn't very keen on that side of marriage. Nobody ever knew, of course. We'd left the district before anything started and it was a very brief affair, but I couldn't let the law get my own daughter, could I? I couldn't do that!"

* * *

Ward Sister Sophie Meecham had taken advantage of the fine afternoon to walk out on to the moor. At this time of year the bracken had a purplish tinge and the edges of the leaves were crisp and brown as toast. She walked briskly, enjoying the frost on the wind, the sensation of being high above the ordinary world. As she neared the gates of the convent she slowed down, her attention caught by the slim figure in grey around whose legs a half-grown alsatian dog gambolled.

"Here, Alice! Good girl!" Sister Joan's clear voice recalled the animal as Sophie Meecham paused and then came on again slowly.

"Good afternoon, Sister Joan." Sophie Meecham spoke somewhat shyly.

There had been a moment during the preceding investigation when she had wondered if it might be possible to make a real friend of Sister Joan, but the moment had passed. Life itself had changed for her.

"Sister Meecham, good afternoon to you." Sister Joan looked cheerful. No doubt her faith had sustained her during the past trying days.

"I hoped that I might run into you," Sophie Meecham said. "I wanted you to know that I think you did the right thing."

"What right thing?" Sister Joan frowned slightly.

"Well, asking all those questions, finding out what had been going on," Sister Meecham said, feeling suddenly awkward.

"There'll be no trial," Sister Joan said.

"Surely that's better all round?" Sophie Meecham ventured. "After all you couldn't possibly have known that Dr Meredith had already taken a fatal dose of the sleeping draught in the whisky he was sipping when you saw him in the residents' unit."

“Justice should be seen to be done,” Sister Joan said. “If I hadn’t left Dr Meredith with the body and driven on to the convent to alert Detective Sergeant Mill I’d have seen him fall.”

“But you couldn’t have done anything,” Sophie Meecham said.

“So everybody told me.” Sister Joan looked unconvinced, then cheered up as she asked, “How is Amy? Have you heard anything?”

“Yes, as a matter of fact I have!” Sophie Meecham beamed at her. “Sister Foster has applied for full custody of her and there’s every chance that she’ll get it. She’ll work flexible hours at the hospital and she has already put down a deposit on a nice little apartment near the infants’ school. Amy’s taken to her wonderfully but that’s to be expected, I suppose, seeing they’re blood relatives. That always creates a bond.”

“Yes, I suppose it does,” Sister Joan said.

“You know I never would’ve suspected Ceri Williams of being a murderer,” Sophie Meecham said. “They call it Munchausen’s Syndrome by Proxy now, of course. The urge to hurt more vulnerable people, usually children, even kill them as a means of drawing attention to their own needs.”

“I know there’s a fancy name for it,” Sister Joan said. “It’s unfashionable to talk of evil.”

"But Dr Meredith wasn't evil surely, Sister!"

"No, he was merely reluctant to believe that Ceri Williams had actually been killing the patients."

"Not to mention putting on a red wig and handing out LSD tablets to people she hoped would end up in St Keyne's!"

"And poor Madge Lee took one." Sister Joan gave a little shiver. "I'm only thankful that Luther wasn't lured into the same situation. At least there's a happy ending for him and for little Amy."

"Also for me, Sister." Sophie Meecham nodded at her in an encouraging way.

"Detective Sergeant Mill told me that you'd resigned," Sister Joan said. "I was sorry to hear that for I'm sure you always did your best."

"In a very difficult situation," Sophie Meecham said. "The long hours, the shortage of staff, the constant form filling and — well, the strain was beginning to get to me, I don't mind telling you. I was going to ask for a transfer but Dr Geeson came up with a solution."

"Dr Geeson?" Sister Joan raised delicate black brows.

"Dr Geeson has been greatly misunderstood," Sophie Meecham said. "Sister Merryl was actually of the opinion that he should have been struck off by the Medical Council!"

"My respect for Sister Merryl's common sense has gone up by leaps and bounds," Sister Joan couldn't resist saying.

Sophie Meecham looked hurt.

"Dr Geeson is a fine doctor with the highest qualifications," she said reproachfully.

"Forgive me but didn't he seduce two women and then drop them flat?" Sister Joan said.

"Even doctors are human when attracted by unscrupulous young women," Sister Meecham protested. "They were clearly after money. Anyway Dr Geeson intends to set up a small private clinic in Devon and has offered me the post of head sister. I shall miss St Keyne's, of course, but I shall remain loyal to Dr Geeson."

"Yes, of course," Sister Joan said, glancing at her with compassion.

"And I will be sorry not to be able to stroll on the moors when my duties permit but there are moors in Devonshire too. Russell — Dr Geeson — says there are some most interesting walks there."

Her eyes were shining and she looked young and eager. Sister Joan knew that words of warning would be both impertinent and futile. Sophie Meecham had temporarily corked up the brandy bottle in the belief she'd just been offered the Holy Grail.

"I wish you luck, Sister Meecham," she said sincerely. "Truly I do!"

"Thank you, Sister. Goodbye then."

"Goodbye. God bless."

Sister Joan watched the other turn and walk away across the moor.

It had been an unsatisfactory affair altogether, she thought. She had been slow to make connections, to pick up on clues.

"I think that about winds everything up, Sister!"

Detective Sergeant Mill drove slowly through the convent gates and stopped, winding down his window.

"Yes." Sister Joan nodded sombrely. "Too many deaths and I got on to the trail too late. I should've checked on the fact that Dr Meredith and Ceri Williams were both from Wrexham. I should've asked who was on duty with Tracy Collet when the old tramp was given his cocoa, and I ought to have remembered that Ceri Williams had just come off duty in the children's unit as Sister Collet took over the reception desk there. Tracy Collet told me that Ceri had gone into the garden to check on the children there. She must've pulled on that red wig and gone and hit poor little Amy, not realizing that Luther had ducked down behind the wall. I ought to have found out things sooner, Alan!"

"Hey, have a bit of compassion on yourself!" he said vigorously. "If you and Mother Dorothy hadn't felt uneasy about Louisa Cummings's sudden death Ceri Williams would've gone on doing away with people whom she considered were useless to society until the cows came home. You did well, Sister."

"Thanks. I'll try to believe you," Sister Joan said, smiling. "You're always very kind to me you know!"

"It's not difficult," said Detective Sergeant Mill, his own smile rueful as he put the car into gear again and drove off across the moor.

THE END

Other titles in the
Ulverscroft Large Print Series:

THE GREENWAY
Jane Adams

When Cassie and her twelve-year-old cousin Suzie had taken a short cut through an ancient Norfolk pathway, Suzie had simply vanished . . . Twenty years on, Cassie is still tormented by nightmares. She returns to Norfolk, determined to solve the mystery.

FORTY YEARS
ON THE WILD FRONTIER
Carl Breihan & W. Montgomery

Noted Western historian Carl Breihan has culled from the handwritten diaries of John Montgomery, grandfather of co-author Wayne Montgomery, new facts about Wyatt Earp, Doc Holliday, Bat Masterson and other famous and infamous men and women who gained notoriety when the Western Frontier was opened up.

TAKE NOW, PAY LATER
Joanna Dessau

This fiction based on fact is the love-turning-to-hate story of Robert Carr, Earl of Somerset, and his wife, Frances.

McLEAN AT THE GOLDEN OWL
George Goodchild

Inspector McLean has resigned from Scotland Yard's CID and has opened an office in Wimpole Street. With the help of his able assistant, Tiny, he solves many crimes, including those of kidnapping, murder and poisoning.

KATE WEATHERBY
Anne Goring

Derbyshire, 1849: The Hunter family are the arrogant, powerful masters of Clough Grange. Their feuds are sparked by a generation of guilt, despair and ill-fortune. But their passions are awakened by the arrival of nineteen-year-old Kate Weatherby.

A VENETIAN RECKONING
Donna Leon

When the body of a prominent international lawyer is found in the carriage of an intercity train, Commissario Guido Brunetti begins to dig deeper into the secret lives of the once great and good.

A TASTE FOR DEATH
Peter O'Donnell

Modesty Blaise and Willie Garvin take on impossible odds in the shape of Simon Delicata, the man with a taste for death, and Swordmaster, Wenczel, in a terrifying duel. Finally, in the Sahara desert, the intrepid pair must summon every killing skill to survive.

SEVEN DAYS FROM MIDNIGHT
Rona Randall

In the Comet Theatre, London, seven people have good reason for wanting beautiful Maxine Culver out of the way. Each one has reason to fear her blackmail. But whose shadow is it that lurks in the wings, waiting to silence her once and for all?

QUEEN OF THE ELEPHANTS
Mark Shand

Mark Shand knows about the ways of elephants, but he is no match for the tiny Parbati Barua, the daughter of India's greatest expert on the Asian elephant, the late Prince of Gauripur, who taught her everything. Shand sought out Parbati to take part in a film about the plight of the wild herds today in north-east India.

THE DARKENING LEAF
Caroline Stickland

On storm-tossed Chesil Bank in 1847, the young lovers, Philobeth and Frederick, prevent wreckers mutilating the apparent corpse of a young woman. Discovering she is still alive, Frederick takes her to his grandmother's home. But the rescue is to have violent and far-reaching effects . . .

A WOMAN'S TOUCH
Emma Stirling

When Fenn went to stay on her uncle's farm in Africa, the lovely Helena Starr seemed to resent her — especially when Dr Jason Kemp agreed to Fenn helping in his bush hospital. Though it seemed Jason saw Fenn as little more than a child, her feelings for him were those of a woman.

A DEAD GIVEAWAY
Various Authors

This book offers the perfect opportunity to sample the skills of five of the finest writers of crime fiction — Clare Curzon, Gillian Linscott, Peter Lovesey, Dorothy Simpson and Margaret Yorke.

DOUBLE INDEMNITY — MURDER FOR INSURANCE

Jad Adams

This is a collection of true cases of murderers who insured their victims then killed them — or attempted to. Each tense, compelling account tells a story of cold-blooded plotting and elaborate deception.

THE PEARLS OF COROMANDEL

By Keron Bhattacharya

John Sugden, an ambitious young Oxford graduate, joins the Indian Civil Service in the early 1920s and goes to uphold the British Raj. But he falls in love with a young Hindu girl and finds his loyalties tragically divided.

WHITE HARVEST

Louis Charbonneau

Kathy McNeely, a marine biologist, sets out for Alaska to carry out important research. But when she stumbles upon an illegal ivory poaching operation that is threatening the world's walrus population, she soon realises that she will have to survive more than the harsh elements . . .

TO THE GARDEN ALONE
Eve Ebbett

Widow Frances Morley's short, happy marriage was childless, and in a succession of borders she attempts to build a substitute relationship for the husband and family she does not have. Over all hovers the shadow of the man who terrorized her childhood.

CONTRASTS
Rowan Edwards

Julia had her life beautifully planned — she was building a thriving pottery business as well as sharing her home with her friend Pippa, and having fun owning a goat. But the goat's problems brought the new local vet, Sebastian Trent, into their lives.

MY OLD MAN AND THE SEA
David and Daniel Hays

Some fathers and sons go fishing together. David and Daniel Hays decided to sail a tiny boat seventeen thousand miles to the bottom of the world and back. Together, they weave a story of travel, adventure, and difficult, sometimes terrifying, sailing.

SQUEAKY CLEAN
James Pattinson

An important attribute of a prospective candidate for the United States presidency is not to have any dirt in your background which an eager muckraker can dig up. Senator William S. Gallicauder appeared to fit the bill perfectly. But then a skeleton came rattling out of an English cupboard.

NIGHT MOVES
Alan Scholefield

It was the first case that Macrae and Silver had worked on together. Malcolm Underdown had brutally stabbed to death Edward Craig and had attempted to murder Craig's fiancée, Jane Harrison. He swore he would be back for her. Now, four years later, he has simply walked from the mental hospital. Macrae and Silver must get to him — before he gets to Jane.

GREATEST CAT STORIES
Various Authors

Each story in this collection is chosen to show the cat at its best. James Herriot relates a tale about two of his cats. Stella Whitelaw has written a very funny story about a lion. Other stories provide examples of courageous, clever and lucky cats.

THE HAND OF DEATH
Margaret Yorke

The woman had been raped and murdered. As the police pursue their relentless inquiries, decent, gentle George Fortescue, the typical man-next-door, finds himself accused. While the real killer serenely selects his third victim — and then his fourth . . .

VOW OF FIDELITY
Veronica Black

Sister Joan of the Daughters of Compassion is shocked to discover that three of her former fellow art college students have recently died violently. When another death occurs, Sister Joan realizes that she must pit her wits against a cunning and ruthless killer.

MARY'S CHILD
Irene Carr

Penniless and desperate, Chrissie struggles to support herself as the Victorian years give way to the First World War. Her childhood friends, Ted and Frank, fall hopelessly in love with her. But there is only one man Chrissie loves, and fate and one man bent on revenge are determined to prevent the match . . .

THE SWIFTEST EAGLE
Alice Dwyer-Joyce

This book moves from Scotland to Malaya — before British Raj and now — and then to war-torn Vietnam and Cambodia . . . Virginia meets Gareth casually in the Western Isles, with no inkling of the sacrifice he must make for her.

VICTORIA & ALBERT
Richard Hough

Victoria and Albert had nine children and the family became the archetype of the nineteenth century. But the relationship between the Queen and her Prince Consort was passionate and turbulent; thunderous rows threatened to tear them apart, but always reconciliation and love broke through.

BREEZE: WAIF OF THE WILD
Marie Kelly

Bernard and Marie Kelly swapped their lives in London for a remote farmhouse in Cumbria. But they were to undergo an even more drastic upheaval when a two-day-old fragile roe deer fawn arrived on their doorstep. The knowledge of how to care for her was learned through sleepless nights and anxiety-filled days.

DEAR LAURA
Jean Stubbs

In Victorian London, Mr Theodore Crozier, of Crozier's Toys, succumbed to three grains of morphine. Wimbledon hoped it was suicide — but murder was whispered. Out of the neat cupboards of the Croziers' respectable home tumbled skeleton after skeleton.

MOTHER LOVE
Judith Henry Wall

Karen Billingsly begins to suspect that her son, Chad, has done something unthinkable — something beyond her wildest fears or imaginings. Gradually the terrible truth unfolds, and Karen must decide just how far she should go to protect her son from justice.

JOURNEY TO GUYANA
Margaret Bacon

In celebration of the anniversary of the emancipation of the African slaves in Guyana, the author published an account of her two-year stay there in the 1960s, revealing some fascinating insights into the multi-racial society.

WEDDING NIGHT
Gary Devon

Young actress Callie McKenna believes that Malcolm Rhodes is the man of her dreams. But a dark secret long buried in Malcolm's past is about to turn Callie's passion into terror.

RALPH EDWARDS OF LONESOME LAKE
Ed Gould

Best known for his almost single-handed rescue of the trumpeter swans from extinction in North America, Ralph Edwards relates other aspects of his long, varied life, including experiences with his missionary parents in India, as a telegraph operator in World War I, and his eventual return to Lonesome Lake.

NEVER FAR FROM NOWHERE
Andrea Levy

Olive and Vivien were born in London to Jamaican parents. Vivien's life becomes a chaotic mix of friendships, youth clubs, skinhead violence, discos and college. But Olive, three years older and her skin a shade darker, has a very different tale to tell . . .